MURDER IN MELUR

MURDER IN MELUR

Stuart Blackburn

RAINLIGHT
RUPA

Published in Rainlight by
Rupa Publications India Pvt. Ltd 2014
7/16, Ansari Road, Daryaganj
New Delhi 110002

Sales centres:
Allahabad Bengaluru Chennai
Hyderabad Jaipur Kathmandu
Kolkata Mumbai

ISBN: 978-81-291-3099-0

First impression 2014

10 9 8 7 6 5 4 3 2 1

Printed at Parksons Graphics Pvt. Ltd, Mumbai

1

As he moved through the weak winter light, Vijayan wondered if it would always feel like this. Voices around him clinked like pebbles against glass, while people passed him without apparent movement of air. Heading toward the tea-stall, he barely noticed a pair of mangy dogs fighting over a banana peel. They growled, yelped, bit and scratched, until one forced the other to retreat, and then both ran off, leaving the prize unclaimed in the dust.

'Puntai! Cunt! Get out of here!' Vijayan heard the words before he saw the speaker. Starched collar, pen in his shirt pocket, creased trousers, a slender plastic briefcase pinched under his armpit, the man stood with legs apart and stared hard at another man on the wooden bench at the tea-stall. The second man didn't respond, didn't even look up and just kept his eyes on his glass of milky tea.

He was small and bony with burnt copper skin, and looked about fifty but could have been thirty. Vijayan didn't know who he was but he knew what he was. A Paraiyar, an Untouchable. His soiled veshti, a sarong-like lower garment, was hiked half way up his thigh to reveal his undershorts. He wore no shirt, only a threadbare towel draped over his slumped shoulder. Thin cheeks, deep eye sockets and hunched back—everything about him was withdrawn, sucked in, protective.

'Paraiyar dogs shouldn't drink here,' muttered the man with the plastic briefcase, throwing a glance at Vijayan. Then he put down his glass of pink sugared hot milk and stomped off down the main road toward the bus station.

Vijayan watched him with a scowl. He knew this sort of thing happened in villages. But he didn't see it often here, in Melur, where everyone had to mix together, in the shops and the schools. That bastard with the briefcase was talking to me, he told himself. What did he want me to do? Beat up the poor devil?

Although he was angry with the man, he felt contempt for himself, for saying and doing nothing. No one, it seemed, had paid attention, not even the man standing beside the steaming urn of tea. Still, he felt humiliated, and he had understood it all so clearly on that day years ago, when he'd met the old man.

Inching forward, almost inside the room, he could see the man propped up on a lumpy cotton mattress laid on an iron-mesh frame bed. A queue of admirers snaked out the door and down the green concrete corridor of the railway station rest house. The old man looked exhausted yet exhilarated. Age was catching up with him, but he had made another six-hour speech. Not for nothing was he called Periyar, 'The Great One.'

Vijayan now stood inside the door and had a good look. He had seen Periyar before, though always from a distance, usually on stage addressing a crowd. His father didn't know he went to those meetings as a teenager and would have been furious had he known. His son shouldn't be associated with those kinds of ideas.

Although Vijayan hadn't grasped all that was said, he was captivated by the oratory, the long phrases that fit together, one by one, erecting a fortress with high walls and right angles, balanced and symmetrical. He liked being swept away by the onrushing words and taken to that place of order and safety.

Suddenly, the old man reared up at Vijayan, who had come forward and was standing next to the bed. 'You're young,' Periyar said. 'Tell me, what's the worst problem in this world?'

Vijayan was startled but managed to recover and repeat, 'The worst problem, sir?'

'Yes. You see the world with young eyes. What's the biggest problem?'

Vijayan thought for a moment and said, 'Caste, sir. Caste is the biggest problem.'

'What's that, young man? Caste?' The old man roared with a throaty laugh.

'Yes, sir. I mean, people…'

'Caste?' the old man bellowed again, now sitting up in bed and fully animated. 'Where is this thing called "caste"? C'mon! Show it to me!'

Vijayan stood speechless and the whole room listened.

'No, of course not. And why not? Because it's all in the mind. Do you understand? Caste doesn't exist anywhere but up here,' he said, tapping the side of his head. 'Only in the mind. That's where "caste" is and nowhere else. That's why we can exist without this barbaric system…'

Fifteen minutes later he fell back onto the pillows. He had covered the consequences of Brahmin domination, the superstitions of religion and the need to recover the true history of the Dravidian people.

The energy and intellect of the seventy-four-year-old man made a lifelong impression on Vijayan after that day. Caste didn't really exist. It was merely an idea, and like all ideas it could be dismantled, discarded and left behind. He would turn his back on it. He would fight it. That's what he said to himself eighteen years ago.

At the tea-stall in Melur, Vijayan watched the man with the briefcase stride down the road. Should have challenged him, he chided himself. Could have said, 'Your attitude is not proper in our modern society.' Something formal like that. Reassured by his imagined riposte, he got up and walked back towards the shop, without noticing that the bent man on the bench had already left.

Going up the main road, Vijayan passed a row of dry goods shops; a pharmacist, a tailor, a photographer, a stationer and a barber, where he went for a shave every fortnight or so. One or two places sold bolts of milled cloth and readymade clothes, mostly shirts and trousers. Then came Tip Top Fancy, with its neon sign, where Melur's sliver of a middle-class could find birthday cards, cashews, baby clothes and sunglasses. Between another tea-stall and a small electrical shop stood the khadi shop.

In five minutes, Vijayan had mounted the three concrete steps and was inside. It was early afternoon, just after the midday reopening, with no customers around, only Muttusami, the shop manager, who grunted a greeting without looking up from his bookkeeping.

Vijayan lifted the panel in the wooden counter, slipped through the gap and moved to the far end. After tidying up the merchandise lying scattered on the counter, he sat down on his wooden stool and looked at a two-day old newspaper.

The counter ran waist high down the length of the rectangular shop, dividing it into two unequal spaces. Behind it, where the glass-fronted cabinets rose up to the ceiling, there was just enough room to turn around. The area for customers, on the other side, was only slightly larger but seemed spacious because it was open to the street. Instead of a door, the shop had green metal shutters that were pulled aside in the morning, while the rest of the storefront had a full-length window, something of a novelty in Melur.

The glass-fronted cabinets behind Vijayan held stacks of veshtis, most were white, though some were dyed green and orange-tan, the colours of the Congress Party, and a few had the newest fashion of a coloured border. Modern shirts, both long and short-sleeved, and also white, with a breast pocket and buttons, lay on other shelves along with the jibas and their deep side pockets.

The bottom shelves contained the small, thin towels, usually white with coloured stripes, worn over the shoulder, tied around the waist or wrapped around the head. Next to them lay piles of brightly coloured lungis, some in the new batik patterns, worn by labourers at work or by others while relaxing at home. Everything in the shop, except a few silk shirts and veshtis, was made of the handspun and handwoven cotton known as khadi.

Raising his head and turning around, Vijayan looked at his smudged image in the glass cabinet. His hairline had receded further, he was sure of it, and his forehead now seemed to reach halfway up his crown. Twisting a corner of his mouth, he patted down his thinning hair and bent over the paper again.

He didn't mind working in the khadi shop. In some ways it suited him, but he resented the way he was sometimes spoken to by customers. He also disliked being part of any programme, and the khadi shops all over the state were a vast government scheme to support a 'cottage industry' that had long since moved out of cottages.

Gandhi began the khadi movement in the 1920s as part of his campaign for Independence. At the time, cotton grown in India was sent to mills in England, shipped back and bought by Indians as finished products. Spin and weave the coarse cotton in India, Gandhi said, and India will achieve economic and psychological self-reliance

In the 1970s, many men in Melur still wore khadi, and in the surrounding villages there was little else. It was inexpensive and it was familiar, but the simple cloth had lost some of its semi-sacred status and was beginning to appear outmoded. Younger men preferred machine-woven cotton veshtis and polyester shirts, while some wore trousers.

Vijayan always wore khadi, though he was far from being a Gandhian. He liked its feel on his skin and the way it breathed in hot weather. While not as smooth as silk or fine Egyptian cotton, it had a reassuring texture. He even liked the knobbly ridges that formed when folding it. Besides, he worked in a khadi shop.

'Time for another tea,' Vijayan grumbled at about five o'clock. Customers had been trickling in, but no one interesting to talk to, and he was still bothered by the incident at the tea-stall a few hours earlier. He hadn't mentioned it to Muttusami. They worked at opposite ends of the counter and didn't talk much.

Each of them had his favourite stool and kept it at his end. The stools were high, and customers who sat on them often felt stranded. After dangling their legs for a minute, they slid off to the safety of a solid floor. Only the regulars, who came in to gossip, sat on them for any length of time.

Turning left down the main road toward the bus stand, Vijayan headed for the tea-stall. The tea and snacks weren't special there, but the benches were. Instead of flat boards on legs, these were more like garden benches, painted a light blue, with armrests and backs to lean against. Vijayan and his friends gathered here in the evenings, when the small market town grew quiet.

'Two cups of tea,' Vijayan said to the man behind the hissing urn. The man knew him by sight, not by name, and made no reference to his earlier visit. He would have liked to eat some parotas, but he didn't have that kind of money. His 280 rupees a month wasn't much, but it was something. A lot of people had less. He'd wait until evening to eat with the others.

Sitting down on one of the blue benches, he took an old paperback out of the side pocket of his jiba. He often read these Ingersoll lectures during the day to give him something to think about. The nineteenth-century essayist used complex English sentences that he liked to puzzle out. They also packed a punch—'demolishing the feeble arguments of religion with the majestic truths of science' is how Vijayan had put it in one of his own, unpublished, essays.

He had worked his way through two paragraphs by the time the tea was ready. A small boy appeared from nowhere, picked up the glasses and started for the shop when Vijayan told him to put a piece of paper over the glasses, to keep the dust out.

Walking back up the main road, they came to the roundabout, from where Melur flung roads out into the countryside, in all directions and at different angles, like the tentacles of an octopus. Five of these country roads met at the roundabout, making it the centre of town and the hub of the surrounding villages.

Entering the khadi shop ahead of the boy, Vijayan smelled the incense. A single stick was burning in front of the framed image of Lakshmi on the back wall. Muttusami lit it every evening when darkness fell.

Pure superstition, Vijayan said to himself. To Muttusami he said, 'Still quiet, I see,' handed him a glass and dismissed the boy with a flick of his head.

'Umm,' the manager muttered, his head bent over a thick ledger. Muttusami was in his late fifties, a thin man with smooth chocolate brown skin. He spent a lot of time on the accounts, mumbling and tapping his pen against the ruled lines. Each morning he lifted the heavy cover and let it fall slowly back on the counter, so that the ledger spread out across the surface like a pair of airplane wings.

Vijayan, the younger man, took his place at the far end and began to put away the clothes that were scattered about on the counter. Muttusami liked to think he was organized and never noticed the mess he left after serving customers. He liked cloth, but he preferred the columns and rows in his big book.

Scooping up the veshtis and lungis, Vijayan turned to replace them in the cabinet behind him but paused to feel the warm weight of the cotton. Then he saw a face in the glass panel.

It was Dandapani. Heavy set and loose-limbed, he took up most of the space on the other side of the counter, where he stood joking with a few men. His hard, flat face, the work of a blacksmith, was decorated with stubbly white whiskers, though he was only in his forties. Short-cropped hair and a thick gold-chain necklace added density to his appearance.

'No, no. The missus knew nothing about it, you see. It was during school time, when I had a "class". She was just a slut, but still…'

His voice trailed off when the High School headmaster came into the shop and asked for a lungi. While Vijayan served the new customer, he saw that Dandapani was sniggering and looking at him. Although he couldn't hear the words clearly, he could guess what the joke was.

They had had only one personal encounter. When Vijayan had been looking for a place to hold a meeting, someone mentioned that no classes were held at the teacher training school on Sundays and a room might be free.

'No classes on Sundays!' someone else snorted. 'There're no classes, period.' Everyone knew about the dusty classrooms in the training school, the most important institution in Melur. Who could be bothered to waste time teaching when you could be gambling or sleeping or, if you were Dandapani, whoring?

But it was a good idea, so Vijayan had walked the mile out of town to the school. It lay on the main road, to the north towards Trichy, but set back behind an iron gate crowned with a crescent-shaped sign in English announcing 'Government Basic

Training School, Melur.' The gate was hinged to a metal pole, and at night it was closed and chained to a second pole. The poles, however, were not connected to any wall or fence, leaving the gate standing on its own. Still, most people walked through that purposeless gate.

Students at the GBTS, as it was called, were high school graduates who trained to be teachers and ended up in a village primary school. Not prestigious, but it was a job, with a government salary and a little status. The training was 'basic' because it followed Gandhian principles. That's what the government claimed, though the only thing Gandhi would have recognized were the spinning wheels.

Even now, twenty-five years after Independence, the 120 boys were supposed to spin cotton once a week on the oversized wooden wheels. One of the sheds was crammed with dozens of them, but like much else at the school, they languished with disuse. Some students enjoyed spinning and worked the wheels during their free time. There was a lot of free time.

Vijayan had stood for a moment, looking through the gate at the low building that must be the office. He walked straight ahead, up two steps to a wide verandah with half a dozen bicycles resting against the wall. Crossing the threshold, he found himself in an ante-room, where a man sat slumped behind a wooden desk.

'I'd like to speak to the principal,' said Vijayan, using the English word. He detested deference yet needed to be polite, so he stood erect and looked directly at the clerk.

The man behind the desk opened his eyes and said nothing. Maybe he's not called 'principal' but 'director' or 'headmaster,' thought Vijayan. He was about to correct himself and then stopped—whatever happened, he would not be obsequious.

'In there,' said the clerk, pointing a stubby finger towards the open door to Vijayan's left.

The principal was an amiable-looking man with large hands stuck on the end of long arms. 'Well, what is it?' he asked after Vijayan entered and stood before him.

'Sir, my name is Vijayan Naidu. I am employed in the khadi shop here in Melur. I would like to ask permission to use one of the rooms for a meeting on the first Sunday of each month.'

'Meeting? I don't know. I'll have to ask the district Department of Education,' he said without even attempting to show interest.

'What kind of meeting?' The question came from behind Vijayan, near the open door. It was Dandapani, the bulky games master.

'Who are you, anyway? Why come here?' The questions were hurled with such force that they threw Vijayan off balance. 'C'mon, son, answer the question. What kind of meeting?'

'It is a meeting of... We've formed a group of people who want to discuss social and literary issues.'

'So what's its name? The "Thinkers of Melur"!' roared Dandapani.

'We've called it "The Rationalist Society" because...'

'Rationalist?' Dandapani sneered. 'Not that rot about getting rid of caste and tradition? You think we're going to let you use our school for that kind of crap?'

The principal twirled a pen and listened.

'This is, I believe, a government institution and so...' Vijayan persisted.

'What day did you say?' Dandapani interrupted.

'Sundays.'

'Not Saturdays?'

'No. Sundays,' Vijayan repeated. 'Mr Principal, sir,' pleaded Vijayan turning to the man behind the desk. 'It's an open meeting. We want to educate ourselves, and we need a classroom once a month, for three hours.'

'I'll have to ask the authorities in Madurai, as I said. Put it in writing, and I'll pass it on.'

'And they'll throw it in the waste bin, where it belongs,' snarled Dandapani.

'Yes, sir. Thank you.' Vijayan turned to leave, when Dandapani blocked his path.

'Vijayan Naidu, huh? You don't even come from our Tamil country, do you? But you bring your rubbish into our towns and villages! Get out now, but one day I'll take care of you and your communist friends. '

Vijayan stepped around him and left the room, only glancing back to see the principal bent over a document, pretending not to have heard. After five months and two letters to the principal, the request was granted and the Rationalist Society of Melur held its first meeting.

That was two years ago and Vijayan hadn't spoken to Dandapani since. The games master and his little band of followers often came to town looking for whatever pleasures it could offer. Liquor was banned in Tamil Nadu, but they could buy a bottle of brandy smuggled in from a neighbouring state. Cheap palm-wine was sold in huts along the roads leading out into the countryside. Prostitutes were not hard to find either, but gathering to gossip in the khadi shop was less expensive.

But it wasn't all talk. Dandapani wore khadi—veshti, shirt and towel around his neck. Now he stood there in the shop, a white pillar of purity who had bullied his way through life and at forty-two was responsible for the physical health of more than a hundred boys.

'Hey! Show me those new lungis.' The order was directed at Vijayan, who still had his back turned and was putting things away in the cabinet. Dandapani used words that would be spoken to an inferior or a child. Although Vijayan was young and a shop assistant, it was still an insult.

Opening a glass panel, he grabbed a stack of brightly-coloured lungis, spun round, held them for a moment above the counter, looked at his customer and let them fall in a heap. 'There, sir,' he said in mock politeness. 'Kindly select your preference from these garments.'

Everyone in the shop was now watching this charade of manners. Conversations ceased and the air bristled with anticipation. As Dandapani leaned threateningly across the counter toward Vijayan, a man darted in from the road and shouted: 'They're coming! The Americans! Listen!'

They all rushed out and looked up at the black conical speaker fixed at the corner of the roof of the electrical shop next door. Vijayan and the others joined a crowd listening to a male voice speaking formal Tamil:

> *...reported that two warships of the United States Seventh Fleet are sailing up the Bengal of Bengal and are now less than 50 miles from Madras. The Government of India has....*

The rest of the All India Radio news was lost in an explosion of voices.

'That's it! War!'

'We made friends with the Russians and this is what we get.'

'But the Americans won't attack us. What've we done?'

'Imperialist nations always fight wars to gain power.'

'Don't be an idiot! Who said those ships are going to attack us?'

'Right. They're probably on their way to Vietnam.'

'Then why are they heading up the Bay of Bengal? Unless Vietnam has been moved recently, they won't get there via Calcutta.'

'They've lost in Vietnam and they're looking for new enemies.'

'Blockhead! They're going to East Pakistan. To keep an eye on the war there.'

'Maybe, but they're going there to support the Pakistani army. Against us.'

The voices grew louder and louder, struggling to be heard above the blaring radio, until another noise drowned them out. Vijayan looked down towards the roundabout and saw an advancing phalanx of red jackets and white trousers, brass horns, baritones and trombones. The shouting men could no longer hear themselves, so they turned around and dumbly watched the Salvation Army march by them.

Muttusami gestured to Vijayan and they returned to the shop.

Inside, Vijayan brooded as he tidied up the counter and put away the scattered pieces of clothing. He had no doubt that America was the enemy of socialism, but he also knew he lacked the charisma to persuade others. Unlike Dandapani, who was still outside holding forth about threats to 'Mother India'.

Vijayan sat down and looked out the window at the other end of the counter. The main road in Melur was always crowded at this time, when it was turning dark. Bullock carts, buses, pedal rickshaws, bicycles, plus the odd auto rickshaw and taxi jockeyed for space with pedestrians on this road running straight through town and connecting it to large cities north and south.

Although some people were going to the bus stand or to their houses in town, many were walking back to their villages, three miles, five miles, even ten or twelve miles away. A bus ticket didn't cost much, but that money could be better spent.

Outside Melur, though, the roads that led to the villages were usually empty. Only at dusk on the market days of Tuesday and Thursday were they busy with people trudging home.

It happened on a Friday. Velan came into town, as he often did, after his shift in the small iron works about a mile away. He went first to the printers to pick up copies of the leaflet for the demonstration next week, and then visited two or three people to make sure they would distribute the leaflets at key places in and around Melur. About 7pm he dropped in at the khadi shop.

He handed Vijayan a stack of the flimsy leaflets, with the black hammer and sickle on a bright red background at the top. They looked good, except that the red ink had run. Still, everyone would know it was the CPM, the Communist Party Marxist.

'Remember to tell your friends. It begins at 9, at the police station,' Velan said, his black bushy moustache moving up and down as he spoke.

'Yes, all right. But…' Vijayan stammered.

'But what?'

'Nothing. I'll be there and I'll tell the others.'

'Good. We need a large crowd, so they'll listen to us.'

Vijayan wanted to say the police might hear, but they'd never act. The labourer they had locked up last month for beating up his contractor would not be freed even if five hundred people gathered and chanted 'Justice for workers!' for five hours outside the station. The man in jail was a Pallar, an Untouchable, while the contractor was a Mudaliar, the same caste as the deputy sub-inspector.

'Look, Vijayan,' said Velan, sensing his friend's hesitation. 'There are bigger things, I know, but we've got to do this. It's here, in Melur.'

'Right. See you next Saturday.'

'Good. It's going to rain. I better go.'

Velan mounted his bicycle and pedalled down the main street, around the roundabout and out on a road leading northwest. He could cycle the eleven miles to his village of Kelalavu in a little over an hour. But that was in the daytime and now it was growing dark.

Every few minutes he glanced behind him. The cotton bag

with the leaflets inside was still there on the back rack, gripped by a strong metal spring. He felt confident about the demonstration. It was what he had to do the following week that worried him.

Velan liked cycling home at this hour, when the heat slackened and lay soft on the skin. As he rode along, the light seemed to retreat in front of him, the huge sky changed colours and he could hear insects in the paddy fields beside the road. He usually saw a bicycle or a bullock cart, but tonight there was nothing.

Ahead of him the narrow road was invisible as it threaded through acres of green. And in some places the heavy black branches of mahogany trees reached across the road from both sides and entangled themselves, forming a tunnel. It was late November, so the branches were thick with leaves and olive green fruit. Velan felt the wind pick up and rush over his bare legs, threatening rain.

He entered one of those tree-tunnels just where the road swung down to the left and over an irrigation channel. He didn't see him right away. It was too dark under the canopy of branches. He saw only the shape of a man standing in the middle of the road. And he didn't see the machete gripped by his side.

Next day, in the late afternoon, a figure approached the same spot, walking slowly and bending down here and there, as if looking for something.

2

When Vijayan arrived in Melur six years ago, it was not by choice. It was a small town, without a major temple, historical landmark or even a railway station. Most people complained about the lack of a cinema, for which they had to go to Madurai, an hour's bus ride to the south.

If Melur was known for anything, it was the metal-tipped ploughs made in small workshops lining one side of the main road, about a mile to the north, near the Government Basic Training School. Some people claimed this useful implement had been invented in the town. True or not, 'famous for ploughs' just about summed up Melur.

The market town was a mix of landowners and farmers, merchants and shopkeepers, agricultural and day labourers, teachers and other government employees, carpenters and blacksmiths, goldsmiths and potters, barbers and washermen.

Although a handful of families lived in two-storey houses, with wide verandahs and thick pillars, no one had a television and very few had a private telephone or car. An audio cassette player or portable radio displayed prosperity. A ballpoint pen was a minor luxury.

One in five people in the town, and slightly more in the villages, was an Untouchable. A Paraiyar, a Pallar, a Chakkiliyar, a Valluvar or a Kuravar. They were the agricultural and manual labourers, grave-diggers and funeral musicians, sweepers and tanners, cobblers and bird catchers, gypsies and fortune-tellers. Barbers, washermen and low-caste priests who served them were themselves treated as untouchable by other castes.

Except for the few who had risen to the rank of government peon or primary school teacher, Untouchables lived in mud-brick houses and huts scattered around the edge of town and in the scrubland beyond. In the villages, they lived in a separate area called the 'colony.' That's where Velan lived, in the colony attached to Kelalavu.

No one had seen him for a week now, not since he had left Melur on his bicycle. His wife didn't take much notice when he didn't come home that night because he was often out on CPM business and sometimes didn't get back until the following day. After three days, however, she asked her brother, Murugan, to look for him.

Murugan knew his brother-in-law had gone to the printers that Friday because Velan had borrowed 35 rupees from him to pay for the leaflets. 'Shakti Printing' lay just off the main road, in a narrow side street where election posters were peeling from walls and shop fronts. A cow licked the still pungent glue from the back of one poster lying torn on the ground.

Murugan stood at the doorway. Two long tables, covered with piles of loose paper, stretched away from him and down the length of the front room. Wooden shelves on all sides were crammed with bundles of printed sheets, posters, cards and pamphlets entitled 'The New Science of Hygiene' and 'The Story of Lord Jesus.' He took a step inside and called out, but the machinery banging away in the back room drowned out his weak voice.

When an elderly man appeared, Murugan noticed he wore shoes instead of sandals.

'I'm from Kelalavu, sir,' he began. 'Velan is my brother-in-law. You know, the CPM activist.'

'What do you want?'

'Did he come here, on Friday, sir? In the evening?'

'Picked up his leaflets. About some demonstration, I think.'

'When was that, sir? What time, I mean?'

'About 6 o'clock, maybe closer to 7.'

'And then he left?'

'Of course, he left. He's not here, is he?'

'Yes, sir. I mean, no, sir.'

'He took the leaflets, hundreds of them, printed on both sides, and left on his bicycle.'

The owner looked at Murugan, his torn veshti, no shirt or sandals, standing silent and uncertain.

'What's all this about? Where's he gone this time?'

'We don't know, sir. That's why I'm here. Trying to find out.'

'Probably off on party business. Or maybe that other business of his,' the old man said with a chuckle.

Murugan took a moment to find another question, but by then the man was already out of hearing among the crashing machines.

At the khadi shop he had to wait for several minutes while customers were being served. Vijayan wrapped a shirt in newspaper, grabbed the string hanging down from a large ball fixed to the ceiling, wound it around the bundle, snipped it off with a pair of industrial scissors, tied a knot and handed over the neat package.

Murugan sidled up to the counter and spoke to Vijayan.

'You know Velan, I think. From Kelalavu.'

'The CPM man? Yes. Who are you?'

'His wife's brother.'

'Tell him I'll be at the demonstration on Saturday. I've got the leaflets, but…'

'It's not that.'

Vijayan looked at Murugan. He was a young man, but his face had already shrivelled into a hard brown nut. Heavy eyelids half-hid his small black irises. He spoke in fragments, his hollow cheeks working like a bellows to push out the words.

'We don't know. Where he is.'

'What do you mean?'

'Not at home. Since Friday. He came here. To Melur.'

'I know.'

'Did you see him Friday?'

'Yes. He came here and gave me some leaflets. Then he left, probably about 7. He didn't make it home?'

'No. Do you think anything's happened?'

Vijayan stared at him and for a moment their eyes locked. Then he pulled away, fiddled with the string trailing from the ceiling and tried to think.

'Well,' he said after a long silence, 'he probably went off to Madurai on business and didn't have time to tell anyone.'

'Maybe. But my sister. What can I say?' Murugan puffed out the words and his cheeks collapsed once more.

'Tell her not to worry. Tell her that he'll come back.'

Murugan looked at him but said nothing. They both knew something was wrong but neither wanted to admit it.

As Vijayan watched him step out of the shop, he tried to remember what Velan had said to him that Friday evening. Something about 'bigger things.'

Three weeks later, in mid-December, Velan was still missing. His bicycle had been found in a ravine not far from the road, about a mile from Kelalavu, and taken to Murugan. The cloth bag with the leaflets was still there, held on the back rack by the metal spring. Nothing more was known.

Vijayan was reading an old newspaper in the room where he and his friends slept. The first-floor room belonged to the family living downstairs and was convenient because it had an outside staircase. But it was small, about five by seven metres, and furnished only with four reed mats. Clothes and a small mirror hung from nails driven into the distempered walls. The two windows, with wooden shutters but no glass, overlooked the lane below.

The front page of Vijayan's paper celebrated the Indian army's victory in East Pakistan, while the international news reported on US losses in Vietnam, Khmer Rouge offensives in Cambodia, and China taking Taiwan's seat on the UN Security Council. Glancing at a report on the growing tension between Tamils and Sinhalese in Ceylon, Vijayan started his hunt for anything on books.

Five minutes later he put the paper down and looked blankly ahead of him. 'What happened to Velan?' he muttered to himself. Then he looked around the room and asked aloud, 'What happened to him?'

Tonight, as usual, Vijayan was in the room with Krishnan, Mani and Raja. Other friends dropped by from time and time, and would spend the night, but these four were the closest. Krishnan, the only Brahmin in the group, worked in a bank. He and his wife and two children lived with his parents in a house nearby, but he liked the companionship of the room. Always neat, he kept his black hair oiled and combed straight back, like a furrowed field.

Mani was a writer. All of them, except Raja, wrote essays, poems and short stories for regional magazines and journals. But only Mani had published a collection of poems, and his stories regularly appeared in Tamil journals. He was slender and taller than the rest, with hair that bunched up on his head like a stiff bush. A clerk in the local tax office, he was married but had no children. He and Krishnan, the two with good salaries, combined to pay the room rent of 75 rupees a month.

The others looked up when Vijayan asked his question but said nothing. They were close friends, close enough to argue about social and political issues, especially topics they agreed on. All of them objected to caste, but not in the same way. Krishnan and Chellappan criticized the system, Mani and Kantan condemned the injustice, while Vijayan felt a visceral anger at the humiliation.

This combativeness had created a strong bond among them and the little room had nourished it. It was their refuge from the outside world, a place where they knew they were accepted and that their ideas, however unconventional, would not be rejected out of hand.

Raja, however, didn't take part in these debates. He was the youngest, only twenty, and spent less time in the room than the others. He often came in to sleep after midnight and was gone by early morning. No one knew who he was, only that he was a Pallar. They had first met him one evening, a year ago, while sitting on the blue benches at their favourite tea-stall.

Mani had been talking about the latest novel by an author they admired. Set in a town in the far south, it consisted of the events—some of them terrifying—witnessed by a tamarind tree.

'But a tamarind tree can't know anything,' interjected Raja, sitting by himself on another bench. They all turned and looked at him for the first time. Handsome and barefoot, he wore a cheap colourful lungi and a dirty sleeveless vest.

'Well, can it?' he persisted, putting down his glass of tea and spreading his upturned palms.

Vijayan pushed his lips into an indulgent smile and said, 'That's right. The tree doesn't know anything. But everything happens around it, so it becomes a character in the story.'

'But it's still a tree, isn't it?'

'Yes, it's a tree. But it's a tamarind tree. You see, tamarind symbolises...'

'Yeah, yeah! I know all about tamarind!' Raja cut in.

'What do you know?' asked Mani.

'Tamarind with tomatoes. Best pickle in the world,' said Raja, his eyes gleaming beneath his thick black hair.

Vijayan laughed and said, 'We're going to have a glass of hot milk before we go. You want one? We'll pay.'

When Raja said no, Vijayan took it as the obligatory first refusal and ordered one for him anyway.

'No. I don't want any,' he insisted.

'You don't like hot milk?' asked Mani.

'I do, but…you wouldn't understand.'

'Tell us.'

'It's just that…well, if I drink it tonight, what about tomorrow? Or, next week? I'll want it again, but you won't be here to buy it for me, will you? I don't want to want things I can't have.'

They shrugged and drank their milk, but Vijayan and Mani remembered what he said that night. They ran into Raja at the same tea-stall later that week, and this time he came back to the room and slept there. Although he didn't talk much, they learned that he did odd jobs, mostly painting and carpentry, but also manual labour. He was often away, sometimes for weeks, working on a house or hotel. He never mentioned his family or where he came from, and they didn't ask.

'What happened to Velan?' Vijayan asked a second time after no one had answered him in the small room.

'Who?' Mani obliged, without interest. He was sitting on a mat in a lungi and vest, his back against the wall as he wrote in a small notebook.

'Velan. The CPM man from Kelalavu.'

'Don't know,' Mani said.

'He's your friend, isn't he?' asked Krishnan.

'Well, we talk politics, how to organize a march, that sort of thing.'

'Then you don't know him at all,' said Mani, putting his notebook down and sticking a beedi in his mouth. He lit the tightly rolled tobacco leaf with a match and added, 'Not if you only talk politics.'

'I do know him,' Vijayan claimed, fixing his large brown eyes on Mani. He recrossed his legs under him on the mat and leaned forward. 'He's defended workers' rights. Been to jail three or four times. He's got passion.'

'And not just for workers,' said Mani under his breath.

'What?'

'Nothing.'

'Anyway, you won't find out what happened to him sitting in this room,' said Krishnan.

'Exactly what I was thinking,' said Vijayan. 'I'm going to his village, first thing tomorrow.'

The others exchanged knowing looks as Vijayan fell back against the wall. Noticing their silence, he added, 'All right then, before noon.'

Picking up a crumpled bundle of cloth, he shaped it into a pillow and lay down on his mat. This was the best part of the day, the end of the day, when he could let his thoughts run free, without anything or anyone in the way.

He opened his eyes in the sunless morning light. With its north-facing windows, the room was never penetrated by direct sunlight, and it felt cold in winter, even with the shutters closed. Krishnan and Raja had already gone, but Mani was still curled up on his mat in a corner. He lay on one side, knees almost touching his chin. It was Sunday, their day off.

'Mani,' he called while shaking him, 'C'mon. Let's go for a bath.' They each took a thin, red and blue checked towel from one of the nails in the wall and threw it around their necks. Wearing a lungi, vest and sandals, they climbed down the narrow steps to the street. Mani clutched his packet of beedis and matches in one hand, a bar of soap, toothbrush and tin of Dr Brown's tooth powder in the other. Vijayan preferred to use a neem tree twig to brush his teeth and to borrow his friend's soap.

Outside, the morning sun had chased off the late December chill and began to warm their bodies as they walked down the main road. After tea, they turned left at the roundabout and headed east on to the road to Devakulam. Although a small village, its temple tower was visible for miles, not because it was tall but because it was surrounded by paddy fields.

The two friends, both in their late thirties, spoke little until they cleared the line of shops, crossed an irrigation channel and saw only fields. Melur was like that. Ten minutes took you right out into the countryside. The tall green stalks on both sides of the road were bent over, top-heavy with grain and waiting for the harvest. When the wind whipped up, Mani wrapped his towel around his head like a turban, which made his bushy hair stick up even higher. Vijayan tied his towel under the chin like a scarf, emphasizing his oval face that tapered to a rounded jaw.

'So, when are you going to get married?' asked Mani with a sidewise glance.

Vijayan was used to hearing this question from Mani and said, 'For a serious person, you don't know how to ask a serious question.'

'But can you answer it?'

'My sister's got another one lined up, I've heard. But why should I enslave another person just because society expects me to?'

A horn sounded and they stepped back, almost slipping into the irrigation channel.

'And she doesn't have to be just my caste. Oh no! She's got to be my uncle's daughter, too. Periyar was right. Caste is a prison of the mind.'

'Marriage isn't like that. A husband and wife…' Mani protested.

'I'm not listening to you ramble on about marriage. How many nights have you slept at home this week? You might as well be a bachelor.'

'Shut up! Don't start on that again.'

'Then don't lecture me about marriage. You don't…'

'Look out!' yelled Mani, grabbing Vijayan's arm and pulling him hard to the side of the road. They hadn't paid attention to the wooden wheels crunching the tarmac and would have been smashed by the heavy bullock cart if Mani hadn't reacted at the last moment.

The water tank, only a few minutes' walk from the road, was deep and about half the size of a football pitch. One end was for men, the other for women. Vijayan took off his lungi and vest, tied a towel around his waist and slipped off his underpants. Mani did the same and they picked their way down the slimy brick steps to the water. Mani put the soap dish on the lowest step, eased his body into the cold green water and floated away. Vijayan couldn't swim and had to let tiny fish nibble his toes while trying to tread water.

Climbing out first, Vijayan stood on the lowest step and soaped his body all over. He worked hard on his feet, rubbing away the dirt that accumulated in the hollow just beneath the ankle bone. After going back in to rinse off, Vijayan washed his lungi, vest and underpants, climbed back up and hung them on a tree to dry. Still wearing the skimpy towel around his waist, he snapped a twig off a neem tree, chewed one end to expose the stiff fibres and brushed his teeth. The sun rose above the trees in the distance and its rays fell on his wet body like warm hands.

He walked a short distance to the men's toilet area, where Mani soon joined him and lit a beedi. When they returned to the tank ten minutes later, their clothes were still drying. Wearing only their towels, Vijayan's dark coffee-coloured body glistened with beads of water, while Mani's smooth skin, a shade lighter, held no moisture. Although they rarely spoke about skin colour, they mocked the popular whitening creams and joked about the latest film star. Both also liked to sprinkle talcum powder on their skin and watch it turn pale.

Having put on their not-yet-dry clothes, they walked back to Melur.

As they approached the roundabout in town, they could see a policeman in khaki shorts, heavy socks and boots standing on the squat circular platform in the centre. They watched him rotate around, to face five different directions, each time raising one hand and gesturing with the other. Bullock carts and cycles gave way to buses and lorries, while pedestrians sailed under his flashing white-cuffed arms.

Passing 'the human windmill,' as Mani called him, they headed for a place to eat. Two idlis covered with watery coconut chutney and a glass of coffee was their normal fare. They sat on short stools at one of the long tables lined up in parallel rows. Sucking the remaining bits of steamed rice cake and sauce from their fingers, Vijayan and Mani folded their glassy banana leaves and headed for the back, where customers threw their leaves into a concrete trough. The trough was set into the wall, half inside and half out, so that scavengers in the lane could reach the discarded leaves.

Mani threw his leaf away, washed his hands and went back for coffee.

Vijayan was doing the same when he heard a yelp. Outside in the lane, a man squatted by the trough, wearing only a torn towel around his waist and foraging through the leaves he had pulled out. A scrawny dog with spots and a pointy nose stood a couple of feet away, its body drawn back like a spring. Fixing a stare at the leaves, it inched forward, low to the ground, nose extended. When it got within touching distance, the scavenger swung back his hand and smacked it. The dog yelped and backed off, then lowered its body and edged forward again. Flailing out with one hand when necessary, the man continued to lick the wet food off the leaves.

Vijayan wouldn't have noticed but for the yelp. The man was almost hidden as he crouched near the low trough, and anyway he had seen this sight before. Seen but not watched. It was all right unless you recognized the scavenger; then you pretended not to notice, tossed your leaf into the trough and walked away. It wasn't hard to ignore, or forget, because it was all done in silence.

That's why the dog's cry made him stop and watch. Rather than throw his leaf into the trough, Vijayan walked through a door into the lane and pitched it against the far wall, beyond the crouching man's reach. The dog saw the unguarded leaf and advanced on it, cringing low as it crept past Vijayan's legs. There wasn't much on the leaf, and the dog licked it off in a few seconds.

Trotsky, said Vijayan to himself as he went back inside. I'll call it Trotsky.

'Where've you been?' asked Mani, sitting at the table smoking a beedi.

'Nowhere. I...'

Mani looked up at his friend. One of his moods, he thought.

Best leave him alone. Then he said, 'I'm going home. When's your bus?'

'Bus?'

'To Kelalavu,' Mani reminded him.

'Oh, right,' said Vijayan, still thinking of the dog.

He walked down the main street near the roundabout where a row of shops sold stationery, schoolbooks, dictionaries, newspapers and printed pamphlets. He liked to read the Sunday paper because it had essays, book reviews and photographs of places he had never seen. He always bought last week's paper. Half-price and the news didn't date.

Buying the paper, he went across the road to a tea-stall he rarely used. It was now late morning and the benches were crowded with men sipping tea, eating snacks, smoking beedis and talking. Seeing Vijayan clutching his paper, they made room for him. Turning the pages, he elbowed the men on either side, but no one took it amiss.

Then he stopped turning. Professor T.K.N. Gopalakrishnaswami had given a lecture at Madras University on the history of Indian languages. Vijayan's lips began to twist as he read the two columns. 'It's the same old story,' he muttered when he had finished. In fact, he'd spoken aloud and heads turned in his direction.

'Don't you see?' he addressed his impromptu audience. 'They still think Tamil is derived from Sanskrit, yet Tamil was spoken in India hundreds of years before Sanskrit appeared. Archaeology alone…'

The heads turned back, a few exchanged glances and others frowned with incomprehension or annoyance. Vijayan shrugged and began to compose a letter to the editor:

Dear Gentlemen,
It has come to my attention that your worthy organ...

No, that's too stiff, he decided. Better use ordinary Tamil.

Dear Editor,
I would like to comment on Prof X's lecture. If he had followed the first duty of a scholar, he would have realized that....

Twenty minutes later, his tea was cold and his newspaper lay scattered on the floor, but his letter was written.

Then he debated with himself about how to sign it. 'Sri Vijayan Naidu, Gandhigram Shop, Melur'? Or 'V. Naidu, writer'?

Ah well, he mumbled to himself, what's the point of composing a letter that will never be printed commenting on a university lecture about a topic that most people don't care about? Velan didn't waste time on these things. He organized marches and demonstrations! Vijayan slammed his palm down on the bench, and this time his neighbours called him 'loose' and turned their backs. Scowling, he strode purposefully to the station, where the last bus had already left for Kelalavu.

December crossed into January with no news of Velan. Vijayan continued to feed Trotsky, and one morning he found himself riding in a bus to Kelalavu. It wasn't that he had made good his promise to go. It was simply that he had seen Murugan when he and Mani had taken one of their long walks.

Although the autumn monsoon had retreated, an overnight burst of rain left puddles and mud that didn't dry in the weak winter sun. They folded their veshtis up above their knees as they walked through town and set out on the road leading to the rocky hills in the west. Clearing the last line of shops, they felt the breeze skip across the open fields. It was growing dark and there was no one about except customers at a stall just off the road. The fermented palm wine served in dented aluminium mugs wasn't strong, but a few mugs added up. Some men bought brandy and whisky, though what was in those Johnny Walker bottles was anyone's guess.

Murugan came towards them, swaying heavily from side to side on the narrow road. 'Oh, darling. I am the bee, for your honey flower!' He pushed out the phrases in a falsetto imitation of the latest film song, wheeling his arms around in a display of desperate passion. Just as Mani and Vijayan stepped aside to let him pass, he lurched in their direction and bounced off Mani, which propelled him down the road at greater speed. Mani didn't recognize him, but Vijayan hadn't forgotten his shrunken body and hollow cheeks.

As he got down from the bus at Kelalavu, Vijayan saw the high rocky hills at close quarters. All around Melur, hills rose in soft brown mounds, but here they jutted up as massive angular blocks piled one on top of the other. In the centuries before Christ, Jain monks had lived up there and left some of the earliest inscriptions in India. Vijayan once spent a whole day scrambling among the rocks searching for those caves and carved letters. Now he was wondering whom he could ask about them when, surrounded by a herd of bleating goats, he realized he was standing in the middle of the road.

He crossed the road towards the Untouchable colony. The village itself, visible beyond a screen of mango trees, had about sixty houses, while the colony consisted of two rows of semi-detached quarters facing each other across a strip of hard ground. The twenty square blocks had been built a decade ago, in the 1960s, when the government undertook a programme of Harijan uplift. Compared to the huts they replaced, the reinforced concrete blocks were a luxury.

Vijayan stood in the open ground between the two rows of identical dwellings wondering why he had come. He had no idea what he wanted to say. The colony was deserted anyway, since it was late morning and everyone was in the fields, trying to get the rice crop in before the Pongal festival.

Walking into the verandah, he called out. Inside the front room on the left he saw a metal frame chair, its seat of red and blue plastic strips sagging almost to the floor. A bicycle rested in a corner of the far wall, and in the opposite corner two reed mats lay rolled up on top of each other. Over his right shoulder, near the door, he noticed Velan's cotton bag hanging from a nail. He saw it was stained dark red. Why didn't Murugan take it to the police? he asked himself before he remembered the ink on the leaflets.

An old woman was sitting in the other front room. She wore a thin sari, faded to a dull maroon, no blouse and no jewellery. Her earlobes no longer held the chunky ornaments that had stretched them. A stick-thin arm waved a rattan fan above a small child lying on a rag in front of her. The fan moved back and forth but generated little air.

'Grandma, is Velan here?' She turned her head towards him, without moving her body or altering the rhythm of the fan. Her eyes were blank, and for a moment Vijayan wondered if she hadn't heard him or couldn't hear at all.

'Where's Velan?' he asked again, and this time she looked down at the child.

'I see. Where's Murugan?'

The bony hand holding the fan dropped into her lap. 'Over there,' she said, tilting her head.

Vijayan stepped across the hard dirt to the other row of

concrete blocks. He peered in through the wooden slats enclosing the verandah, pushing his nose into one of the diamond-shaped gaps in the lattice work. The house looked empty, so he rattled the cheap lock on the door and called Murugan's name, but there was no response.

It was getting hot and Vijayan was glad to find a bench under the tamarind tree near the tea-stall at the bus stop. Four or five small, weather-beaten cradles hung from its branches, put up by childless women hoping for a baby.

'Come from Melur?' asked the tea-stall man.

'Yes. I...have you seen Velan?'

'Him? Wish I did. Owes me a lot.'

'Not only you,' said another older man who had crossed the road from the colony. His clean but worn clothes hung loose on an erect body.

'Tell me about him,' Vijayan said and ordered a tea for him.

It was served in a small earthenware cup that would be thrown away because this man from the colony drank from it. Vijayan had been given a glass that would be washed and used again. He winced and was about to say something but bit his lip. It was still like this in villages, he knew, and it wasn't going to change in a day.

'He told us he'd get a well dug,' said the old man. 'Then we'd have our own water. We gave him 400 rupees. But there's no well. Said he spent it, paying for the plans and all.'

'Spent it on his little whore in Madurai, more like,' snorted the tea-stall man.

'Lots of us would like to tear a piece out of him,' said the other man.

'If he ever shows up,' added the tea-stall man.

Bumping along in a bus on his way back to Melur, Vijayan felt deflated. He had found nothing, only rancour and mistrust, and what was Velan to him anyway?

It was an old bus, with no glass in the windows, only pieces of canvas to roll down in case of rain or wind. Through the open windows, he could see the rocky hills again, with their rugged boulders and irregular outcroppings. Most of the sharp angles were blurred by blue-black shadows, while the hilltops held a pale golden light. Trying to visualize the ancient caves and inscriptions up there, Vijayan fell asleep.

3

When Velan's body was found five days later, there wasn't much left. It had lain under a low bridge, in an irrigation channel, about 200 metres from where his bicycle had been recovered. Hidden in this culvert, no one had seen the body during the day or thought much when the jackals howled at night. Only when the debris snagging on the skeletal remains slowed the flow of water did it attract attention. The police came and the corpse was taken to the government hospital in Madurai, where an autopsy noted severe lacerations on the head and upper body, probably caused by a heavy instrument.

In Kelalavu a week later, what remained of Velan was draped rather than dressed in white silk and laid on a charpoy outside his house. Then the funeral songs began. His widow and other female relatives linked arms behind their backs and shuffled around in a circle. Dipping their heads in towards the centre and then rearing back, they sang:

For you, oh husband, a young white bullock,
and a black horse runs wild.
For you, a mango tree grows by the river,
and fruit hangs from the branch.
For me, oh sister, the lightning strikes,
and thorns pierce my skin.
For me, the tree stands barren,
and the dry earth is cracked.

For an hour their thin bodies clung together, swaying and

circling, singing songs of loss. From their repertoire, they chose the phrases that seemed to describe Velan. Confident, committed and now dead. Death was terrible. And they didn't think about transcendence.

Soon a troupe of Paraiyar drummers and singers appeared from another village. The men played huge frame drums, which hung by a cord over the shoulder and reached the waist. Striking the buffalo skin with thin bamboo sticks, they pranced around and sprung into the air, off one leg and then the other, all the time keeping a steady beat.

Suddenly, as the frenzy peaked, the drummers stopped. Velan's relatives stepped up to the charpoy and dropped a few grains of cooked rice into the hole that had been his mouth.

The body was lifted on to a rattan bier and covered with marigold flowers. Led by the drummers and singers, and accompanied by male relatives, the corpse was carried to the burial ground outside the colony. At the edge of the scrubland, one of the singers delivered a formal speech, asking that the deceased be allowed to enter the world of the dead. Then Velan was lowered into the earth. Wood for a funeral pyre was too expensive.

Vijayan didn't go to the funeral—no one outside the Paraiyar community did—but Murugan had asked him to come to the hospital to help identify the body. When the sheet was drawn back, Vijayan didn't recognize the half-decomposed body. It had been cleaned up, but he couldn't look for more than a second. Although he had seen dead bodies before, dressed up for burial or cremation, this was not a corpse with a face, but a skeleton with a skull.

Identification was possible only from a thin brass ring on a bleached bone of the right hand. Murugan recognized the embossed pattern of leaves on the outside, a set of little ridges that Velan used to rub with the index finger and thumb of his left hand.

On the evening after the funeral, a group of men gathered as usual at the tea-stall beside the khadi shop. They sat on benches arranged around an oil drum with an iron grill on top and a wood fire roaring inside. Warmed by the heat radiating from the drum, they relaxed, conversing quietly but keeping a wary watch on the progress of their meal.

They knew each step of the sequence that would produce a flaky, layered pastry filled with potatoes or minced meat or topped with an egg. Suddenly the dough was flung high and talk ceased as their eyes followed the airborne disc. Only when it landed safely on an outstretched fist did the men exhale and resume talking.

'Did you hear? They found Velan's body.'

'Umm. In a culvert, near Kelalavu.'

'Not much left of him, they say.'

'Yeah, the body was cut up something awful.'

'Buried him yesterday.'

'So Velan's dead.' Dandapani's voice cut in like cold steel. 'That's no great loss. Probably one of his own CPM madmen did it.' He roared with laughter and two or three others followed suit.

From inside the shop, Vijayan heard their bellowing voices. He had tried to put Velan out of his mind, telling himself that it had nothing to do with him. But these words, coming from outside, broke through his defences.

He was murdered, he said to himself with a shudder, only an hour or so after talking with me.

Vijayan admired rather than liked Velan. He was one of the few people with whom he could debate issues on more or less equal terms. Although Vijayan had more information, Velan could cut to the quick; the more complicated the topic, the more Vijayan talked, only for Velan to tie it all up with a concise conclusion. That kind of confidence had impressed and unsettled him.

Probably killed for what he said and did, Vijayan reflected. With his elbows propped up on the wooden counter, he reached for the string trailing from the ball attached to the ceiling, wound it around his index finger, let it unwind and watched it sway back and forth. That's what's wrong with me, he thought, grabbing the string again. Never felt for anything strongly enough to act.

He was sitting there, string wound around his finger, when Muttusami returned and said it was time to shut up shop

The three friends walked north up the main road, Vijayan and Mani holding hands, Krishnan ambling beside them. It was the first Sunday of the month, when the Rationalist Society of Melur held its regular meeting. That was the intention, though it was more like every other month.

Outside the town, beyond the shops and small workshops, the road was lined with tamarind trees. Planted during the first years of Independence, they stood nearly 30 metres high, dense with knotted brown pods hanging from leafy branches. The commercial harvest would begin soon, but local people would get there first. Climb up the trunk, poke the branches with a long pole, throw stones, use a slingshot—they'd do anything to bring down the sour fruit.

Vijayan remembered climbing tamarind tress when he was a boy. Not here, but further south in the 'black soil' country where cotton grew. His ancestors were itinerant bangle sellers who had migrated from the river plains north of Madras to the Tamil-speaking area in the south. Just after the turn of the twentieth century, his grandfather settled down in Madurai and travelled all over the southern districts with his wooden cases of bangles.

Vijayan's father, only a boy at the time, often accompanied him on these trips, which lasted for weeks, even months. After his grandfather's death, his father set up a small jewellery shop in Virudhunagar, a town south of Madurai, in the heart of the black soil country.

That was where Vijayan was born—a dusty, sprawling place, more like a cattle town in the American West than a Tamil temple town amid paddy fields. And like a prairie town, it had sprouted up in the nineteenth century, except it wasn't cattle that led to its growth. When factories in England needed a new source of raw cotton, after its supply from the southern states of America had been cut off by the Civil War, the black soil district was the beneficiary. Cotton acreage doubled, then tripled and soon covered the entire region in order to meet the rising demand from overseas. The new crop turned a profit, middlemen arrived and the small town became a prosperous commercial hub.

Virudhunagar was still a traders' town. A large market and several warehouses near the bus stand formed the centre, beyond which sprawled a grid of residential streets, clean and wide with whitewashed houses. Vijayan's older sister lived in one of those houses.

He had two sisters. Meenakshi, the younger one, was born with a deformity of the legs and was married off at an early age. His older sister, Pushpa, was tall, almost stately, and practical, some said shrewd. After high school, she wanted to go to a teacher training school but settled for a Home Science certificate and got married to a cotton merchant in Virudhunagar. Now she had three children of her own.

Vijayan was unmarried, which at thirty-six was not unusual, but he rarely thought about it, which was. He didn't mind being alone and, like Raja, had little connection with his family. Although he visited his elder sister and her family in

Virudhunagar from time to time, sometimes to borrow money, there was little rapport between brother and sister. Neither knew where their younger sister was.

As a child, Vijayan used to go to the back of the shop and examine his grandfather's now abandoned bangle cases, marvelling at the gleaming circles of silver, gold and glass, each in a separate niche. When he was fourteen, his father took him out of school and put him to work in the shop. Two years later, after his father died, the business was taken over by a cousin from Madras, and his mother moved in with Pushpa and her family in a better part of Virudhunagar.

That was when Vijayan left home, half-educated, penniless and without a plan. Had he known what a 'writer' was, that would have been his ambition. Instead, he wandered from place to place, finding and leaving jobs, which is when he began to enjoy travelling by bus. For him, the sensation of moving without physical or mental effort was enhanced by passing through places and leaving them behind.

People in other castes, he knew, lived their whole lives within a few square miles, working the land, going to market and back to the same village. Unlike them, he didn't have a dense network of cousins and uncles. His ancestry of bangle-selling merchants, which he detested, had both spared him the Lilliputian bonds of kinship and prepared him for itinerancy, though he didn't realize this at the time.

He was working for a publisher when he got his older sister's telegram. As the only son, he would play a prominent role at his mother's funeral, though he hadn't even known she was ill. Arriving on an overnight bus, he reached the house just in time, and Pushpa ushered him into the front room, where their mother lay in a white sari under a bed of flowers. Two Brahmins chanted verses in Sanskrit. His brother-in-law, swathed in a gold-bordered silk veshti, glanced at him and frowned, crinkling the dried sandalwood and turmeric paste on his forehead.

At the cremation ground, he lifted his mother onto the criss-crossed stack of wood and walked around it several times, sprinkling the body with water. Just before he lit the kerosene soaked pyre, he was given a hammer and cracked open her skull, to release her soul.

Two days later, sitting on the edge of a bed, alone in his sister's house, he looked down at the coir matting and the tears rolled out. He didn't know if he had loved his mother—he hadn't loved anyone as far as he knew. He only knew he hadn't known her. How could he when they hardly talked about anything? But after the funeral he understood that he had loved her, and loved her more deeply than he had imagined was possible.

Each morning, she had dressed him for school. He stood as she buttoned his shirt and adjusted his satchel so that it rested in the centre of his back. When she had made sure the leather belt was buckled, she sent him off like a toy soldier. Walking down the street, to join other boys, he knew she was proud of him.

Later, he sensed that he confused and disappointed her. It wasn't that he was a failure, and she admired his intelligence. But he had no proper job, seldom came home and said things she didn't understand.

She didn't show her disapproval, but he knew. His sister made sure of that: 'Mother's angry with you. Can't you settle down? Why don't you ever come and see her?'

'At least she's got Pushpa,' Vijayan had consoled himself. 'And grandchildren, too.' But it was with her son that she felt a rapport. His dark brown eyes drew her close in a way that Pushpa's straight lines and sharp edges never did.

One day he remembered well. They were alone in the late afternoon, on the back verandah of the old mud house. She was grating a knob of ginger on a sharp-edged, curved knife stuck into a block of wood, and he was looking at his schoolbook.

'Amma, want to hear the best poem? I learned it this morning,' he said.

'Yes. Let me hear it.'

You are my light, I am your vision.
You are my harmony, I am your music.
You are my love, I am your heart.
You are my scripture, I am your knowledge.

Her head was bent forward, pushing against the blade, as she listened. Although they never spoke about it, then or later, this inarticulate sharing held them together, no matter where he went.

After his mother's funeral, Vijayan left Virudhunagar and went back to Madras, but he didn't last long at the publisher's office, or in any job where he took orders from men he considered his intellectual inferiors. He felt at home only when working in the New Century Book House in Madurai. Behind its large glass front sat piles of Tamil, English and Hindi translations of Russian classics, plus various dictionaries and other reference books. The modern shop in the city centre attracted a mixed clientele with whom he could be himself and express opinions that didn't prompt thin smiles of indulgence.

Those two years in Madurai, in his early twenties, changed Vijayan. Reading Gorky's *The Mother* in Tamil translation overwhelmed him as he lived with the characters during the monsoon rains. That's when he decided he would try to be a writer. At the same time, he became involved with the Self-Respect Movement. Political rallies were nothing unusual in that populous, bustling city, but one made him stop and stare.

Hundreds at the front of the gathering wore black shirts instead of the white cotton or saffron veshtis that were meant to cloak these events in purity. On the temporary outdoor stage stood a tall man, with large round glasses and a cane. Even from a distance, Vijayan recognized him as Periyar, with his high forehead and half-bald crown shining under the lights. His expansive face was encircled by fluffy white hair, as if he had stuck his head through a pillow.

Vijayan stood at the back for more than three hours and listened to the stream of phrases flow without interruption. He didn't remember much except that he was mentally exhausted, trying to fit causes to conditions and follow the logic of proposed solutions. But he did remember one thing.

The speaker seemed to have concluded his speech when he let his outstretched hand with raised index finger fall to his side. But as Vijayan turned to leave, he heard the old man roar:

'There is no god. He who invented god is a fool. He who propagates god is a scoundrel. He who worships god is a barbarian.'

The audacity of the statement turned Vijayan inside out, and he kept repeating its rhythmic phrases in his head. 'There is no... He who...' It reassured him that he hadn't been wrong, all along.

He began to read Periyar's books and later met him face-to-face in the railway station rest house, when the old man explained that 'caste' was a mind-forged manacle. That was the final piece of a puzzle Vijayan had been trying to fit together. From then on, he felt he understood the empty eyes and bent bodies around him. Understood, yet felt powerless to alter anything.

Ten years later, he swallowed his pride and let his sister's husband find him a permanent job. Selvan's uncle had a relative who knew the head of the government organization that oversaw the khadi industry. That was six years ago, and he was still in Melur, frustration feeding the self-reproach that surfaced in his scowling face.

Vijayan was thinking about those years in Madurai as he,

Mani and Krishnan walked to the Rationalist Society meeting. Each of them wore a freshly laundered veshti and shirt or jiba, with a fountain pen clipped in the breast pocket. Krishnan, the shortest of the three, carried the small brown leather briefcase that he took to his job at the bank. The cotton bag slung over Mani's shoulder held notebook, beedis and matches. Vijayan's handwritten notes were stuffed into a pamphlet carried in his right hand, swinging loose at his side.

The tarmac road leading north out of Melur had wide verges, where the tamarind trees stood, so they walked side-by-side. Keeping in step, they spoke quietly, despite the occasional rumbling lorry or bus. The damp, sweet smell of freshly-cut wood told them they were close. Passing the sawmill, Krishnan glanced at his watch and said they were on time, only ten minutes after the scheduled time of 3 p.m. Turning off the road and through the wall-less gate of the Government Basic Training School, they saw students playing volleyball and lounging on verandahs.

Numbers for the meetings varied. Vijayan, Mani and Krishnan were the self-appointed officers of the unregistered society, and they could count on about ten others to attend. One of the regulars was Chellappan, who was standing on the steps to the single-storey building where the meeting was to take place. Seeing the three friends enter the compound, he held his palms together high above his head.

'Thinks we're swamis,' mocked Vijayan under his breath, and the others pretended not to hear.

Chellappan was a teacher, in a primary school about 12 miles west of Melur. He liked to read the Tamil classics and fancied himself an expert on a fifth-century collection of maxims. The ancient author had been the darling of English missionary-scholars in the nineteenth century, as well as Tamil nationalists in the twentieth century, because he was not a Brahmin and his aphorisms hinted at shortcomings of the caste system. After Independence, the saintly sage became an icon of Tamil identity. No classroom in the land, no matter how humble, no public speech, no matter what the topic, could escape his words of wisdom.

Chellappan had memorized most of the more than one thousand couplets and had several ready for every occasion. His underfed students, clutching their slates and chalk, might not have been averse to hearing their master intone his favourite verses as they dozed through a lesson. Members of the Rationalist Society were less obliging, though it was a rare meeting when he could resist declaiming the poet's best-known maxim: 'The world is my home and everyone is my family.' Admirable, and occasionally apt, but they had heard it too often

The three men swept past the little teacher, who followed in their slipstream. After Vijayan fished the key out from the side pocket of his jiba and opened the formidable lock, they entered the classroom. It was empty except for a desk on a small dais and a blackboard at the far end. Pale green paint was peeling off the concrete walls and the shuttered windows, which looked out on the compound. Sitting down on the concrete floor, each man began to prepare for the meeting.

Soon another of the regulars arrived. Kantan was a big man, with a square face, broad shoulders and barrel chest. 'Vanakkam! Hello friends!' he called out in his hearty voice. Although he was only in his forties, he laughed with the wheeze of an old man and had silver-grey hair. Kantan was a small landowner with seven acres of sugarcane and paddy in a village north of Melur. While still a young boy he had been put to work in those fields, which he later inherited from his father. Now he worked the land himself, hiring others only during the harvests.

He joined the CPM at the time of the notorious killing of

seventeen agricultural workers in a wage dispute. Since then he had worked with Velan, organizing demonstrations and holding meetings, as well as lending him money from time to time.

Kantan read little, except political pamphlets, but he liked these Sunday meetings. Among the Rationalist Society members, only he knew what agricultural labour was like, especially in the sugar cane fields—chopping down the thick stalks, avoiding their sharp serrated leaves and hauling heavy loads to the sugar press.

By 3:30 about fifteen men were sitting in the room. The meetings were open to everyone, but most were from low and middle castes—Kallars, Tevars, Mudaliyars, Naickers—no Untouchables, and Krishnan the only Brahmin.

Vijayan opened the meeting, speaking in semi-formal Tamil, coupling phrases together with an extra syllable and elevating his vocabulary.

'This afternoon we are convened for the thirty-first meeting of the Melur Rationalist Society. As usual, we will hear a short lecture, followed by a discussion, which is open to everyone and which is intended to provide an opportunity for us to explore ideas that will lead to a correct understanding as well as improvement of our Tamil society.'

Some of the younger men lit Gold Flake cigarettes, while others, including Mani, puffed on beedis. Only one, an older man, began to prepare betel nut. Opening a container the size of a sardine tin, he selected a small leaf, placed it in the palm of his left hand and smoothed it out with the thumb of his right. After several firm applications had flattened the ribs of the leaf, he looked up and heard Vijayan continue.

'Today's presentation will be made by me. My topic is "The Revolutionary Poetry of Subramania Bharati." I shall begin by reading two of his poems, followed by my own commentary on them and then we shall begin the discussion.'

The old man smiled to himself. Unlike others in the room, he had been a young man when Bharati wrote the poems that electrified the Tamil literary world and made him famous throughout India.

Although A.K. Perumal Tevar was in his seventies, his frame was firm and his mind alert. Poet, pamphleteer and provincial scholar, he had a large collection of palm-leaf manuscripts, some of which he had written himself. As a boy, he had learned to cut the stiff palmyra leaves to a prescribed length, let them dry for a day or two and then polish the surface by rubbing it back and forth against the bottom of his foot. Mastering the shorthand script adapted for inscribing palm leaves was more difficult, but he soon learned to press the tip of a long nail on the softened surface with just the right force and guide it along with his thumb. Now he was one of only a handful of men who could produce these palm-leaf manuscripts.

As Vijayan began to read the first poem, Perumal Tevar dug some lime paste out of his tin container and spread it on the flattened betel leaf. Then taking his knife out of the waist-fold of his veshti, he cut thin shavings off an areca nut and watched them drop onto the leaf. Finally, he folded the leaf, tossed it in his mouth and began to chew.

Halfway through Vijayan's recital of the second poem, the old man stood up and walked to the open window. Pressing two fingers against his parted lips, he formed a narrow aperture through which he propelled a dark red stream of juice out the window and on to the ground below.

'In my opinion,' Vijayan said in conclusion, 'the key line is "the rain ran red on the soil". Given the historical situation of the poem's composition in 1917, I would suggest that this image is a direct reference to the revolution in Russia and, furthermore, that it conveys the poet's hope that such an upheaval would usher in a new and more equal society, not just in the far away land where it took place but also in India and in our Tamil land.'

'Yes, yes,' enthused Krishnan.

'Very likely,' conceded Mani, raising his right hand and turning it palm upward. 'However, we must also consider the words themselves, not just the events surrounding them.'

'Go on,' said Vijayan, grudgingly.

'Well, the phrase "rain ran red" has internal rhyme as well as a rhythm that moves the poem forward, like a river flowing towards...'

'Social unity, of workers and peasants,' Kantan burst out and looked around at everyone with a tentative smile.

'Towards the sea, actually,' continued Mani in a low voice.

'Might I also suggest that the line is not entirely original with this poet?' Chellappan's chirpy schoolmaster voice rose above the others. 'Indeed, it derives, I would argue, from the much earlier...' A groan broke out to protest against yet another recitation from the *Tirukkural*. Undaunted, Chellappan soldiered on but paraphrased rather than quoted. 'There's a maxim,' he said, 'in which rain is said to be a raja's gift to his people.'

'Yes. There are earlier references to rain, possibly hundreds of them in Tamil literature,' Vijayan agreed, pre-empting another unscheduled lecture by Chellappan. 'But the question I am asking is, what did this poem, written in 1917, mean to the poet at the time? Its revolutionary meaning is undeniable. Despite the reactionary society Bharati grew up in, and despite his marriage at fourteen to a seven-year-old cousin, he had a radical vision for the future.'

No one responded directly to this pronouncement, although many turned to their neighbours and commented in lowered voices. Then a new voice rose above the murmur and addressed the whole group.

'This image of rain running red on the soil has another

meaning,' said Perumal Tevar. 'A meaning that includes the others you've mentioned, the sea, social unity and even revolution.'

Moistening lips already stained purple from betel nut juice, he recited a poem from nearly two thousand years ago:

What could my mother be to yours?
What kin is my father
to yours anyway?
And how did you and I ever meet?
But in love,
our hearts have mingled
As red earth and pouring rain.

'That's what this poem refers to. Mixing and combining, in love and in life, so completely that differences disappear.'

There was a collective intake of breath before heads began to wag in affirmation and voices rang out: 'That's right!' 'Well said!' Vijayan joined in and declared the meeting closed.

Conversation among the men bubbled and eddied into small pools. Pretending to listen to Krishnan prattle on about monsoon rains, Mani eyed the old man.

A.K. Perumal Tevar wore no shirt or sandals, only a veshti held up by a thick leather belt and a towel over the shoulder. His mahogany body seemed lit up by the white hair on his head, eyebrows, moustache and bare chest. Small brass rings gleamed in his earlobes, and a thick wooden umbrella lay like a weapon on the ground beside him.

Although the old man came to most meetings, Vijayan and his friends knew little about him. Even his name puzzled them. They knew that 'A' referred to his native village and 'K' to his father's name. But they also knew that Tevars were a low caste that was not supposed to use 'Perumal' or any of Vishnu's names. What they didn't know, however, was that he had taken the name

'Perumal' in defiance of that taboo and that his family had then disowned him.

After wandering for a year, he attached himself to a poet-scholar at the court of a minor raja, and under his tutelage, during the 1920s and 30s, he absorbed the tradition of Tamil classical literature. After Independence, he had settled in Melur, where he rented a room and put up a sign: 'A.K. Perumal Tevar. Poet, scholar, editor. Tuition available.' Mani had often looked at that sign and wondered who this modest polymath might be.

Everyone at the meeting stood up and prepared to leave. Perumal Tevar lodged his umbrella in the crook of his elbow and, since the temperature had dropped, wrapped his towel around his head. Mani watched him walk out to the main road and march towards Melur with long strides, the umbrella's black cloth flapping around his legs like bats.

Mani fell in with Vijayan and Krishnan as they gathered to walk back along the same route. When Kantan joined them, Vijayan turned and asked the gregarious farmer why he hadn't said much in the meeting.

'Well, while you were discussing that line…about the rain and earth…'

'You mentioned something about unity,' Krishnan prompted him.

'I did, but then, well, I thought of him. Velan.'

'Velan? Why him?' Mani asked in a casual voice.

'You see. It was the rain.' Kantan's normally hearty voice wavered as he spoke. 'Remember, it rained the night he…was killed. So I saw him. In my mind's eye.'

Vijayan could see him, too. They had all heard about the death, but he had been with Velan just before that savage attack. He saw him in the shop that evening, leaning over the counter, his wiry body bristling with energy and his black slab of a moustache rising and falling as he spoke.

And he had seen his battered body in the morgue. It must have been a heavy machete, they said. Not the short sickle used in the paddy fields, but the two-foot-long one with a broad blade for cutting wood. As Vijayan tried to push the image of Velan's body from his mind, it merged with those of red earth and rain in the poems, the ancient one about love and the modern one about revolution.

4

When Vijayan awoke, Mani and Krishnan had already pulled a comb through their hair and were collecting towels, soap, toothbrushes and powder. Raja was still asleep in a corner.

'Coming?' asked Mani as he slipped into his leather sandals and stood with Krishnan at the top of the outside stairs that led down to the street.

'Go on. I'll catch up later,' said Vijayan, prone on his mat.

After they left, he pulled himself up and sat cross-legged for a moment. He was about to flop down again when his eye fell on a magazine beside Raja. *Stars and Screen* had the latest gossip about film stars with dozens of colour photos. Vijayan crept over and picked it up. While he sat there turning the pages, Raja opened one eye.

'Anything good?' he asked, to tease Vijayan.

'Huh? No. I…,' Vijayan said and handed it back.

Raja smiled but turned his head so Vijayan wouldn't see. 'Do you like films?' he asked.

'Yes, a lot. But…'

'Then let's see one, in Madurai. You can pay. I'll let you.'

'Right. And I'll let you pick the film. Any film at all. But it has to star Shivaji.'

'Him? He's old enough to be my grandfather.'

Raja slid back down on his mat, pressing his face against a make-shift pillow, and mumbled something else.

'What's that?' asked Vijayan.

'I said someone came here last night asking for you. When

you and Mani were out walking.'

'Who?'

'Don't know. Seemed funny, though.'

Vijayan suspected it was one of his sister's spies. Cousins and uncles seemed to turn up at regular intervals. 'Just passing through Melur and thought I'd say hello' was what they said, but he knew they were sent by Pushpa to check up on her wayward brother. Was he dressed properly? Any problems at the shop?

He didn't resent them. It was his sister who angered him. You'd think she would've had her hands full with three children and a husband who ate enough to keep a kitchen staff busy from morning to night.

But Pushpa liked to hover about and straighten out problems others didn't even know existed. Although she complained that she was 'run off her feet,' that was how she liked it. Bustling around, she felt she was in control, beating back the bushfires of unpredictability.

The man waiting at the shop that morning, however, did not look like one of her spies. Arriving late, Vijayan stood on the step for a second and studied him. He was perched on one of the high stools, his right foot secure on the support bar, his left dangling with toes just brushing the floor. He was talking to Muttusami but kept swivelling his head towards the door.

'Are you Vijayan?' he asked as he stood up.

'Umm,' Vijayan grunted and walked past him, lifted the panel and moved to the far end of the counter.

The man slid off the stool and followed on the other side of the counter. Lowering his voice, he said, 'I think you know P.S. Velan.'

Vijayan had begun to arrange clothes in one of the tall glass-fronted cabinets. Turning around slowly, he looked at the man. Trousers and a dark blue polyester shirt, thin lips, no facial hair, a high forehead and thick glasses.

When Vijayan didn't respond, he continued, 'I know he's dead.'

'So why come here?'

'He said you were his friend.'

'I see. So who are you?'

'I'm also his friend. My name's Pandian, from Madras. Velan and I worked together.'

'CPM?'

'No, not exactly.'

'What then?'

He adjusted his black-rimmed glasses, pushing the bridge back up his nose and said, 'Let's just say we had common interests.'

Vijayan remained silent and he elaborated. 'We shared a desire to improve the condition of the ordinary men and women in our Tamil society.'

'What do you want from me?'

'Velan spoke highly of you.'

'Me?'

'Yes. He said you were intelligent, a good writer. And intelligent writers are very useful.'

'"Useful"? Excuse me, but I'm busy.'

'Yes, of course. Perhaps we could talk somewhere…'

Vijayan stiffened. 'No. I don't think so.'

'Look,' the man said leaning across the counter, 'if you'll only…'

'I'm not interested.'

'Right. Sorry for intruding. Here's my card. If you ever come to Madras, please come and see me.'

Vijayan took the stiff card and put it in his shirt pocket. As soon as the visitor left, he took it out and read the small black type, Tamil on one side and English on the other:

Mr S.K. Pandian, M.Sc.
Universal Life Assurance
144 Mount Road Near Gemini Theatre
Madras Tel. 46389

He put it back in his pocket and played with the string hanging from the ceiling, winding and unwinding it around his finger.

'Who was that?' asked Muttusami without looking up from his sprawled ledger but failing to hide his curiosity.

Muttusami regarded his assistant with a mixture of incomprehension and respect. Not as punctual as he would have liked. Not exactly lazy, but not what he'd call dedicated either. Of course, he's a writer, Muttusami told himself. Can't expect him to be completely normal. Besides, he's honest and courteous. But moody, almost angry.

'Oh, a friend, from Madras,' Vijayan answered.

'He was here, waiting, when I arrived. At 9:30,' Muttusami said, emphasizing the time. 'Asked about Velan, and then you.' To himself he added, and he didn't appear to know you, let alone be a friend.

'Did he?'

Muttusami raised his head and looked towards the far end of the counter. Working with Vijayan for the past six years had been an experience. It was the first time he had got to know someone so different from him and know him well enough to care about the difference. Vijayan wasn't unusual like the Malayalis or Bengalis, with their strange hairstyles and clothes, or like the other outsiders who came through Melur on their pilgrimage to the sea at Kanyakumari.

He speaks and dresses like everyone else, Muttusami reminded himself. But he doesn't fit in. Except those few friends. Muttusami bent his head back down to the ledger. A minute later he raised it again. Yes, that is strange. He never talks about his family.

Vijayan ate his midday meal of rice and vegetable curry at the usual place. When he had finished, he folded his banana leaf and carried it between pinched fingers to the back of the shop, where he saw Trotsky in the lane. Calling its name, he tossed his leaf outside the trough so the dog could get at it easily. He watched it finish his leaf before returning to those it had already dragged out of the trough.

Today there was no scavenger to compete with, so the dog took its time selecting which leaves were worthy of attention. Trotsky poked its black-and-white spotted nose between the folded halves, pushing until the leaf fell open, sniffed at the offering and then made a decision to eat it or not. Although the supply of leaves seemed endless, the animal was always hungry. Vijayan counted the ribs showing through its hairless skin. Six of them, bowed and thin, similar to Velan's, only smaller.

Back at the shop, friends and customers were chatting away when a white Ambassador car glided by, windows curtained, horn blaring, flag fluttering.

'Looks like...what's his name...the minister for family planning, on his way to that conference in Madurai,' said Kantan, who was sitting idly on one of the tall stools. 'Probably got a carload of radios in there.'

Everyone knew about the government scheme to encourage vasectomies by giving a transistor radio to men who volunteered for the operation. Newspaper reports claimed that gangs were 'dragooning innocent young men', taking them to the clinics by the taxi-full and giving them ten rupees for the radio that they would sell for 250.

'My brother got a radio last month,' offered another man in the shop.

'Pretty soon your whole village is going to be full of eunuchs listening to the news,' said another and everyone laughed.

That evening Vijayan went back to Kelalavu to see Murugan and ask him about Velan. Through the open window, he saw those high rugged hills, their tops gathering a sand-yellow light and the rest lying in purple-black shadows. He passed the spot where Velan's bicycle had been found lying beside the road, just the black cycle with his bag of leaflets. He didn't know which culvert the body had been in. He could find out but didn't want to.

The sun was gone when he got down from the bus. Walking to the tea-stall, he asked the owner if he had seen Murugan.

'He's there. In the colony.'

'Right,' Vijayan said and started to cross the road.

'You asked about Velan before, didn't you?'

'Yes.'

'Well, I remembered something.'

Vijayan came back. In the darkness, the man's face was half-lit from below by a gas lantern hanging from a corner of the stall. His sharp cheek bones formed a diamond shape.

'Before he died…' the man began.

'How long before?'

'I don't know. Maybe a week.'

'Right. What happened?'

'A man used to come and sit, on the bench here. Two or three hours every day, drinking tea, smoking, reading papers.'

'Is that all?'

'I'm coming to that. He came five or six days in a row. In the morning one day, evening or afternoon the next. Like that.'

'I see.'

'On the first day he asked about Velan. Wanted to know if he lived here. In the colony, I told him. But he didn't go find him. Just sat here.'

'Okay.'

'And another thing. He talked funny.'

'Like what?'

'Hard to say. Just sounded different.'

'Probably from Madras, where they speak mixed-up Tamil.'

'No. I know what that sounds like. He spoke something else. Like...like...I don't know.'

'Right. He came several days in a row. Then what?'

'Didn't come back. Next day, or maybe the next, Velan disappeared and...you know.'

Vijayan looked at the man for a moment, said nothing and turned again to cross the road towards the colony.

'Wait. There's something else.'

'What?'

'His leg.'

'Leg?'

'Couldn't tell when he was sitting. But when he got up, you could.'

'Could what?

'See that he dragged it. The left one I think.'

Heading for Murugan's house, Vijayan wondered who this man could be. Pandian was his first thought, but he spoke Madras Tamil and this stranger spoke something else. Besides, he didn't remember him with a limp.

Murugan was sitting on his front step with his arm around a young boy. Murugan didn't recognize him in the pitch blackness, so Vijayan spoke first.

'How are you? All right?'

'Oh, it's you. Welcome.' Murugan threw his palms together in front of his eyes and gestured to his guest to sit beside him. He had been drinking, but his words were clear enough.

'Get some palm-wine for uncle,' he said and released the boy. 'And more for me.'

Then to Vijayan, 'What's up? It's late.'

Vijayan hesitated, not sure what to tell him, how much to reveal.

'Ah…I met someone who knew Velan, from Madras.'

'Yes. He went to Madras. "On business" he said.' Murugan pushed out the words, his cheeks inflating and deflating.

'CPM work?'

'I guess so. He went there a lot, before he died. Maybe once a month, near the end.'

'Did he ever mention a man named Pandian?'

'Pandian? Don't think so.'

'When did he last go to Madras?'

'Not sure. A month ago, I think.'

'Did you notice any strangers around here then?'

'Strangers? Who's a stranger here?' said Murugan with a laugh that turned into a cough.

The boy emerged from the house, where Vijayan could hear Velan's widow and her children moving about. Taking the mug of palm-wine, he continued, 'No strangers at the bus stop?'

'People go to the village. Not the colony.'

'So nothing unusual happened?'

'Don't remember.' Murugan's speech was starting to slur. 'But something happened, after he disappeared.'

'What's that?' Vijayan asked with flutter in his voice that made Murugan turn toward him.

Neither could see the other's face as they sat side by side on the step looking straight ahead into a darkness broken only by uneven rectangles of light suspended in the houses opposite.

'A letter came, for Velan. About two weeks after he died.'

'So?'

'Not much of a letter. More like a telegram.'

'From whom?'

'That's just it. No name.'

'Can I see it?'

Murugan went inside and came back with a thin blue sheet folded so that the address was written on the outside and the message on the inside. There was no separate envelope.

'Why didn't you mention this before?' asked Vijayan, looking at the letter. Turning it over, he saw the Madras postmark.

'Didn't open it at first. Didn't think it mattered. Just put it away. With his things. The police came. Asked questions. I didn't say anything.'

'When did you open it?'

'My sister moved in with us. After the funeral. "We should help the police", she said. Tell them everything. I didn't. But I opened the letter. I can't read. But I saw. There's no name.'

In the funnel of yellow light from a torch Murugan held, Vijayan read the brief message written in formal Tamil:

> *This confirms our plan. You will arrive in Colombo on the date agreed and meet us at the agreed time and place.*

'Did Velan ever go to Ceylon?' asked Vijayan.

'Don't think so.'

'Never?'

'Never.'

'Anyone in your family ever go there? Or work there?'

'No. Why?'

'The letter says Velan was going to Colombo to meet someone.'

'Meet who?'

'I don't know. It doesn't say.'

The two men turned towards each other in the darkness. Muffled voices floated out of nearby houses, and the wheels of a bullock cart creaked on the tarmac road.

Vijayan could hear his own thoughts. Why would Velan go to Ceylon? What's this got to do with his death? Confusion hardened into irritation as he asked himself why he had got involved in the first place. He held out the letter.

'No,' Murugan said, with unusual firmness. 'I can't do anything.

Keep it. Find out who killed him.'

5

Vijayan viewed the five-hour bus journey with mixed emotions. He liked travelling to the far south—he was taking a consignment to the khadi shop in Nagercoil— but he would have to get off and visit his sister either now or on the return journey. If anyone saw him pass through Virudhunagar without stopping, the news would reach Pushpa. He might not be seen, of course, but he would never hear the end of it if he were spotted. Besides, he liked his nephew, the oldest of Pushpa's three children. In the end, he decided to delay the inevitable and stop on the way back to Melur.

His bench had only one other passenger, so he leant against the window, let his body slide down and closed his eyes. But he couldn't sleep. Each bench had two detachable seat cushions covered with a dark green vinyl, stuffed with cotton and backed with cardboard. The cushion under Vijayan didn't fit in its space, so when he shifted his weight, it popped out and left him sitting on the exposed edge of the metal frame.

After Madurai, the landscape changed. Swaying ribbons of paddy gave way to regular rows of bushy cotton plants and then to slender palmyras with their stiff spiky leaves.

As the bus cruised south on the smooth road, Vijayan watched the mountains on his right move closer and the land in front of him funnel down. By the time the bus snaked along a winding street into Nagercoil, everything seemed to slow down in the haze that gathered at the tail end of a day, when heat rising from the earth mixed with dust in the slanting light.

Vijayan slept late, delivered the consignment by noon and went to the bus station. He saw a driver shovel cooked rice into an old hub-cap and coax a small dog to eat. Then his bus pulled in and he joined the crowd ready to board it.

'You've got to buy another ticket!' the driver bellowed at someone.

'But we're only two,' a gypsy man protested, waving towards his wife.

'You need a ticket for that,' insisted the driver, pointing to the wooden birdcage in the man's hand.

'For the parrot?' asked the gypsy.

'Yes. Give me another two-fifty or you don't get on this bus.'

Whether from impatience or sympathy, the crowd began to shout at the driver, 'Let 'em on! They're only two!' A minute later they forced their way on, everyone found a seat and the bus slid away.

The gypsy woman in a calf-length embroidered skirt and half-blouse perched among women in saris, who tolerated her like a leper. The man, who wore a lungi and a scarlet turban, sat next to Vijayan. Placing the parrot cage under his feet, he adjusted the creased leather bag hanging over his bare shoulder so that it rested in his lap.

Vijayan was curious, but managed to wait for ten long minutes before asking him where he was going.

'Muppandal,' the man answered.

Another five minutes passed.

'What's in your bag?'

'In there? All sorts of things. For my work.'

'What sorts of things?'

'Tell you what. Put your hand in and see what you find.'

The man angled his bag toward Vijayan, who slid his right hand under the flap and pushed it down. He dug inside, brushing by several small objects, before landing on a smooth, round surface. Looking up at the man, who showed no expression, he lifted his hand out. It held a small skull.

'Well done! Best thing in there,' said the gypsy.

'What is it?' asked Vijayan, turning the whitened object around in his hand.

'A fox skull. The most intelligent animal, the *nari*. That's why we're called Nari Kuravars.'

'How'd you get it?'

'Oh, this one I shot myself. But look closely. See anything?'

'No.' Vijayan felt ridiculous holding the skull and handed it back to the man.

'Maybe you wouldn't notice. But it's missing its two horns on top. That's where the brains are. I filed them off and kept them.'

'Kept them?'

'Yes. Pounded them and put the powder into this,' he said, fingering the small aluminium cylinder that hung from a short black cord around his neck. 'It's good luck. Want one?'

'Ah. An amulet...with fox brains?' Vijayan stammered, unsure where this was leading. 'No, I mean not now.'

'Only 25 rupees. And it's good luck.'

'Oh, no! I don't have that much,' said Vijayan, relieved.

'All right, 15,' said the gypsy as he took a small cylinder from his bag and put it in Vijayan's hand. Vijayan gave him a ten-rupee note and dropped the amulet into his breast pocket. That skull's too small for a fox, he thought later. Probably a cat or something.

On the way to his sister's house in Virudhunagar, Vijayan walked through the main bazaar to the residential area where single-storey terraced houses lined broad streets. As Vijayan turned on to one of those streets, an elephant led by a trainer ambled along and dropped large clumps of dung with bits of straw in it. Two pedestrians went out of their way and stepped into the moist, sweet-smelling mounds to clean their feet. Some of the houses were decorated with vertical red stripes, like candy cane, and most had a verandah enclosed with wooden lattice-work. Open sewers ran along both sides but at a depth to maintain hygiene. Three concrete steps bridged the sewer and led to each verandah, forming a row of little white arches all along the street.

'Anyone home?' he called out, walking inside and placing his bag down beside a wicker chair.

Pushpa came out from the kitchen. Her hair had been freshly oiled, parted down the middle and plaited in a single braid that hung down to the small of her back. Although not pretty, she was an attractive woman, tall with a proud bearing. The severity of her straight nose, heavy eyebrows and unyielding eyes was relieved only by full lips. She wore a lemon-yellow polyester sari with a blue diamond pattern and a white choli. A fan-shaped gold nosepin sparkled on each nostril, and two or three silver bangles jingled on her wrists.

'Oh, it's you! When did you arrive?' she smiled at her younger brother, whom she hadn't seen for months. She came forward, fingering the thali hanging around her neck, but none of her limbs appeared to move.

'Just got off the bus, from Nagercoil. Back to Melur tomorrow.'

'That's fine. Come and have something to eat. The children are at school, and he's at the office.' She never called her husband by name.

Vijayan sat cross-legged on the kitchen floor and leant back against the wall while Pushpa arranged three cold idlis in a stainless steel plate with a raised edge, like a shallow pie pan, and ladled warm sambar on top.

'I'll cook some rice, too, and then you can take a nap,' she said, placing the plate in front of Vijayan. 'How's everything in

Melur? Shop all right?' she asked while Vijayan ate.

Don't trust your spies, do you? was what he wanted to say. But between mouthfuls he replied, 'Everything's the same. Nothing ever happens in Melur.' Pushpa was the last person he was going to confide in about Velan.

Yes, and you don't change either, she thought. Still the same old misfit. To him she said, 'The children will be excited to see you, especially Arun.'

Arun, her oldest, was twelve. He would have had three sisters if her first-born had survived. The baby's death, at four months, had thrown Pushpa into a deep depression and she refused her husband for three years. When Arun was born, she treasured him even more than a first-born son. He had saved her. That's what she told herself.

Then the two girls came. Vanni was a gangly girl of ten with buck teeth, who moped about and showed little initiative at home or school. Kalyani, the clever younger sister, was just seven but had more confidence and better features. All the family's hopes, however, were pinned on Arun, a bright boy who was mature for his years. He stood about half his father's height, but erect and always with a pen in his pocket.

As Vijayan listened to her describe the children's latest achievements, deficiencies and illnesses, he remembered Velan's letter, the stranger in Kelalavu and Pandian. When the rice was cooked, he ate a large plate with more sambar and then fell asleep on the cot in the room opposite the kitchen.

The house had been built in the 1930s. The kitchen, which led outside to a half-enclosed bathing and washing area, was where the family ate. Across the hallway from the kitchen was the small, windowless room where Vijayan stayed. Further down the narrow hallway two bedrooms faced each other, one for Pushpa and her husband, the other for their children. But the centre of the house was the spacious front room, where they gathered in the evening.

Awakened by sounds of children shuffling around in the kitchen, Vijayan got up, patted the wispy hair on his balding crown, slipped his shirt on over his vest and tightened his creased veshti around his waist.

'Uncle! When did you come?' called Arun and Kalyani in unison, while Vanni watched. Five minutes later, when they were all in the front room, Vanni handed Vijayan a small porcelain cup of milk coffee and a plate with crispy snacks. Then she backed away, with her toothy grin and stooping posture.

Pushpa sized up the situation. 'Arun needs a new satchel. Go out and get him one, all right?' she said to Vijayan, not trying to disguise her command as a request.

Taking the ten-rupee note she handed him, Vijayan led Arun out the front door and down the street. It was dusk, when the paraffin lanterns on handcarts and stalls suffused the air with murky amber light. Soft-edged figures gaped at shop windows, surrounded pavement sellers and stood in faceless groups, while others moved in packs that surged one way, then another, split apart and dispersed.

Arun stared through the window at the statuesque ladies draped in expensive saris. While he knew they were fake, the symmetrical lines and perfect smiles fascinated him. Vijayan stopped in front of a display of watches twinkling behind glass. He'd never had one, but he liked the way they looked on a man's wrist.

They walked on, bumping into people and dodging horse-drawn jutkas, bicycles and rickshaws. Just as a bullock cart carved its way through the throng, Arun stumbled and reached out for his uncle's arm but fell forward and hit the ground. Vijayan gave a cry, pushed people aside and hauled him up. Carrying him to the side of the road, he inspected the scrape on his knee.

'Does it hurt?'

'No,' said Arun through tightened lips.

'Good. Now let's find you a satchel,' he said and put his arm around the boy's shoulders.

His quick response, after a moment of panic, had surprised Vijayan. He couldn't remember another time when he had helped someone in danger, even if this wasn't serious. He looked down at Arun, who was again eagerly scanning the shop windows. He's my nephew, I guess that's why, Vijayan said to himself. But this explanation unsettled him.

They found a shop with satchels and studied the different types hanging from hooks. Leather, plastic, canvas and cloth; heavy buckles and straps; a variety of pockets and zips. Most had a picture printed on the front. An open-petalled lotus, Gandhi at his spinning wheel, Ganesa, an airplane titled at an angle, Nehru's face superimposed on a map of India, a film star with fez and sunglasses. Arun chose one with a temple tower.

'Why'd you choose that?' asked Vijayan.

'Mother says temples bring good luck. Living near one or walking by one is good. And now I'll have one on my back,' he said, with a little grin.

'Right, but you know...' Vijayan started and then checked himself.

'What, *mama*?' Arun asked, looking up at him.

'Oh, nothing. Just take good care of the satchel. That'll please your mother.'

Vijayan reached into his shirt pocket and took out the gypsy's amulet. Clasping it in his hand, he considered giving it to Arun but decided against it. His mother would never let him wear it. Too crude. He opened his hand and let it drop to the ground, where it was trampled underfoot and split so that the fox skull powder mingled with the dust.

Vijayan left for Melur the following evening. It was dark in the bus and he felt drowsy. Not a bad visit, he summed up to himself, except for his heavy-jawed brother-in-law, Selvan. They had nothing in common and neither attempted to pretend otherwise. Pushpa was the same, as pushy as ever, but his expedition with Arun had shifted something inside him. Later he reflected that his sister had been calculating in her decision to send him out to buy the satchel.

It was almost midnight when he reached Melur. Pieces of paper whistled past his legs as he walked up the deserted main road towards the roundabout. The unevenly spaced street lamps spread pools of pale light on the tarmac, darkening the shadows everywhere else. It was late January, when the heat of the day did not survive the night.

He turned off the main street into the lane leading to the room. A man stood at the top of the outside stairs. Fifty metres further down the lane a single bulb shone. Bending forward from the waist, the man peered in through the open door of the room and seemed to gesture; then he quickly descended the steps and disappeared down the lane.

Vijayan hadn't moved. Must be one of Mani's or Krishnan's friends or relatives. But he knew that wasn't right. He went up the stairs and looked inside the room. Mani and Krishnan were fast asleep.

If that person knew Mani or Krishnan, why didn't he wake him? he asked himself. Why'd he go away without saying a word?

Vijayan slipped silently into his space under the window and stretched out on his mat. Face upward, eyes open, he knew the answer: he left because he was looking for someone else.

Turning over on his side, and bunching up a pile of clothes into a pillow, he tried to sleep. A lorry rumbled along on the main road and scavenger dogs howled in the distance. Then a window shutter started banging in the wind. It was three houses away but sounded like it was above his head. Wood slammed against wood, but not in any kind of pattern, and that's what unnerved him. If he could anticipate the sound, he wouldn't listen for it and it would recede into the background. Random noise, like other things he couldn't control, kept him on edge.

6

Vijayan didn't speak to Mani or Krishnan in the morning. As usual, they had hurried off to work before he was fully awake. Sitting in the empty room, he was unable to ignore it any longer. He was frightened.

Velan had been murdered. A stranger had spied on Velan at Kelalavu. Pandian knew Velan and had come to Melur. Someone had stood outside the room late last night, probably looking for him.

He repeated these facts to himself, one by one, trying to break it all down. This was his way of thinking through a problem, but this time it failed to calm him. He had no plan and nothing to guide him. Although he often doubted his ideas or actions, this was different. A friend had been killed and he was involved. Murugan had given him that letter, asking him to find out what he could, yet he had done nothing.

At the shop that day, he periodically stopped what he was doing and looked outside. Vehicles passed at different speeds, crossing in a blur of colour and sound. Slipping into that stream, he let himself be swept away, out of the shop, out of Melur, beyond what he knew, where he no longer felt the ball of fear inside him.

'What's up?' Mani asked as he entered the shop at closing time.

'Pongal, that's what,' said a cheerful Muttusami. Everyone was in a good mood because the New Year festival was about to begin.

'You going to catch one this time?' teased Mani, referring to the main event when young men wrestled bulls to the ground.

'Definitely. As soon as this famous writer over here gets married!' said Muttusami, nodding towards the far end of the corner, where Vijayan bent over a newspaper.

'That means you've got at least ten years to prepare yourself,' said Mani. 'And given your physical condition, you'll need all ten.

'What about it, Vijayan? Are ten years enough for this youngster to get ready to take on a bull?' continued Mani.

'What? Oh, Pongal,' Vijayan replied, finally looking up from the paper. 'Well, no. I wouldn't hold my breath on anything involving this old geezer.'

His jocularity sounded off key and Mani noticed it.

'Seriously, Vijayan. Why don't you come and spend Pongal with me?' asked Muttusami. He had noticed that his assistant had been in one of his moods all day long. 'Even if I don't manage a bull this year, there's always the food.'

'And girls look their best at Pongal,' Mani said, attempting to lift his friend's spirits.

'Oh, shut up, Mani. For a poet, you're not very original,' said Vijayan in an angry voice that he didn't try to hide.

'All right. All right. Let's go for a walk. It's getting dark,' Mani said and went over to his friend. 'What's so absorbing in the paper?' he asked and angled his head to read the front page headline:

Maoist insurgency claims 33 lives in Ceylon

'What's that all about?' Mani asked.

'Mostly Sinhala youths, unemployed and frustrated, it seems.'

'Any Tamils involved?' asked Muttusami.

People in Melur had a vague sense of the political situation in the island only a short boat ride away from the coast. After Sinhala nationalists had won the recent elections, Tamil demands for language rights and autonomy had grown louder. Anyone who even glanced at a newspaper knew that tensions had reached a danger point.

'Tamils? A little. The CPM are giving lip service to the movement, but most parties in Madras are staying quiet,' answered Vijayan.

Abruptly he folded up the paper, slapped it hard with his palm and said, 'Nothing we can do about that. Let's go.'

Mani and he turned left outside the shop and headed towards the roundabout, when they heard noises in a side street. Going closer, they saw about thirty or forty men chanting. Streaks of white ash across foreheads, arms and bare chests contrasted with black veshtis, shirts, beards and hair. It was the season when thousands of devotees like them would make the pilgrimage to Sabarimala, high in the western mountains

Turning their shoulders sideways, Vijayan and Mani edged in front and saw the bed of coals set up in the middle of the lane. Although not red-hot, the smouldering coals lay a few inches deep and about fifteen or twenty feet long, like a dull grey carpet with ruby red highlights. The heat was palpable and stoked the already fierce passion of the men in black cloth and white ash.

The devotees stood at one end of the bed of coals, chanting and shuffling about in little knots, while a crowd of men and women shouted blessings and cheers. One or two of the devotees began to twitch and then pranced around in short, jerky steps. The crowd raised its voice, encouraging those who were now possessed by their god.

One devotee approached the burning coals and began to walk over it. He placed one bare foot in front of the other, in measured steps, not running or hurrying; and when he reached the end, the cheering crowd embraced him. Another man stepped on to the coals, and then another.

When a fourth man lost his balance and fell, he was dragged away quickly, but the smell of burnt flesh lingered in the air. More men completed the ordeal, until all had demonstrated that they were blessed by their god and felt no pain.

Just as the crowd was dispersing, a final coal-walker appeared. Barefoot but without any of the pilgrims' trappings, he was no devotee. Walking slowly across the coals, this man in rolled up trousers and vest, chanted his own blessing:

'There is no god! He who invented god is a fool. He who propagates god is a scoundrel. He who worships god is a barbarian!'

He stepped off the coals at the end and proudly showed the crowd his unblistered feet. Most were dumbstruck, but one man found an explanation and screamed, 'He repeated the word "god." That's what protected him.'

Others grumbled or shouted abuse, but a triumphal satisfaction surged through Vijayan. That man had done what he always wanted to: put his ideas into practice, in public. Then he noticed someone staring at him. It was Dandapani. He wore black and had cheered the fire-walkers but hadn't crossed the coals himself. The ferocity of his stare made Vijayan turn his head.

Later, they sat on a bench and sipped milky tea in the evening chill.

Mani looked at his friend's face, sealed up like a vault.

'What's the matter?'

'Oh, nothing really.'

'It's the news, isn't it? About Ceylon, I mean.'

'Well, sort of.'

'What?'

'I didn't tell you everything.'

After seeing the unsigned letter to Velan, Ceylon had been added to the list of topics that Vijayan hunted down in the newspapers he read every day.

'There's a new group, the Tamil Student Front. They held a demonstration, demanding that Tamil be named a national language.'

'Nothing new there, is there?'

'No. But sixteen protestors were killed, shot down by the police.'

'Ceylon, the Buddhist paradise!' Mani cried. 'As peaceful as our beloved India.'

Vijayan unconsciously began to pump one of his legs, the knee rising and falling in short, rapid strokes. 'The DMK government in Madras condemned the killings,' he said. 'But others are demanding more active support.'

'I see.'

'Thing is,' said Vijayan, who turned and scrutinized Mani's face as he spoke, 'some reports say Colombo is targeting groups here who support the Tamil movement.'

'Targeting?'

'They send agents to "eliminate" groups here, in Tamil Nadu.'

'C'mon! They can't be worried about a handful of people. '

'No. But they're afraid of the Tamils in Ceylon joining up with the Maoists.'

'That's not going to happen,' Mani said.

'You're probably right. The Maoists are low-caste and unemployed Sinhala men. Anything Tamil or Hindu is their enemy, or that's what they think.'

'That's what I'm saying. Both have grievances, but they're never going to be allies.'

'Maybe not. But if they did join together, they could overthrow the government.' The words came out before Vijayan knew he had formed the idea.

Mani wanted to ask if he was joking, but Vijayan's stone-hard face checked him. 'Come on,' he said instead, standing up and throwing away his beedi. 'Let's take that walk.'

From the roundabout, they took the road leading west, through the prosperous part of town, including the Brahmin quarter, and out towards the high hills. Passing a school and a bicycle repair shop, they crossed over an irrigation channel and entered open countryside.

'By the way, did anyone come to the room last night?'

'Last night? No. Why?'

'Oh, I thought I saw someone on the stairs, when I came back. You and Krishnan were asleep.'

'And?'

'Well, I don't know. He just stared, like he was looking for someone.'

'Probably one of Raja's friends.'

'Hmm. Where's Raja anyway?'

'In Madurai. Big job in a hotel.'

A stiff wind blew across the fields, making Mani's hair stand up even higher than usual. Although the image of the man on the stairs stayed in Vijayan's mind, he said nothing more. Must've been one of Raja's friends, he reassured himself. But he knew that wasn't right. The unknown visitor had been looking for someone who wasn't there.

Chellappan finished his night meal of rice and eggplant sambar. Pouring water from a tumbler, he rinsed his right hand over the rimmed plate, drank the rest of the water, gave a little belch and stood up.

'I'll be back soon,' he called through to his wife and mother in the kitchen and hurried towards the front door.

'Papa, you said you'd help me,' pleaded his ten-year-old son.

'Just be careful when you copy out the verses from Kampan. Don't forget the "joining" rules,' commanded the little teacher, who couldn't resist the temptation to supply several examples of the abstruse conventions for writing Tamil in longhand.

Twenty minutes later Chellappan was sitting on the small, square verandah of a red-tiled house in the Brahmin quarter. Six or seven others sat with him watching a middle-aged man and his daughter a few feet away. Krishnaswami, the music teacher at the Government Basic Training School, was tuning his violin, or fiddle as he called it, preferring the English word but pronouncing it more like 'piddle.' His daughter, Saraswati, on his left, was arranging the hem of her sari. When she was satisfied it formed a neat circle in front of her; she adjusted the jasmine flowers in her braid and began to warm up with short phrases.

Father and daughter came from a three-hundred-year-old lineage of musicians and singers patronized by rajas in a famous temple town. Now he was a government employee, drawing a meagre salary, in a small market town. Teaching bored him and he disliked the boys at the GBTS, who preferred volleyball to the violin.

Tonight their host was Sivaramakrishnan, headmaster of the Middle School, whose family and a few women from the neighbourhood sat inside and watched through the open door. The half dozen men on the verandah were packed together so tight that their knees touched. Two or three others stood next to a wooden pillar or squatted on the narrow steps.

The only light came from a chimney lamp with a cotton wick sheltered by a smudged glass cover. Saraswati began by elongating single notes in a wavering voice. The violin underneath was barely audible, but then she stopped and her father angled his head towards the rosewood throat of his instrument.

Chellappan loved the human-like sound of the violin. Someone told him it had been introduced to India by the British in the eighteenth century, but he didn't believe that—it was part of ancient Tamil tradition. Now, on the verandah, he closed his eyes, leant back against the wall and let the music flood through his body.

When he opened his eyes, he saw Vijayan and Mani standing in the street. He waved to them to join him on the verandah, but they signalled that they preferred their less conspicuous position.

'I didn't know you came to these concerts,' said Chellappan later, as the three men walked home.

'We don't. We were just walking and heard the music,' Mani said.

'Beautiful. That's all you can say,' enthused Chellappan. 'What'd you think, Vijayan?'

'Vijayan only looked at the daughter, so don't ask him,' joked Mani.

'By the way, Vijayan, I want you to meet someone. Why not come to my school tomorrow?' Chellappan asked.

'What for?' Vijayan said rather than asked.

'A teacher there. He knows something about Velan,' Chellappan explained, looking sidewise at Vijayan as they continued to walk.

'So? Why should I come?'

'I thought you wanted to find out more...about him. That's all.'

'No. Not anymore. Besides, I won't be able to get off work tomorrow.'

Next day he was on a bus to Chellappan's school. A fine, steady drizzle had been falling since early morning and Vijayan sat hunched up beside a man holding two chickens in his lap and another with a large sack wedged between his splayed legs. As the hills came closer, the rain thickened and the canvas window flaps were whipped aside by the wind.

'Why am I doing this?' Vijayan muttered to himself, jamming his hands between his legs to keep warm. But some instinct urged him on. Don't stand still, it warned. If you do, you'll sink down and never get up.

Getting down from the bus, he looked around. He knew where he was, but it felt like the middle of nowhere. Beside the road was a shack selling cigarettes, matches and betel nut, a tea-stall with a sagging bench and a man squatting under palm leaves waiting to repair sandals. That was all.

A 100 metres away were mud-brick houses huddled together in a haphazard pattern, as if they had no idea why they were there. Behind the houses, on a path leading to fields of sugarcane, Vijayan spotted the school.

The low-lying brick building had three rooms arranged in a U-shape around a courtyard. A shallow verandah, overhung by rafters with ochre-coloured tiles, stretched along the front of the main room in the centre and the two smaller ones flanking it. Faded green shutters swung on loose hinges, and the windows bared their iron bar teeth. A flagless pole in the middle of the courtyard was encircled by stones once painted white, but now weathered to a dark grey.

The high triangular gable above the entrance to the main room was the only feature that might have reminded local people of its grand opening, ten years ago, when a cavalcade of cars rolled into the hamlet. With two classes and one teacher to each room, this primary school had close to a hundred students. Most came only during breaks in the agricultural season and largely for the hot rice lunch, provided through an American loan scheme.

Vijayan entered the courtyard and heard the children. 'It-is-a-cat! It-is-a-cat!' they screamed again and again, thrilled with their vocal powers.

'Come! Come!' Chellappan shouted almost as loudly as the children, who watched in astonishment as their teacher jumped up and raised his hands high over his head in an exaggerated greeting. Vijayan stood just inside the door, unsmiling.

'All right. Copy the paragraph about the cat ten times on

your slates,' Chellappan commanded and led Vijayan outside to the verandah.

'I'm glad you came. Wait here. I'll call Periyaswami.'

His colleague was a thin young man with a ledge of hair extending over his forehead. He had dark, almost black, skin and spoke with soft, liquid sounds. Vijayan, who didn't miss the shiny watch on his wrist, liked him at first glance.

They walked over to a small grove of mango trees and squatted at the base of one. It had stopped raining but the moist air was chilly. Periyaswami lit a beedi and began to tell Vijayan what he had told Chellappan.

'It was about a week before Velan disappeared. Maybe two. I was in Madurai for a meeting.' Periyaswami was a leading figure in the local unit of the DMK, the governing party in Madras.

'I was coming out of the office, when I saw Velan. He was talking with the district head, and two or three others I didn't recognize. They were in a side room, but the door was open and I saw him. I was about to say hello, when someone inside shut the door.'

'You sure it was Velan?' asked Vijayan.

'Oh, yes. It was him all right.'

'It's a little strange for Velan, a CPM man, to be in a secret meeting with DMK people.'

'Yes. But I forgot about it, even when I heard Velan had disappeared. Then Chellappan told me he'd been found, and I remembered.'

'When exactly did you see him?'

He pulled a diary from his shirt pocket. 'It was 10 November, last year.'

On the short bus ride back to Melur, Vijayan tried to make sense of what he had learned. Velan had met with DMK leaders about two weeks before he was killed and three weeks before he was supposed to go to Ceylon. But why was he going there?

Vijayan had his midday meal in the usual place. The men beside him on the wooden bench ate with rapid, repetitive movements. Propping their left elbow on the formica table top, forearm and hand pointing straight up in the air, they leant forward, squeezed the rice and sambar into tight balls with their right hand and tossed them towards their mouth. As soon as one ball went in, the right hand returned to the plate and worked up another. Servers milled around with metal buckets shouting, 'Rice? Sambar?' and ladling out as much as the men wanted.

The men around him finished, licked their right hand clean, drank a small tumbler of water, folded up the banana leaf and took it to the trough at the back. Vijayan finished and folded his leaf but just sat staring straight ahead. When he finally got up, he stepped on someone's foot and apologized by gesturing towards the man's foot and then his own head. Tossing his leaf out at the back, he saw the scavenger but not Trotsky.

'Have you seen that dog? The one that's always there,' he asked one of the servers in a diffident voice.

'Dog?' the man screwed up his face in disgust.

'Yes. It's always there, at the trough.'

'He's asking about a dog!' the man snorted.

Several heads turned and watched Vijayan leave. Although the sun was shining, large puddles lay like paving stones in the main road. Men hiked their veshtis up above their knees and women lifted their saris, revealing the hem of petticoats. Too preoccupied to pay attention, Vijayan crossed the road as a bus sped by.

When he entered the shop, with his scowl and mud-stained veshti, Muttusami looked up and gave him a silent sideways glance.

Vijayan lifted the panel and slid into place behind the counter.

'Half-day leave,' he said in response to the unasked question.

'All right. I'll put it in the book,' said Muttusami, who looked again at his assistant. 'You feeling all right?'

'No, I mean yes. Everything's fine. Just got caught in the rain,' Vijayan said and turned away.

About four o'clock people began to come in and soon all the stools were occupied. The murmur of conversation was suddenly interrupted by an angry voice, 'Hey! I gave you ten rupees! Where's my change?'

Everyone turned and saw a man thrusting his open palm at Vijayan.

'I...I,' stammered Vijayan.

'Just give me the money!'

'Yes, of course,' Vijayan said. The whole shop watched as he drew a five-rupee note out of the cash drawer and gave it to the man, who snatched it and stomped out of the shop.

When heads swung back and the patter of voices resumed, Vijayan kept his face down, pretending to fold a shirt but held there by shame. Everyone makes mistakes, he said to himself. No one in the shop gave it a second thought, but he prided himself on being better than a shop assistant. And it was humiliating in front of customers. He unfolded the shirt, shook it out, laid it on the counter and folded it again. Still not right, the edges didn't match up, until he pulled one corner, then another and patted the little pile into shape.

'Do you have a khadi veshti with a red border?' The voice was measured and flat, as if reading a newspaper aloud. Vijayan looked up to see a short man, with a flabby face and small eyes, shifting his weight around on the stool.

'One moment,' Vijayan said and turned to the glass-panelled cabinet behind him. He placed two folded veshtis on the counter and slid his hand inside one to display its texture.

'This one's a bit thinner, finer. But the other's a little warmer, especially in this weather,' Vijayan advised.

'What's the price?' asked the man, not examining either veshti and looking straight at Vijayan. When he chose the thinner one, Vijayan wrapped it in newspaper and tied the bundle with the string hanging from the ceiling.

'Here you are,' he said.

'Right. Goodbye,' said the man as he slid off the high stool with his parcel. His stomach pushed out a polyester white shirt, the bottom of which cut across his dark trousers just below the waist.

Doesn't look the khadi type. Strange accent, too, thought Vijayan.

Turning towards the cabinets, he stopped and spun around. He couldn't be sure. The strides were too short inside the shop, so he continued to watch as the man walked down the steps and across the street. It was slight but unmistakable. His left leg stayed behind for half a second as the rest of his body waited for it to catch up.

Seen from a distance, the caravan moved soundlessly against a background of yellow-brown hills. Dozens of carts mounted on wooden spoked wheels nearly as tall as a man, and pulled by bullocks a little taller, creaked along the narrow country road.

The animals' brightly painted and flower-festooned horns swept upwards in a three-foot arc as they tripped along on muscular, graceful legs. Decorated with stalks of sugarcane and rippling with banners of blue, green and gold saris, the carts became chariots.

They were heading to a small village outside Melur, where each January, on the second day of the Pongal festival, large crowds gathered for the bull-catching. The village had only three or four hundred people, but that day it played host to several thousand who came to watch young men pit themselves against the bulls.

While the event was celebrated all over the region, here in Nattam it was famous. The animals were bigger, the horns sharper and the money to be won greater. Twenty-, fifty-, even one hundred-rupee notes were tucked inside the cloths tied around the bulls' necks. You only had to get close enough to untie them.

By mid-morning the crowd in the open space outside the village hummed with anticipation. Vijayan had arrived the day before with Muttusami and spent the night in his brother's house. He was alone now, with Muttusami involved in a family ritual.

He looked around, shielding his eyes from the sun. A space the size of three or four football pitches was encircled by the crowd, and behind it a pen held several dozen bulls. On the inside edge of the circle, a handful of men stood ready, veshtis hiked high above their knees or pulled between their legs and tucked in at the waist. Some dispensed with the veshti altogether and just wore shorts. Many had wound towels around their head like turbans. Most were young and all were nervous.

A huge cry went up when the first bull raced down the passage that opened up through the crowd and into the circle. Stopping in the middle of the open ground, the powerful animal turned around, confused. It stood there, motionless, and then tossed back its head.

Four men approached, crouching and advancing step-by-step. When they came within a few metres, the bull pawed the ground and lowered its head, horns almost scraping the dry earth. The men stopped and inched forward. Suddenly the bull reared up and charged, scattering the men, who hit the ground and rolled away to safety. The bull ran towards the crowd provoking screams of panic and then veered away, only for the crowd to taunt it.

A second bull was released, and another, and soon six or seven were being chased in the circle.

A large black bull thundered close to the crowd, and a shaven-headed man grabbed one of its horns. Trying to grab the other, he was thrown high in the air; the crowd gasped. Three men wrestled the bull to the ground, tore the cloth off its neck and waved it to loud cheers.

Another bull trotted near a crouching man, who threw his arms around its neck and swung himself up on its back. A minute later he slipped off and the bull gored him with its long, pointed horns. When dragged clear, his body was streaked with dirt and blood. The bull stood still for a moment and then advanced on the crowd, which scuttled backwards, though not before the enraged animal had ripped through the flesh of several men.

Transfixed, Vijayan didn't notice the disturbance next to him until he heard, 'Motherfuckers! Stay away from that bull!' The speaker knocked a man to the ground and shouted, 'Now suck my cock, you bastard!' Another man kicked the fallen man in the back and a third spat on him. Vijayan stood speechless as the beating continued and then raised a hand to protest.

Someone shoved him aside and knelt down beside the man on the ground. Looking up at Vijayan, he screamed, 'Give me a hand!' Before Vijayan could react, two burly policemen arrived in knee-length khaki shorts and beat away the onlookers with batons.

Three hours later, all the bulls had been caught, all except one. Last year Maharaja had gored one man to death and sent three to hospital. Everyone now watched this final drama.

Maharaja was exhausted. Chased for the better part of an hour by different groups of men, it walked rather than trotted but kept its magnificent horns high in the air. Patches of yellow turmeric and white ash, with which the proud owner had decorated his bull, ran in streaks of perspiration down its sleek, black body.

A group of six men surrounded it, keeping a distance of about five metres, still gauging its strength and mood. If they got closer, the bull dropped its head and threatened to charge. As they circled around, Maharaja turned and tilted its head, fixing them with dilated eyes.

The stalemate was broken when a man crawled forward on his stomach, leapt up and threw an arm around the bull's large hump. Another man grabbed its tail and a third caught one of its horns, while others piled on and the bull was wrestled to the ground.

When the men untied the cloth and retreated, Maharaja scrambled back on its feet and ran off in a final show of defiance. One of the men held aloft their one-hundred rupee reward as they merged with the cheering crowd.

Walking back to Muttusami's brother's house, Vijayan thought about the past four hours. Eleven people had been injured, five seriously, and one would probably die. Seems we're little different from our primitive ancestors, he mused, though that idea ran counter to his belief that, over time, people gained knowledge and became more civilized. But he had read somewhere that our minds and bodies have not changed much since we hunted with clubs. Kicking at a stone in the path, he managed to stub his toe.

The threshold to Muttusami's brother's house was decorated with a flower design. Lines radiated out from the centre, looped around, headed back to the middle and got lost in the criss-crossing pattern. Every threshold in the village displayed a similar design, drawn with rice powder pinched between finger and thumb and released as the hand traced the design. The patterns were all different, and each was scrutinized by neighbours and passers-by, like flowers in an English village fête.

Muttusami's relatives and a few friends filled the small front room of the house. His elderly parents sat in plastic weave chairs.

The room was undecorated except for a large format calendar that hung on one wall and a smaller astrological calendar, with one day per page, on another.

When the women and children left, the men and older boys sat down to the afternoon feast. Cross-legged, backs against the wall, two groups faced each other across a green concrete floor. A large, freshly washed banana leaf was placed in front of each guest and heaped with pongal rice, combining ginger, dhal, cumin seeds, curry leaves, ghee and cashewnut, all of it laced with jaggery.

A silk sari with silver threads swished as Muttusami's niece moved around the room, bending down to serve each person in turn. Vijayan kept his eyes lowered while eating but managed to see the brick-red dye on her feet. After the pongal came payasam, the sweet soupy dish of rice vermicelli, jaggery, raisins, cashewnut and cardamom. Now he saw her properly. Jet-black hair and an oval face. Not beautiful—something about the skin—but he liked her eyes. Outlined in black, the whites held dots of soft velvet.

Coffee was followed by a special preparation of areca nut, sugar and spices wrapped in a betel leaf and held together by a toothpick. As the men chewed the aromatic blend, they began to talk. A new bridge was needed over the irrigation channel; a calf had been found dead in a well; Balan's wife was pregnant. Then came the events of the morning.

'Bloody Kallars should've kept their hands off our bulls,' bellowed one of Muttusami's relatives. Their Naicker caste was only slightly higher in status than the more populous Kallars.

'Did you catch any bulls?' asked Muttusami's nephew, sitting beside Vijayan.

'No, you see…'

'What?'

'We don't have bull-catching where I come from,' he said.

'Where's that?' asked Muttusami's father, who had been

helped back into his chair.

'Virudhunagar, sir.'

'I see. Cotton country. How many acres do you own down there?'

'Sixteen of paddy and ten of sugarcane.' Plucked out of the air, these numbers took Vijayan by surprise but sounded plausible even to him. Muttusami looked at Vijayan with astonishment. This was the first piece of information, invented though it was, his friend had divulged about his family.

Later that day Vijayan and Muttusami left for Melur, each laden with a packet of pongal rice, enough for two or three days. The family stood outside the door, as if posing for a photograph. 'Come again! Come again,' they called and the teenage boy caught Vijayan's eye. He looks like Arun, Vijayan realized. Same expression that could be worry but was only concentration.

Vijayan said goodbye and started to walk away but stopped. The daughter, taller than her brother and mother, stood smiling behind them. Vijayan took several steps to catch up with Muttusami, then turned and looked back. But only the boy was there, squinting hard in the slanting sunlight.

It's impossible, he told himself as he walked on. She was of a different caste, and he knew that 'love-marriages' usually ended in disaster, often in debt and sometimes suicide. It would be stupid. He had no money and no real prospect of getting any. Only a dead end job. Besides, marriage would mean family pressure, Brahmin priests, temple rituals, Sanskrit chants—and he couldn't bear that.

Bumping along beside Muttusami in the bus, he looked at the fields flashing by in the failing light. It felt cool, almost dewy, so he crossed his arms on his chest and hunched himself up like a midget. He wished he had brought a towel, like Muttusami, to wrap around his balding head. A peacock perched in a barren tree spread its fan of feathers and let out a piercing shriek. Vijayan squeezed himself tighter and tried to push the image of her eyes out of his mind.

When Vijayan reached the room in Melur, Raja was turning the pages of an old film magazine.

'Where've you been?'

'Muttusami and I went to his brother's village, for Pongal.'

'Oh. How was the food?'

Only then did he realize that he had left his packet on the bus. 'Good. So, where've you been hiding?'

'Working in Madurai. Painting rooms. Three rupees for twelve hours.'

'Can't eat much on that.'

Raja grunted and turned his attention back to the glossy pictures of plump ladies in tightly wound saris.

'Raja, do you have any friends…with a limp?'

'What?'

'Nothing. Forget it.' Vijayan flapped a hand aimlessly in the air, and Raja looked at him, wondering if he would ever understand this man.

Later that week, Vijayan and Mani went to bathe at the tank on the way to the village with the temple tower visible in the distance. Returning to town, they avoided the road and took a footpath that cut through harvested paddy fields. Snow-white egrets stood on the bunds and picked their way through the stubble, lifting thin black legs and probing the shallow water with yellow beaks.

Whenever Vijayan and Mani got close, the egrets straightened up, extending their long necks and turning their spear-shaped heads one way and then the other. If they sensed danger, they unfolded their wings and flapped them twice before floating soundlessly away to the next field.

Soon the path ran alongside millet fields yet to be cut. The stalks stood a man's height or more, topped with helmets of dark grain. Entering a small clearing with a low building, they heard singing.

Inside, four women in ragged saris and no upper garments sat on the ground turning flat grinding stones. Gripping a short wooden handle stuck in a hole of the top stone, they turned the grey-pitted disc. With the other hand they guided millet into the centre, where the grains were caught between the stones and ground to a coarse powder. They bent their bodies forward when they swung the top stone away from them and straightened up as they pulled it back towards them. And all the time their chunky cube earrings swayed from elongated lobes.

Standing outside the shed, Vijayan and Mani heard the raspy voices soar above the scraping stones:

I was married far away in the north,
Where thorns grow on the path.
I picked bitter fruit there,
Where paths are lost in the forest.

As the phrases rolled out, Vijayan listened closely, trying to follow the story he thought must be there. But when he and Mani walked away, all that remained were the voices and the sound of stones.

Vijayan turned to Mani and said, 'There's something familiar about that song.'

'Yes. A woman and her children. Suicide, I think,' Mani suggested, although he preferred to remain silent and let the song stay inside him.

7

It was a fine, cloudless Sunday, but Vijayan awoke late and lay on his mat. Hauling himself up, he saw he was alone and began to rub hard on the palm of his right hand with the thumb of his left. After a few minutes he stopped and examined his palm but was unsure if his life line had been lengthened. Then he remembered there was a Rationalist Society meeting that afternoon.

Back in the room, after a bath, he found Raja and Krishnan talking loudly about the split in the ruling party in Madras. Ignoring them, he sat down, got out his notebook and tried to write down the song he and Mani had heard the day before.

He needed to get it all down, not just the words but also the pain in the women's voices. But the fragments that came to him looked meaningless on the page.

'Will you two shut up?!' he exploded at Raja and Krishnan.

Too stunned to reply, they looked at him in silence. Before anyone could speak, Vijayan grabbed his notebook and stormed out of the room. He walked a long way and sat down on a low bridge over an irrigation channel, where he tried again but couldn't remember much of the song.

When he returned to the room after lunch, it was empty so he lay down for a nap.

'Vijayan, wake up!' It was Krishnan. 'Time for the meeting.'

'Right,' murmured Vijayan as he sat up and rubbed his eyes. 'Sorry about this morning…it's just that…'

Krishnan stood looking at him, waiting for an explanation that never came.

Vijayan got up and pulled a clean veshti off a nail in the wall. Wrapping the khadi cloth around his waist, he adjusted the length so that it fell just above his instep. Then he tightened it and tucked one end into the fold at his waist. He checked the length again and, satisfied, tilted his head to tell Krishnan he was ready.

At the meeting Perumal Tevar gave a long, rambling talk on the significance of the mango in Tamil literature. His command of sources was impressive and his enthusiasm undeniable, though not inspiring enough to prevent half his audience from nodding off. Mani lit his first cigarette only a few minutes into the forty-minute oration. Vijayan feigned attention, but his thoughts were far away.

During the discussion that followed, Chellappan chipped in with an aphorism that compared consuming mangoes to hearing Tamil poetry. Kantan observed that today's mangoes were not as succulent as those in his youth, while Perumal Tevar added that the English word 'mango' was one of the few in that language derived from Tamil. After others cited dubious examples of fruit symbolism in various texts, the discussion meandered.

Time to end this anaemic event, Mani decided and looked at Vijayan sitting near him at the front of the room. But his friend was staring towards the windows and showed no sign of recognition.

Krishnan cleared his throat and addressed Vijayan, 'Dear friend, I believe it is time to conclude this meeting and announce the date for the next.'

The room fell silent and all heads swung around to Vijayan, who looked back at Krishnan with vacant eyes. A lorry rumbled by on the main road, and rooks squawked in nearby trees. Mani leaned across to him, said something and then announced in a calm voice, 'He's lost in thought, contemplating our stimulating debate on the mango.' A few laughs relieved the tension.

Vijayan smiled weakly and everyone, except Mani and Krishnan, felt the atmosphere return to normal.

On their way home, Mani, Krishnan and Vijayan said little. Several times, during the twenty-minute walk down the main road under the tamarind trees, past the sawmill and the plough workshops, Mani wanted to break the silence.

Back at the room, they decided to go out for a dosai. Vijayan said he didn't feel well and would stay behind. Before they separated, Krishnan forced himself to speak.

'Anything the matter?'

'Not really. I heard a song yesterday.'

'The women's grinding song? Mani mentioned it.'

'Yes. I want to write it down but can't remember enough.'

'But surely...'

'It's important,' Vijayan said sharply. 'I don't know why. But it is.'

Krishnan and Mani looked at him, wondering what had happened to their friend. Vijayan glanced at them and turned away, though not before they saw his darkened brow.

After they had left, he took stock of his situation and realized how isolated he felt. Frightened and anxious, he would also be alone. His friends would be polite, of course. They would include him in conversations and walks, but that was on the surface. People in the street would also acknowledge him, while inside they would withdraw. He could see that already. Even Muttusami wasn't as congenial as usual.

It's worse than physical isolation, he reflected. You're with people, the same as always, but not part of them. In prison, they say, you can draw on some kind of inner strength. But if people shut you out emotionally, you lose strength. It ebbs away, and when it goes, you are alone.

Fragments of the women's song, images of rain and memories

of Velan's corpse flitted through his mind. Then he recalled the man outside the room and the other man with the limp—or were they the same? He saw Murugan giving him the letter and Pandian visiting the shop. And there was something Velan said that evening before he was killed. He could put two or three pieces together, but when he added another, they broke apart and scattered.

'There is no god. He who....' The atheist's credo came to his lips but faded away. Nothing could help him create the coherence he craved. He had to go back to the women who sang that song and write the whole thing down. Then he might understand.

Next morning, he walked to the grinding shed just outside Melur. It was deserted, but an old man chopping firewood nearby directed him to the millet fields. He found the women and asked if they would sing for him.

'What for? Who are you? Some kind of raja?' they jeered.

'No. I just...' Vijayan faltered.

'Don't be stupid, fancy pants! We've got work to do.'

'I'll pay you,' Vijayan announced before he realized he had only a few paisa with him.

'What'll you pay us, moneybags?' the women cackled.

'I'll...I'll come back tomorrow and pay you,' he said, not even convincing himself.

'Get lost! Go masturbate.' They hurled more insults and drove him off.

As he passed the shed, the old man put down his axe. 'What'd you want with them?' he asked, his two remaining lower teeth wobbling as he spoke. 'I've seen you in the khadi shop. They owe you something?'

'Nothing like that,' Vijayan explained. 'I just wanted to ask about a song. I heard them singing it yesterday.'

'Song? What song?'

'I don't know. They sang while grinding. Something about a woman and her children, I think.'

'That one? It's called "The Good Sister." It's a true story.'

'What's the story?'

'You never heard "The Good Sister"?'

'No. Can you tell me?'

'Well, it's not very long,' he said, rubbing the stubbly white hair on his head. 'I can't sing, mind you, but I'll tell you about it.'

The old man led the way to a battered bench resting against the shed wall. His face was a riverbed of ruts, with his eyes set deep in their sockets.

He fumbled in the waist-fold of his veshti and drew out a paper packet. Opening it, he selected a betel leaf, smoothed it on the bench surface and smeared a little lime paste on it. With a thin knife he carved a half-used areca nut, letting the shavings fall on to the leaf. Then he folded the leaf, put it in his mouth and chewed.

Wiping his hands on his towel, he turned to Vijayan with another toothy smile. Watching the man's hardworking jaw, Vijayan wondered how his few feeble teeth would cope with the betel nut. After a few minutes, the old man puckered his lips, leaned to the side and let fly a long spray of red juice. Having got rid of that first bitter mouthful, he was ready.

'Selvi, that's her name. She got married when she was only ten. Then went to her husband's village, a long way away,' he began. 'Somewhere in Ramnad, I can't remember where. Like I said, it really happened.'

He glanced at Vijayan and continued, 'Anyway, after she left, her brother got married and continued to live with their parents, until they died. They were very close, Selvi and her brother.'

Vijayan began to take notes, writing down facts and phrases.

The old man spat and said, 'Over the years Selvi had children, seven of them. Then—this was about twenty-five years ago—there was a famine. The monsoon failed two years in a row and there wasn't anything to eat. Cattle died, goats died. Selvi's husband left her. Just took off and disappeared. She and her children had nothing to eat. She was as thin as a stick and the children no better. So she decided to go back home, to her brother's house.

'She and the children walked for four days. Across dry land, without water or food. They arrived at her brother's house, half-dead. Just lay down at the door. When no one came, Selvi called for her brother, but her voice was faint.'

Vijayan continued to write though he wanted to ask questions.

'He wasn't there, you see. He'd gone to the fields. The sister-in-law was inside. She heard the cries and knew who it was. But she didn't want to let her in. She never liked her and…I mean, how was she going to feed eight more mouths? So she stayed inside and kept quiet.'

'They had food?' asked Vijayan. 'Wasn't there famine there, too?'

'Not so bad. They had some food. Not a lot, but enough. You see, the sister-in-law wasn't a bad person. But she didn't like Selvi. She was jealous of her husband's affection for her.'

Vijayan wagged his head to show he understood and the old man resumed.

'Selvi lay there and cried for help. But the sister-in-law didn't open the door. Then Selvi prayed, "If I'm a good woman, let the door open; if I'm not, let me die!" The door swung open and Selvi sobbed, "Give us some food, sister. My children are dying. Help us!"

'Still the sister-in-law said nothing. Then Selvi called for her brother. When he didn't come, she thought he'd abandoned her. You see, she didn't know he wasn't in the house.

'That's when she lost hope. She dragged herself up and

stumbled away, leading her children. She came to a well and looked down. It was dry, only rocks at the bottom. She stared at those rocks, took the oldest child and threw it down the well. Then the next, and the next, until she'd killed all seven. At the end, she jumped in herself. That's what happened.'

Vijayan looked up from his notebook. The old man bent forward, spat on the ground and fell back against the shed wall. He held his head at an angle, as if to deflect the pain that had narrowed his eyes and tightened his lips. He crossed his arms, shield-like across his chest.

Vijayan started to speak, but the old man cut him off. 'The well's still there, they say. In that village.'

'Where? Ramnad District?'

'That's right. One of those women was born near there. She'll tell you the name of the village.'

Vijayan didn't relish another interview with those women, so he found someone else in the hamlet who knew the story and where it had happened. It was in Manakkadu, not far from the Pearl Coast on the Bay of Bengal.

'Another half-day leave?' Muttusami made it sound like an accusation when Vijayan entered the shop after midday.

'Yes.'

Muttusami made an entry in a notebook, Vijayan took his place at the far end of the counter and neither spoke another word.

The afternoon slid by until the loudspeaker attached to the electrical shop outside crackled into life:

> *This is All India Radio, from Madras, with the news at 5 o'clock.*

A handful of men were sitting outside on benches, but they all swivelled their heads up towards the conical speaker when they heard the announcer continue in formal Tamil:

> *Seven Tamils were killed by police yesterday in Colombo. They were part of a large crowd demanding that the government of Ceylon declare Tamil a national language, alongside Sinhala. Thirty-four others were injured in the riot that ensued when the police opened fire.*

Listening on the steps of the khadi shop, Vijayan went numb. The horror of the killings was compounded by a fear that events in Ceylon were closing in on him.

In the room that evening, he took out his notebook and looked at what he had written about 'The Good Sister.'

'Did you hear about the killings in Colombo?' asked Krishnan.

Vijayan murmured assent.

'Things are moving fast there. With DMK support, Tamils will soon be demanding a separate state in the north and east,' said Mani, raking a hand through his shrub of hair.

'Yes. They're already demanding national language status for Tamil and quotas in the universities,' Krishnan agreed.

'They need a leader, that's for sure,' said Raja. The others turned to the young man, who rarely spoke about current affairs. Unsure of himself, he added, 'I mean they need someone to bring them together.'

'That's right,' said Mani and Krishnan at the same time.

'So what are you doing?' Vijayan flung out the words, not caring whom they struck. 'Just sitting around and talking like you have the answers. That's all.'

The other three looked at each other and continued their discussion in lowered voices.

'What are you writing?' Mani asked softly after a few minutes.

'The song we heard. I got the full story from a man there,'

said Vijayan. As he told Mani the story in his own words, the sister's loss hit him with even greater force.

'Sad story,' Mani said, partly out of sympathy for his friend, who he could see was shaken.

'It's a true story, Mani.'

'Are you going to write about it? An essay or something?'

'No, no. I've got to find it,' said Vijayan fixing him with his dark brown eyes.

'Find what?'

'The well. Where she killed herself and her children.'

'What do you mean "got" to find it?'

'I…I can't explain it. I want to see it, not just know about it.'

'Right,' said Mani, unconvinced.

'Listen, Mani. It really happened. She killed all her children. Threw seven of them down a well. It was cruel, but she didn't do it because of caste oppression or class exploitation or religious superstition.'

'Yes,' said Mani. 'It was sheer poverty.'

Vijayan stiffened and looked at his friend. 'No. It wasn't that, Mani. She was alone. All alone. That's why.'

Pandian dropped into his wooden swivel chair. Lifting his feet, he slid his hands down over the thick knobs at the end of the chair's arms and spun himself around. He knew he had to do something soon. Using his feet, he stopped the chair, and grabbed another cigarette.

The alliance between the Maoist and the Tamil movements in Ceylon was no closer than when he began his plan three years ago. Although the government in Madras was speaking out in support of Tamils there, and he had access to senior officials, he needed people on the ground to bring the two movements together.

He crushed his cigarette in the sand bunker of a ceramic ashtray and reassured himself that it was still possible. Tamil groups had become more militant, and though the Maoist revolt had been defeated, its cells were active.

An alliance would bring credibility to both groups, and then the money will flow, Pandian said to himself, repeating what he had been thinking for weeks. But I need someone to make them see their common interests.

He got up from his chair and looked out the window of his first-floor office. 'Together, they could topple the government,' he said aloud. 'And we could build a society where everyone is equal.'

Below he watched people on Mount Road hurrying down the street, looking at shops, standing, waiting. He needed two or three men now, before the opportunity slipped away.

He had lost three agents in Ceylon. One killed, two disappeared. And Velan had been murdered in Tamil Nadu. That's what alarmed Pandian. Velan had the perfect credentials: CPM activist, efficient, articulate, committed. That's probably why they had risked coming to India to kill him, and not waited until he went to Ceylon.

Pandian turned around and trained his eyes on the buff folders stacked on the desk. One of them contained his list of contacts, which he had been through three or four times already this morning. Competent but dull and predictable, every one of them. He needed someone with spark, an independent thinker, not a follower.

He ran a finger along his lower lip. Yes, maybe he would be just right, he thought and reached for a pen.

8

'When are we going to Madurai?' asked Raja.

'What?'

'To see a film. Remember?'

'Right. I...,' Vijayan stuttered and looked down.

Alone in the room, in the early morning, they faced each other.

'That's all right. Nothing good showing anyway.' Raja's voice affected indifference.

'We'll go,' Vijayan promised.

An hour later, when Vijayan entered the shop, Muttusami was crouched beneath the counter, routing around in the shelves. 'Got to find space for that shipment coming in today. Did I tell you? You have to meet the bus from Madurai at about 4.'

'Right,' said Vijayan, happy to have an excuse to leave the shop.

The morning crawled along, with fewer customers than usual and little to prevent his thoughts from swirling around in circles.

'I said, will you take this packet to the bank and deposit it?'

'The bank? Yes, of course,' Vijayan said, but not before his manager glowered at him in exasperation.

Stepping outside, he saw five women striding up the road. Their long white robes swung around their legs and their black headdresses flapped up and down on their shoulders as they hurried along in single file.

Must be from Father Pinto's, thought Vijayan as he watched the procession of nuns, who rarely left their school and church compound. Passing him, their faces flashed resolution rather than piety.

He had met Father Pinto once, when he accompanied Krishnan to apply for his son's admission to school. The Roman Catholic school, built in 1810, was the best in Melur, and the discipline and high standards, especially in English, justified the fees. Nuns taught the upper classes and laywomen the lower ones, while Father Pinto taught theology to the older students, though it wasn't compulsory.

Vijayan had planned to go back and ask Father Pinto about something that had been bothering him. Could a person be both scientific and religious? After all, Christianity was a modern religion. Instead he went to the church one Sunday, sat in the back and watched Father Pinto conduct mass in formal Tamil, with something else mixed in that didn't sound like English and wasn't Sanskrit. The candles, brass vessels and incense in the dark interior reminded him of a Hindu temple, though not the altar boys dressed like little priests. Walking out into daylight, he felt as if he had been in a different world, not ten minutes from the shop.

But now, looking at the nuns heading north up the main road, Vijayan could see they were integrated into local society. Different, but they fitted in, perhaps more than he did.

Where are they going? he asked himself as he crossed the road to the State Bank with its sky blue lettering on a white background. Waiting in the queue to deposit the month's takings, he overheard the answer.

'It's Dandapani, at the Government Basic Training School,' said one man.

'What's he up to now?' asked a second.

'They say he insulted one of the lady teachers from Father Pinto's. In the market.'

'I see. Looks like they've set the nuns on him.'

'I wouldn't want to face them.'

'No. Strong as an ox, only without the balls.'

Walking back to the shop, Vijayan saw Murugan coming towards him and ducked into a shop. 'Yes?' asked the man working a sewing machine with his foot and feeding a thread through the needle.

'Ah, I need…a shirt. Yes, a shirt.'

'Got to bring the cloth, young man. I can't make it out of air, you know.'

'I'll bring it…tomorrow,' Vijayan said, backing out on to the road.

Back in the khadi shop, Muttusami silently took the receipt for the bank deposit and looked for the right column to enter the details. 'By the way,' he said casually, 'Murugan came by just now. He's looking for you.'

'Really?' Vijayan asked weakly. The handful of customers, gossiping among themselves, perked up their ears.

'He came to tell you something.' Now Muttusami looked straight at Vijayan and spoke in a low voice. 'His sister died. You know, Velan's widow. Seems she took rat poison. Murugan found her this morning.'

'Terrible,' Vijayan said, while others in the shop seized on this revelation and chewed it over in excited voices.

'Rat poison? That's painful.'

'Those Paraiyars are too stupid to do it any other way.'

Vijayan wanted to tell them to shut up but only cringed and began to wonder about Velan's children. That nice-looking son, maybe eight or nine. Wasn't there a daughter, too?

He shoved his stool into his corner and worried about what he would say if he saw Murugan. Reminding himself he'd done nothing about the letter, his lips tightened and his face darkened. Why am I involved in this, anyway? I hardly knew Velan. Got to forget the whole thing.

The khaki-uniformed postman entered the shop and called out 'V. Naidu?' Without even looking at the postmark, Vijayan knew who it was from. When he slid it unopened in his breast pocket, the disappointment among the customers was audible.

The next thing he knew Muttusami was shouting: 'It's 4! That bus'll be here soon!'

On his way to the bus station, Vijayan pulled out the letter and saw the Madras postmark. I could just tear it up and throw it away, he told himself. Letters go missing all the time.

'How are you?' Kantan's hearty voice made Vijayan turn around. The burly farmer clapped a meaty hand on his shoulder as he caught up with him and they walked side-by-side to the bus station.

Pulling Vijayan aside, he said in a subdued voice, 'Bad news about Velan's widow, isn't it? Who's going to look after those children?'

'Murugan?'

'No. He's taken to drink again.'

Vijayan mumbled something and looked down.

'She just couldn't cope,' continued Kantan. 'He didn't earn much. But it was enough to get by on. Her daily wage was only half his. And that wouldn't feed four people, not after he was gone.'

'What are the police doing? About Velan's death, I mean.'

'That's what I'd like to know! They tried to bully Murugan into a confession. Right after they found the body. Haven't been seen since.'

'But they'll find...the killer. They've got to.'

'One more dead Harijan isn't going to worry them.'

'Umm. I guess not.'

'But what can we do?' Kantan shouted as he dashed to climb on the moving bus.

'Well,' Vijayan said half-aloud as the bus pulled out on to the main road, 'I could go to the police with Velan's letter.'

In the room that evening, he opened the letter delivered to him earlier in the day. He was careful not to tear the thin paper since the message was written on the inside of the folded envelope itself. Vijayan read:

> *Dear Friend,*
> *I am well and wish the same for you.*
> *I kindly ask that you come to Madras and visit me.*
> *I would like to discuss with you a matter of mutual interest.*
> *Please call for me at the above address at your earliest convenience. <u>Do not, however, write to me at this address</u>.*
> *Sincerely,*
> *S.K. Pandian*

Vijayan glanced at the top of the letter:

> *3/C 2nd Cross Street*
> *T. Nagar Madras*

He looked at the address again. It seemed different to the one on Pandian's business card. Rummaging through his shoulder bag hanging on a nail, he found the card and read the address: 144 Mount Road. That must be his office, he reasoned. And T. Nagar must be his home.

Looking back at the letter, he wondered about the 'matter of mutual interest.' Velan was the only thing that connected them. But what did Pandian want?

'Another love letter?' Raja laughed, looking up from a magazine.

'What? No, no. From my sister, in Virudhunagar,' he said, but his feeble cover-up was obvious. Mani, who was writing in the corner, shot a glance at Vijayan.

Alone when he awoke next morning, he felt immobilized. Things were happening around him yet he remained motionless. Looking again at Pandian's letter, he considered going to the police and showing them the letter written to Velan. But that letter proves nothing, he thought. Besides, Kantan's right—the police wouldn't be interested. Still, I've got to do something.

Vijayan walked into the shop and found Muttusami purring over his ledger. Before the manager had a chance to upbraid him for being late, yet again, he made his announcement.

'I'd like to take a week's leave, with your permission.'

'What?' Muttusami's head jerked up, his eyes narrowed.

Vijayan repeated his request.

'A week? Well, it's not busy now, after Pongal. All right,' said Muttusami, eager to sort out a problem he had discovered in the accounts. Half an hour later, he shut the heavy cover of the ledger with a smile of satisfaction.

'So, when do you leave?' he asked.

'Tomorrow, if that's all right.'

'Okay. Where to?'

'I'm...still planning the trip,' he said, trying not to lie.

'I see,' said Muttusami, unconvinced. He admitted that writers are more spontaneous than shopkeepers. Even indecision, they say, can be creative. While he liked this explanation, he didn't believe it.

That night Vijayan packed what he needed. Mani and Krishnan, talking about the upcoming elections, saw his preparations without actually looking. The usual easy banter was gone, and they no longer knew how to approach Vijayan. Finally Mani asked, 'Are you taking a trip somewhere?'

'Yes,' said Vijayan, who had now worked out an answer. 'I'm going south, on shop business.' He decided this half-lie was all right.

He didn't know exactly where Manakkadu was or how many buses it took to get there. The early March sun had just risen and patches of dark mauve shadows still lay on the land like ink stains. On the move, and gently rocked by the bus, Vijayan's body relaxed.

At Madurai, he changed buses and headed southeast toward the coast. There, in the early sixteenth century, the Portuguese had brought Christianity, horses and guns. The last two were traded inland and became de rigueur for aspiring rajas and nawabs, but the stone churches remained, their spires piercing the sky all along the coast, where men with names like Roderigo and Antonio fished, made salt and climbed palm trees to collect sap.

Paddy stubble gave way to tall millet stalks with their knobbly heads. Here and there, the cut stalks were laid out on the road, forming a thick brown carpet twenty or thirty yards long, so they would be threshed by the wheels of buses and lorries. Small batches of red chillies also lay drying by the roadside.

Dry scrubland appeared after about two hours. The wide, flat tracts were dotted with tall palmyras, whose tight fists of purple-black fruit hung high under a canopy of thick fronds. When the bus stopped in the middle of nowhere, Vijayan saw a cluster of brown tents and open fires, men wrapped in blankets and women scrubbing blackened pots. When three men wearing trousers, climbed on, their wary eyes confirmed Vijayan's suspicion that this was a resettlement camp for Tamils deported from Ceylon.

Vijayan knew Manakkadu was close when the soil became sandy and he smelled salt in the air. Getting down at Nazareth, a small market town, in the mid-afternoon, he found a cheap room and looked for somewhere to eat.

'How far is Manakkadu?' he asked as he paid the man sitting in a chair on a low dais.

'About five or six miles. Turn right at the post office,' he said, cocking a curious eyebrow.

'Any buses?'

'Three or four a day. Last one's gone, though.'

Vijayan rented a bicycle and rode down the narrow tarmac road lined by slender areca palms swaying in the coastal wind. Reaching a string of shops, he saw a group of houses set back about twenty metres from the road in a palmyra grove. Most were single storey and mud-brick with red-tiled roofs, though some were huts covered with stiff palmyra leaves.

Resting his bicycle against a tea-stall, Vijayan asked where everyone was.

'Gone to collect salt or toddy. That's what most people do here.'

'I see,' said Vijayan, looking around.

'Looking for someone?' the man asked, scrutinising Vijayan, who clearly wasn't a local man or itinerant merchant and didn't look like an official.

'I'm a newspaper reporter. I heard about the story of "The Good Sister." Thought I'd find out more.'

'You mean the well?'

'Yes. Where is it?'

'Over there, in those palmyras behind the shed.'

Vijayan swivelled around and saw a low-lying building and the trees beyond. 'Does it belong to anyone? Now, I mean.'

'No. It's dry, now as then. But you're in luck.'

'Luck?'

'The festival starts tomorrow. For Keni Amma, Goddess of the Well.'

'You mean…the woman who killed herself?'

'That's right. She and her seven children. Come, I'll show you.'

The low stone wall of the well was more or less intact. So were the wooden posts that rose above it to hold the metal rod from which the rope and bucket would have hung. But the posts now reached up towards the sky like empty arms. Vijayan bent over but couldn't see the bottom. His eyes crawled back up along the stonework inside, so dry not even a weed grew.

'Most people don't go that close,' said his guide. 'They're afraid the spirits in there might attack 'em. Only during the festival they feel safe.'

'Where do you hold the festival?'

'Right here. Where you're standing. You'll see it all, tomorrow night.'

Vijayan stepped back. Off to the side, at the base of a palmyra, he saw a row of stones. They stood upright in the sandy earth. One, two, three…eight stones. One about two feet high and the others half that.

Following his eyes, the man said, 'There's one for the brother, too. Over there.'

'When did he die, the brother?'

'A few years after his sister. Just lay down and died.'

'Will there be songs at the festival?'

'Of course!' the man said, dropping his guard and relaxing with the stranger. 'It'll be Punkani. She's the best, the sweetest voice. And she knows the story backwards and forwards,' he added with pride.

Vijayan sat down on the wall of the well and began to write in his notebook. 'This is where it happened? Right here?'

'Yes. That's why we have the festival. So she doesn't turn against us.'

The suicide had made her a local goddess. It's sheer superstition, he assured himself that night staring up at the ceiling. But he couldn't deny the power of the story. Those stones—for the sister, her children and brother—each represented a god or goddess who would possess someone in the crowd. He began to turn the story over in his mind, wondering why it captivated him, too.

The next day he was cycling at dusk along a deserted road to an interior village where he knew no one. Streaks of rose-peach ran across the horizon, and the land lay under a pale light. He felt relaxed, eager to see the festival, the singing and the well. But when he saw Velan cycling on another road, the colours drained from the sky, and he pedalled hard, trying to drive that image from his mind.

Vijayan heard the singing before he reached the well. A low stage had been erected next to the well, with loudspeakers and a string of light bulbs. Stumps of banana trees flanked the stage and arched over it with their fan-like fronds. In front, a small bamboo structure was decorated with white jasmine and the spidery tendrils of the areca palm. Smaller garlands of marigolds hung on each of the eight stones, which had been freshly white-washed and smeared with vermillion. The other stone, for the brother, stood undecorated.

Punkani, the singer, sat on stage behind a six-foot-long hunting bow. The curved wooden limb of the bow rested on the stage floor, arching upward, so that the bow string stretched horizontally in front of her. She struck the taut string with a pair of rattles, which shook the metal cowbells hanging from the string. One of the men beside her played a large earthen pot by striking its side with a piece of wood and slapping its mouth with a palm-leaf fan. Others played a small hour-glass shaped drum, wooden blocks and brass cymbals.

Sixty or seventy people were packed close together on the ground in front of the stage, men on one side, women and young children on the other. Must be half the village, Vijayan estimated, still standing back near the shed.

The audience didn't clap or tap out the throbbing beat of the pot and drum. In fact, they hardly moved at all, but they were listening to the fast-moving story. Punkani sang a line, which the chorus of men repeated, and then she sang another, a new line every ten seconds.

After an hour, Punkani's pretty face shone with sweat and excitement. She tossed the rattles high in the air, flashed her black eyes at the audience, caught the rattles and continued singing. When the drum-beat grew more insistent, her voice rose higher and higher, pulsing with the pain of famine, barren land and dying animals.

Now the crowd stirred, bodies tensed and heads twitched. The sister was rejected at her brother's door, and the children were thrown down the well. Two people stood up and began to dance, a man prancing with little leaps and a woman swaying from the waist. The garland was taken from the sister's stone and placed around the woman's neck, while one from the children's stones was hung on the man's. More men and women joined them, dancing with flowers from the other stones.

Although they gyrated in unpredictable patterns, the possessed dancers appeared to be in control. They demanded coconut milk, cigarettes and brandy, which were provided by the crowd, happy to serve their gods. Vijayan watched in mounting fear as the dancers swerved closer and closer to the well. The one possessed by the sister circled round and round, her head thrown back, her mouth open. Suddenly she bent forward over the wall, and Vijayan gasped, but someone drew her back.

A heavy metal chain dangled from the hand of a male dancer whose bulky body gleamed with perspiration as he stomped wildly around the open space in front of the well. Then he stopped and began to strike himself with the chain. Once, twice, three times he swung it high over his shoulder and then down onto his back.

Blood trickled through his sweat as he danced on. Again and again, he struck himself, and several times, when he seemed out of control, he was doused with a bucket of a little sandalwood paste diluted with coconut oil.

Long after midnight, when the music had stopped, the dancers sat down exhausted. But their work was not finished. They were still possessed by Keni Amma, the Goddess of the Well, and her children. People pressed around them, asking questions. 'Will my daughter have a baby?' 'Is my buffalo dying?' 'Will my son pass his exams?' Brief answers were supplied with a pinch of sacred ash.

Perched on the edge of the empty stage, Vijayan watched the dancers, these ordinary men and women besieged by people wanting answers. He wanted to speak to the woman possessed by Keni Amma but couldn't bring himself to feign belief in her prophetic powers. Then a middle-aged woman noticed him.

'Not from around here, are you?' she asked. Her sari, like her face, was clean but worn.

'No. I came to hear the singing. She's good, very powerful,' he said tentatively.

'She knows the story. That's why. Most singers just sing whatever comes into their head.'

'Do you hold this festival every year?'

'Yes, every year. But Keni Amma is always here.'

'What do you mean?'

'She's always here to help. I come to the well and the stones whenever I have problems.'

'And she helps you?'

'Yes.'

'How is that?'

The woman hesitated and then said, 'She was my aunt. Her brother was my father.'

Vijayan stared at her, and she looked back at him, pulling up one corner of her mouth into something like a smile.

When Vijayan returned to Melur and climbed the stairs to the room, it was nearly midnight. Sliding down on to his mat under the window, he listened to Raja and Mani breathing softly. All the way back on the bus he had written down what he had seen in Manakkadu. The well, the stones, the festival and the woman whose aunt had killed her children.

He hadn't looked at Pandian's letter since he left Melur almost a week ago. Nor had he thought about Velan or anything connected with his death. It was easy when he was moving, outside Melur, away from the shop, going someplace, doing something. Now, back in Melur, motionless and without a plan, the sediment began to settle and he couldn't avoid seeing what he had been doing. Chasing a story about an abandoned sister.

So what? he asked himself. Why should I bother with Velan? Or Pandian? But no matter how hard he tried, he couldn't escape the feeling that he was running from something.

Mani turned over in his sleep and opened an eye. He saw Vijayan flat on his back, staring at the ceiling, arguing with himself. He wanted to ask what was troubling him but feared he would only get brushed off. Making a mental note to talk with him tomorrow, he turned over and went back to sleep.

In the morning, Muttusami greeted Vijayan's arrival with surprise.

'You're back? But today's only Wednesday. You've got two more days' leave.'

'Yes, well, I…finished my business quickly.'

'Listen. I've sent the letter to the head office. Take those two days now or lose them.'

'I see,' said Vijayan, who understood little about his terms of employment. 'All right, then, I'm off,' he said with uncharacteristic gaiety and left the shop.

Stars sparkled in a moonless sky as Vijayan walked alone that night on the road leading to the western hills. For him those hard bright lights always had a cold beauty, and now their distance soothed him. Although he had few ambitions, he did want to make a difference. The Rationalist Society was something, he would admit, but the men at the meetings were already thinking about new ideas. It was others he wanted to change.

Mani always said he could do it through writing. That's probably true, Vijayan conceded. But face-to-face, personal contact was better. The problem was he wasn't gregarious and didn't like crowds, or even most people. He realized that he was the wrong person to achieve his own goals.

Returning late, he stood outside the room for a moment, worried about the decision he had made.

9

Pandian paced up and down. Not only had his network of Tamil agents been depleted, but yesterday his key associate had been questioned by the Military Intelligence Corps in Colombo. Subbiah had telephoned him the previous night, a thing he was told never to do, because he was frightened.

'They wanted to know about the meeting last month in Galle,' Subbiah had explained. 'They showed photos and asked me for names. They named Balan and Victor. I think they know a lot more…about you.'

'They may think they know, but we can work around them. Be very careful. And don't call me again. I'll be in touch the normal way,' Pandian had said hurriedly and put down the telephone.

He stopped pacing, fell into a chair and grabbed a cigarette. He felt safe in Madras and knew that Subbiah wouldn't compromise him. But maybe Colombo already had him under surveillance.

Vijayan got off the overnight bus to Madras and found his way to T. Nagar. Only the occasional car or auto rickshaw disturbed the quiet street, and few pedestrians walked on its narrow pavement. Vijayan admired the substantial late-nineteenth century houses, now divided into flats, in this garden suburb. Verandahs sagged and paint was peeling off walls, but such defects were screened by trees of fire-red blossoms, dangling yellow tassels and delicate white tracery. On a corner, Vijayan saw his favourite flower, the nagalingam, with its cluster of light pink and yellow stamens in a cave of deep scarlet.

Pandian's building was a pale green four-storey structure, surrounded by neem and mango trees. An outside staircase led up to a small landing and his door on the third floor. Vijayan stood amid pots of marigolds, wondering why he had come. Then the door opened and Pandian stood there, facing him, his large eyes steady behind black-rimmed glasses. For a moment neither spoke. Pandian's pinched lips relaxed and, without smiling, gestured him inside.

A hallway led to a spacious room, with windows on three sides. Vijayan had never seen anything like it. Tall trees, green and glassy, were within touching distance just outside the windows. Faded Persian carpets lay on the wood floor, with stuffed cushions and wicker chairs around a low coffee table. Vijayan's eye was drawn to a sharp-edged object poking out from a pile of papers and pamphlets. Leaning closer, he saw it was a miniature Eiffel Tower.

Two tall cabinets filled with books and files flanked a window. On another wall hung a large reproduction of a painting, a woman's body broken into geometric shapes of blue and red. Vijayan was looking at it when Pandian offered him one of the chairs and himself sat in another.

'When did you arrive?' asked Pandian, still expressionless.

'This morning, by overnight bus.'

'Where're you staying?'

'I don't know. Probably near the bus station.'

'How many days?'

'One or two.'

'You're a writer, aren't you?

'Ah…'

'You write books?'

'Yes.' Vijayan saw no reason to add that the books hadn't

been finished let alone published.

'Velan mentioned you organized a writers' group.'

'I set up the Melur Writers' Association,' said Vijayan, again not bothering to correct Pandian's information.

'Have you ever been arrested?'

'No.'

'You're not married, are you?'

'Look, what do you want? Who are you?'

Leaning forward, Pandian pushed aside the papers on the coffee table, found an engraved sandalwood box and took out a cigarette. Cocking a look at his guest that said, 'You don't smoke,' he grabbed the Eiffel Tower statue, flicked open its spire, rolled the little wheel hidden inside and lit his cigarette with the flame that emerged.

'I'm a Tamil patriot,' he answered, adjusting his glasses so he could look straight at Vijayan. 'Do you know what the new constitution in Ceylon says? Sinhala is the national language and Buddhism is the national religion. Our people are struggling, some are dying, to gain equal rights.'

He spoke with determination and without expending energy. Leaning further forward, he said, 'I need someone to help us.'

'Help do what?'

'Achieve justice for Tamils in Ceylon, equal status for our language and culture.'

'But what can I do?' asked Vijayan, pulling back from Pandian's prominent face.

'I need someone who's intelligent and can write pamphlets, letters, essays, speeches. Someone who can write proper Tamil and speak it, too.'

Vijayan relaxed a little.

'Someone who's independent, who can make up his own mind and act.'

'I'm not sure...' Vijayan began to object, when a woman appeared from another room carrying a tray. She was a little older than Pandian, maybe forty-five or fifty, and wore wide pyjama-like trousers and a loose tunic. Strong features marked her handsome face, set off by jet-black hair combed straight back and falling to her shoulders.

'This is Jeya,' Pandian said. 'She's part of our group.'

'Welcome,' she said, placing the tray with little ceramic mugs down on the table. Vijayan poured in milk and sugar, while Pandian and Jeya drank the coffee black.

Pandian resumed. 'We've very little money, and the work is not without danger. That must be understood at the very beginning.'

'What do you mean?'

'I mean that the Military Intelligence Corps in Colombo are attempting to break up our organization. They carry out surveillance on Tamil groups and often arrest people.'

'But we're in Madras, not Colombo,' protested Vijayan before he remembered that Velan had not been in Ceylon.

Pandian unlocked his gaze from Vijayan and looked towards one of the windows, as if he had heard something. Vijayan followed his eyes but saw only green foliage.

Pandian turned back to Vijayan. 'I need someone to go to Ceylon. To work there, from time to time.'

'Is that what Velan did? Work for you in Ceylon?'

'Yes.'

Vijayan fidgeted under Pandian's fixed stare. 'What would I do?'

'We can discuss that tomorrow.'

'Tomorrow?'

'I want you to think this over, in general terms, and meet me tomorrow.'

'I'm…I'm not sure.' Avoiding Pandian's unmoving eyes, he looked down at his leg, which was pumping up and down, unbidden. He stood up. 'All right. What time should I come?'

'We won't meet here.'

'Why not?'

'Best not to meet at the same place twice. It's safer that way,' said Pandian. 'Meet me at the Modern Coffee House. On the Marina, opposite the university library. 12 noon.'

Vijayan wagged his head in agreement.

'One more thing,' Pandian said in lower tone. 'Don't go back the same way you came here. Take a different route.'

Vijayan looked at him but didn't have to ask why. He went down the outside staircase and, instead of going down the street, turned at the corner. A man came out of a small shop and followed him. At the first intersection, Vijayan climbed on to a bus jammed with commuters and shoppers, without caring where it was going. He was just able to grab one of the frayed leather straps hanging from an overhead horizontal pole.

The bus hurled itself through traffic, lurching to avoid lorries, weaving around taxis and forcing auto rickshaws to pull over. Starting again after each stop, it groaned and expelled a black plume exhaust. More and more people crammed on until several men had only one foot on the running board and one hand on a pole. When the bus swerved or turned, they swung out and back like a hinged door.

At one stop, a large group disembarked and carried Vijayan with them. He tried to clamber back on, like a drowning man, but had to give up. Looking around, he saw the area wasn't a suburb or a commercial centre and was vaguely familiar. From a bridge over a railway line, he saw a massive building with triangular pediments resting on black columns. Fort St. George looked out of place, but he was impressed by its cold stone symmetry.

Then he raised his eyes, to the sea beyond, and tried to visualize Ceylon floating on its surface.

Should I go? he asked himself. He remembered that Pandian said he wanted to 'achieve justice.' Vijayan liked 'neethi', the word for justice, and said it aloud twice, listening to the cadence of a long syllable followed by a short.

Pandian also said it was dangerous work and used the English words 'Military Intelligence Corps.' Vijayan thought he had heard correctly and that he understood what they meant. 'Spying' is how he translated it in his head. But spying for whom?

He continued to wander, and found a bookshop, where he looked at translations of Tolstoy and Turgenev. Too expensive, so he turned to fiction and the latest romance by a bestselling novelist. The cover showed a young woman standing up to her waist in a pool of water screaming for help. More interesting was an autobiography by an Untouchable man, though Vijayan doubted he had written it himself. In the end, he bought the latest issue of a literary periodical because one of the essays highlighted on the cover was 'The Politics of Protest: Tamil Writers in Colombo.'

Pandian stood up and walked to a window, an unlit cigarette in his mouth. Jeya came and stood beside him, struck a match and lit his cigarette and then hers. She put a hand on his shoulder and leaned against him.

'You think he's the right person?' she asked.

'I don't know. But his hesitation makes me think he might be,' he said. 'I'll meet with him tomorrow and see. If he agrees, then I'll contact Subbiah.'

Both drew heavily on their cigarettes and looked out at the fading light. Mynah birds squawked in the top branches, and shrieking parakeets darted through the dense foliage. Noises rising from the street joined with raucous crows circling overhead and drowned out the voices right below their window.

The food-stalls along the Marina were doing a good business. Families on a day out and young men with nothing to do strolled along the broad promenade. It was low tide and the sandy beach stretched back for nearly a hundred metres from the water. Dozens of catamarans had gone out in the early morning and returned with the catch. Logs lashed together and curving to an upturned prow, the boats lay sunken in the sand like bleached whale skeletons.

Laundry was laid out on the beach or hung on makeshift clotheslines. Women and girls of all ages played in the surf at the water's edge, lifting their saris and skirts to meet the onrushing water. Their laughter was lost in the roar of the waves and the wind, as were the shouts of young men playing volleyball.

Vijayan watched these strangely silent scenes, though it was the limitless sea and sky that drew his eye. Above him, in front and on both sides, there were no boundaries, nothing to measure oneself by. His eyes followed the sea out as far as he could, out to the horizon, where even that line wavered and disappeared. Closer to shore, the water's surface was broken into sequins flashing silver and white.

The Modern Coffee House had a terrace that extended over the beach, and there he saw Pandian seated at a table. After they ordered coffee and snacks, Pandian spoke.

'This is the situation. Tamil groups are demanding a separate homeland. That will not be granted and civil war is coming. We need to defend ourselves.'

He lit another cigarette and continued, 'We have agents in the eastern and central districts. They're working to build an alliance between the Tamil groups and the Maoists. Together, they will overthrow the government and create a new society, based on equality for all. That's our goal.'

'But…how will you achieve it?'

'Look at East Pakistan. They fought a civil war with powerful West Pakistan and they won. Now they have their own country, with their own language.'

'Right,' Vijayan said, uncertain of the comparison. 'But what do you want me to do?'

Pandian leaned in close and spoke with unhurried resolve. 'Our people will take you to a base outside Madurai. Someone will come to Melur for you. He'll use my name. That's all.'

'And then?'

'You'll receive three weeks' training.'

'What training?'

'Mostly operational practices and communications. We use code for important messages.'

'Code?'

'Yes. Each Tamil letter has a number,' explained Pandian.

Vijayan was trying to visualize this when Pandian said, 'You'll need to read a lot about Ceylon, too. History, geography, politics.

'When would I go?'

'When you're ready. You'll go across on the ferry from Ramesvaram. As a researcher working on marine life.'

'Marine life?'

'Yes, that won't attract attention. You'll have to learn about that as well.'

'What about my job in Melur?'

'We'll take care of that.'

'"Take care"?'

'Listen. We have government support at the highest level. Not officially, but in practice. The khadi shop is government-owned, so they'll make sure everything's all right.'

'I see. But what happens when I get to Colombo?' Vijayan asked with rising anxiety.

'You'll be told all that, at the end of your training.' Pandian gave a thin smile and stared at Vijayan with unblinking eyes.

Vijayan looked down at his coffee and then out at the sea, searching for some discernible point in the distance. After a minute, he jerked his head back and asked, 'Who killed Velan? The Military Intelligence Corps?'

'Almost certainly.'

'So you want me to replace him? Now that he's dead.'

'That's up to you.'

'I don't know,' said Vijayan. 'I support your goals and I appreciate your confidence in me. But this is a serious decision that I cannot make without further consideration.' He liked the sound of his rehearsed words.

'I understand,' said Pandian. 'But our movement cannot stand still. I can give you ten days.'

'Ten days is fine,' said Vijayan, not knowing whether it was or not.

'That's agreed, then. You'll contact me by 1st April,' said Pandian, rising from the table and glancing at his watch. 'One last thing. Don't mention this conversation to anyone. To no one. Do you understand?'

Vijayan thought he saw hesitation—or was it fear—flash across Pandian's face. 'Okay, but how should I contact you? In your letter you said not to write.'

'Write to me, but not at my T. Nagar address. Use the Mount Road address on my business card. Do you still have it?'

'Yes.'

'Good. That's all.' With a slight tilt of the head, Pandian stood up and left the terrace.

Vijayan watched him reach the promenade and walk briskly away. At that moment, a crow swooped down and tried to snatch a pakora but only succeeded in knocking over Vijayan's coffee.

When Vijayan returned to the lodge and asked for his key, the man at the desk said, 'Your brother has it. He took it about an hour ago.'

'My brother?'

'Yes. He said you knew he was coming.'

'What did he look like?'

'Your brother?'

'Ah… I have three brothers and they're all coming to see me…eventually.'

'I see. He's short, shorter than you, anyway.'

'Did he have a limp?'

'What? Oh, you mean his leg. Yes, I think so.'

'Right. That must be Suresh,' Vijayan said and turned towards the stairs. He took his time, trying to calm himself. Probably no one there now, he reassured himself.

On the third floor, he slid rather than lifted his feet down the corridor towards his door, though what difference this silent approach would make he didn't bother to consider. Instinct had taken over. He stared at the door and his hand shook as he reached out. Gripping the handle steadied him.

Inside nothing appeared to have been disturbed, though the window was closed. He had opened it, he remembered clearly, in the morning because it felt hot and there was no chance of someone climbing in this high up. Someone had closed it.

'Suresh never liked open windows,' he said with a little laugh. Relieved, he picked up his shoulder bag and looked inside.

Everything was still there—toothbrush and powder, soap and dish, extra veshti and shirt—everything except the magazine he had bought the day before, with the essay about Tamil writers in Ceylon.

He sat on the bed and tried to think. The man with the limp had been here. He had also been in Kelalavu and in the shop in Melur. How did he know he was in Madras? And staying in this lodge?

He considered telling Pandian what had happened. But he didn't want to. He didn't want to tell anyone. He wanted to keep it all inside him, where it would remain a memory and not become a reality.

When he left the room fifteen minutes later, another man was sitting behind the desk.

'Your key?' he asked politely.

'My brother's in the room. He'll be down in a few minutes.'

Vijayan hurried out the door and down the street, clutching his shoulder bag close to his side. They won't harm me, he said to himself. They're just watching. He quickened his pace but couldn't run, not in floppy sandals.

The dense crowd of evening commuters and shoppers hemmed him in. He squeezed and darted between people until, looking back over his shoulder, he ran straight into a woman. She screamed and fell, but he kept going until he jumped into a cycle rickshaw and had to catch his breath before saying 'central bus station.'

The overnight bus he wanted didn't leave for another hour, so he took the first one going south. Inside, he looked around at the other passengers and took a window seat. His eyes swept back and forth across the bus station. Satisfied, he leaned back and closed his eyes. The bus eased out of the congested city and into the long shadows of the countryside.

10

'Welcome back,' said Muttusami as Vijayan entered the shop. 'Any adventures in Madras?' he asked without looking up from his ledger.

'No. Nothing really. Just seeing the sights,' muttered Vijayan.

Something in his voice made Muttusami look up, and he saw a different man. Vijayan's face had the same scowl and his body hadn't changed, but he seemed to move in his own space. As if the shop, the counter and the stools weren't there. He didn't knock into them but appeared to avoid them without knowing where they were there.

Bent down over his books, Muttusami continued to watch from the corner of his eye. Must be money problems again, he concluded, though he wasn't sure. Once or twice he opened his mouth but no words came. What could he say? 'Do you have a problem?' That would embarrass Vijayan if he was in trouble and sound stupid if he wasn't.

Vijayan, too, said nothing as he drifted ghost-like through the morning. With no customers around, Muttusami could stand the tension no longer and blurted out, 'Getting hot, isn't it?' The words seemed to travel across the room before penetrating the bubble around Vijayan, who looked up as if he had heard a knock on the door.

'Hot? Ah, I guess so,' he answered.

Vijayan stared outside and saw black umbrellas, not because it was raining but because the sun was beating down. He always estimated the heat by how many people carried umbrellas and how many crossed to the shady side of the street. Only March but it seemed like May, especially in the cramped shop. The ceiling fan had broken down years ago and, despite repeated requests to the head office in Madras, no money had been sanctioned to buy a new one.

Customers entered the shop. 'A long-sleeved shirt.' 'Let me see the new lungis.' 'A veshti, with a green border.' He pulled out the soft cotton clothes, unfolded them and waited, folded some up and put them back. Carefully wrapping the chosen article in newspaper, he tied it with the hanging string and handed it over.

His mind was racing. They knew who he was and where he was. The shop was safe. And someone was usually with him in the room or when he went for a walk. But not always.

'How are you?' He was facing the tall cabinets, with the counter and customers behind him. The voice was familiar but he didn't identify the speaker until he saw Murugan's face reflected in the glass.

Towel around his head, no shirt, torn veshti and no sandals, he stood out. No one said anything or showed discourtesy, but the contempt was palpable. Ignoring it, Murugan's sunken eyes looked straight at Vijayan.

'Come, we'll get some tea,' said Vijayan, getting a sign of approval from Muttusami.

The two men sat side by side on a wooden bench at the tea-stall outside the shop. Glass in hand, they looked down at the hard earth.

'What's new?' asked Vijayan trying to sound casual.

'The police came again. Yesterday,' said Murugan, blowing out his words in short bursts. 'Asked questions. Who Velan knew. What they were like.'

'Umm,' Vijayan grunted, wondering if his name had been mentioned. 'Did they write down what you told them?'

'They didn't write. I didn't say much. They talked.'

'What'd they say?'

'They know who did it. They think.'

'What?'

'Yeah. Periyaswami. The CPM organizer. Teacher at the primary school. In Nattampatti.'

Vijayan remembered him, Chellappan's colleague, who said he had seen Velan at a meeting with DMK leaders in Madurai a few weeks before his death.

Murugan continued. 'He was jealous. Of Velan. The police said. Velan borrowed money. From him.'

And not only from him, Vijayan thought and then said, 'I see. Any hard evidence?'

'Evi…what?'

'Evidence. I mean, why do they think he did it?'

'They argued. That's what they said.'

Vijayan wanted to tell him about the man with the limp and about Pandian. And that Velan had almost certainly been killed by an agent from Colombo.

'Why are you telling me this?' he asked instead.

Murugan turned to face Vijayan. Trying to focus his hollow eyes, he said, 'You were his friend. You came to see me.'

'Yes, but I…'

'You took the letter. Said you'd find out.'

'Where are his children now?' asked Vijayan to change the subject.

'They're gone.'

'Gone where?'

'A lady came. She took them.'

'What lady?'

'From a hostel. In Pasumalai. Church of South India. They're fed. Given clothes. A bed, school.'

'When are they coming back?'

'Coming back? What for? I've nothing to give.'

'They'll become Christians and forget you, their uncle.'

'So what? They won't be Harijans, will they?' Murugan said in a flash of anger.

Vijayan was going to tell him about the separate pews in churches and the caste divisions among Christians, but what was the point?

Without thinking, he asked, 'Do you think Periyaswami killed Velan?'

'I don't know. What do you think?'

'Me? What would I know?'

'You're educated. You can speak, to people. I thought...'

'What?'

'You'd go. To the police. About the letter. Tell them.'

Vijayan flinched with shame and turned away.

'What kind of police came yesterday?' he asked after a brief silence.

'What?'

'Did the main person wear a uniform?'

'Yes.'

'What did he wear on his shoulder?'

When Murugan looked blank, Vijayan persisted, 'How many stars?'

'Stars? Can't remember.'

'Did he give his name?'

'Yes. Joseph. Melur station. That's what he said.'

'Inspector? Sub-Inspector?'

'Don't know.'

'All right. I'll find him and tell him what I know. About the letter,' Vijayan said.

He lay awake that night, trying to think. Only eight days

before he had to answer Pandian. He had two choices. Go to the police or accept Pandian's offer. If I go the police about the letter, he said to himself, they'll ask more questions. Then what'll I say? That Velan worked for Pandian? That he was killed by an agent from Colombo? Can't do that. It would be dangerous for Pandian, and maybe for me.

On the other hand, accepting Pandian's plan might get him killed. He could always do nothing—his usual way—but he sensed that would only be waiting for danger to strike. As the uncertainties mounted and spun out of control, there was something else he didn't want to face. He was being watched, and pursued.

Vijayan fell asleep in the early hours, his breathing blending with that of the others in a concord they couldn't achieve during the day. Then a loud rapping on the open door woke them.

'You know a Raja?' shouted the small man in a khaki uniform.

'Umm,' grumbled Mani.

'Come with me. Quick.'

Vijayan, Mani and Krishnan threw on shirts and veshtis, found their sandals and followed the man down the stairs.

In fifteen minutes they reached the government hospital on the southern edge of town, a two-storey concrete block unrelieved by texture or colour, except damp stains on the walls. Inside, they were led to a high-ceilinged room, with ten or twelve beds separated by wood-framed cloth screens.

Two nurses in light blue uniforms stood beside one of the beds, white-winged caps on their dark hair. As the three friends approached, one nurse warned them not to tire the patient and then withdrew with her colleague.

Raja lay flat on his back, his head and most of his face covered with bandages. Tufts of his thick black hair stuck out through gaps in the dressing. One eye was closed. The other stared at his visitors.

'What happened, Raja?' asked Mani.

He spoke slowly, in a hoarse voice they could barely hear. 'Went to work. A house in Kallampatti. Kallar family. Painting windows.' The words exhausted him, and he had to catch his breath.

'When was this?' asked Vijayan.

'Yesterday. Started in the morning. Rested in the afternoon. She brought me rice and sambar. That's all.'

'Who did?'

'His daughter.'

'How old is she?' asked Mani, beginning to catch the drift.

'Don't know. Fourteen, fifteen.'

'Then what happened?'

'Nothing. I left when it got dark. They followed and attacked me. On the path to the main road.'

'Who attacked you?'

'Her brothers. Four of them. With a metal rod.' Raja's open eye closed. Mani shuddered and Krishnan looked away, while Vijayan stared at Raja's face, a scowl darkening his own.

'Called me a bastard. Said I showed no respect. Because I ate their food,' Raja said, thrusting his head forward and then falling back.

'That's all right,' said Mani. 'Just rest now. We'll take care of everything.'

The matron told them that Raja had been brought in after midnight. Fortunately, someone had found him lying on the path from Kallampatti to Melur and he had been brought straight to hospital.

'What are his injuries?' asked Mani in a low voice.

The matron fixed her large black eyes on him and said, 'He has a broken jaw and eye socket. The operation to reset his jaw will take place this afternoon, as soon as the doctor is available.'

'And the eye socket?' asked Mani.

'That should heal naturally, over time.'

They turned to go when the matron spoke. 'He awoke about an hour ago and said he had no family but told us where to find you.'

Not knowing what to say, they all shuffled towards the door.

'Such a good-looking young man. So brave,' she continued. 'He hasn't complained or said one negative word. Does he really have no family?'

Mani looked at the others and then at the seated woman. 'We don't know. We're his friends. We look after him.'

She took off her thick glasses and laid them on the table. 'Yes, but his mother and father. Where are they?'

'He doesn't speak about them. That's all we know,' said Mani, who pursed his lips in a half smile and left with the others.

The blue and green shop fronts looked dull grey in the early light. Huddled under thin shawls, figures crouched in the shadows of doorways. Only at the roundabout, with its open spaces, was the air tinted yellow by sunlight. At a tea-stall, the friends watched hawkers set out their goods on the pavement in front of unopened shops.

'What should we do?' Krishnan asked.

Mani lit a cigarette from the slow burning rope that hung from the edge of the stall. Vijayan glared straight ahead.

'I guess we'd better go to the police and report it,' Krishnan suggested, answering his own question when no one else did.

'What for? Do you think they'll take this seriously?' Vijayan asked.

'We can prepare a statement for Raja to sign,' Mani said.

'Right! And when the police question those brothers, if they ever do, who's going to pay the price? They'll make more trouble for Raja. He'll never work for a Kallar family again.'

No one responded to Vijayan's outburst.

'I'll go back at midday, during my lunch break, and see how he is,' Krishnan said. 'I'll get my wife to make him some food.'

'Good idea. I'll bring something in the evening,' Mani said.

'I wonder when the operation will be,' Krishnan said.

They both looked at Vijayan. Down the main road, towards the roundabout, he was watching a man drag two dogs by a metal wire put through the dead animals' mouths. He knew what this meant. At the beginning of the month, the local government paid 25 paisa for each dead dog brought to its offices. They said it reduced the pack of feral dogs that ran through the town, feeding on rubbish and spreading disease. Another man came into sight, heading the same way and dragging three dogs. Seventy-five paisa for him, Vijayan sneered.

'We're going to bathe. You coming?' Krishnan asked as he and Mani rose.

'No, not today. See you later.' The other two shrugged and left him sitting on the bench.

Got to find out what's troubling him, Mani reminded himself while Krishnan rambled on about problems at his bank.

When they were out of sight, Vijayan got up and walked to the place where he ate his afternoon meal. Although it had just opened, the long tables were filled with men pushing idlis and dosais into their mouths. Vijayan walked past them towards the back, to the concrete trough into which the banana leaves were thrown. He went through the door and stood outside in the lane, where two dogs were pulling leaves out of the receptacle. There was no Trotsky, and he never saw the dog again.

Entering the shop later that morning, he noticed the

formidable umbrella leaning up against the counter before he saw the man perched on a stool. Perumal Tevar swung adroitly around when Vijayan came in, hopped off the stool and executed a dramatic greeting by lifting his folded palms above his head.

'Greetings. How are you?'

Vijayan tilted his head in acknowledgement and returned the old man's smile with a grimace.

'You haven't heard, I guess,' said Vijayan stiffly.

'Heard what? That we Indians have landed on the moon?'

'No. About Raja. He was beaten up last night. Badly. He's in hospital.'

'Aiyo! Poor boy! What happened?'

Muttusami stopped his work and waited for Vijayan's answer.

'Seems he took some food from a Kallar girl, while working in Kallampatti. Her brothers attacked him. And he's still in pain. The operation is this afternoon, we hope.'

'Kallars are too proud,' said Perumal, whose Tevar caste was only a notch above them in the local hierarchy.

'And violent,' added Muttusami, a Naicker about on equal standing with Tevars.

'We're taking food to him. That's what he needs now,' said Vijayan.

'I'll go visit after I leave you,' said Perumal Tevar, levelling his eyes at Vijayan. 'First I need your help in a minor literary matter.'

When Vijayan didn't take the bait, he plunged on. 'You see, I've edited three ballads of not inconsiderable historical significance. I've corrected the mistakes that inevitably creep in when manuscripts are copied over and over again by less able people. Now, one of these ballads…'

'What do you want from me?'

'You're an intelligent man,' Perumal Tevar said, raking his long white hair back from his temples. 'A writer. Therefore, I would like your assistance in preparing an introduction to the ballads.'

'What exactly do you need? Help in writing it?'

'Oh, no my friend. Only that you cast your trained eye over the manuscript and point out any infelicities. If indeed any should exist.'

'All right.'

'Good. I'll call again tomorrow or the next day, when the manuscript is ready. Now I must go see our poor Raja.'

That night Mani and Vijayan sat with their backs against the wall on opposite sides of the small room. Vijayan's prematurely balding head was bent over a literary magazine, while Mani was reading yesterday's Tamil paper. Mani had already explained that when he went to the hospital, Raja had been transferred to Madurai because his jaw operation required special equipment.

The bare light bulb overhead flickered, then shone fully, flickered again and went out.

'Another powercut!' Vijayan snarled, throwing down his magazine.

'We need a new bulb,' said Mani, who got up and looked outside to check if all the lights were out in the neighbourhood. They weren't.

'Let's go for a walk,' he suggested.

Mani was determined to find out what was bothering his friend. He valued their companionship, built up over the past five or six years on shared literary interests and social ideals. Although Vijayan wasn't subtle when it came to literature or politics, he had a stubborn streak that often produced original ideas. The main difference was that Mani could be detached, while Vijayan's reactions were visceral. Caste injustice was anathema to Mani, but it didn't generate the heat that smouldered in his friend.

Underneath it all, though, was a deep rapport. They could

be together, in the same room or walking at night, and not say a word. When they did talk, they discussed everything from novels and local elections to medieval poems and the Cold War. Formulating and expressing these ideas took them beyond the little world of the shop, the office and the roundabout. Literature and politics were not just topics for debate—they filled every bone and sinew of their bodies.

'How was your trip down south?' Mani asked, after they'd left the town and entered the countryside.

'Good. I found the well.'

'Really! Why didn't you say so?'

'I…I didn't think it was important.'

'Tell me about it.'

By the time Vijayan had described what he saw in Manakkadu, they had gone more than four miles.

'Let's turn back,' said Vijayan.

'Sure. You also went to Madras, didn't you?' asked Mani, knowing he was probing a little closer.

'Yes.'

'And?'

'And what?' snapped Vijayan.

'Something's bothering you, isn't it?'

'I'm fine. Just tired. That's all.'

'Is it…something to do with Velan's death?'

'Why do you ask that?'

'Because you've been acting strangely. You're anxious and…'

'What do you mean?'

'You asked about someone who came to the room. Strangers have come to see you. You chase after that story about the well. A letter delivered to the shop. Then you go to Madras.'

'How do you know all this?' demanded Vijayan, anger rising in his voice.

'I was concerned, that's all. So I asked Muttusami. He says you're not your usual self.'

'Oh, he does, does he?'

'What's bothering you? It's Velan's death, isn't it?' Mani asked more directly.

'No, not at all.'

Mani stopped in the middle of the road and stared at him. 'Then why are you…'

'Look, Mani. It's nothing.'

'But…'

'But what?' Vijayan shouted. 'Stop this. Leave me alone!'

'Vijayan…'

'Get lost! Do you hear? Just fuck off!'

Mani stood in shock and watched him stomp off into a darkness so still he could hear the water running in the irrigation channel beside the road. Not wanting to meet Vijayan in the room, he spent the night at home with his wife.

Propelled by the ferocity of his feelings, Vijayan didn't slow down until he reached the roundabout. He didn't want to go to the room, either, in case Mani was there. There were the shop verandahs where night watchmen and beggars slept, but he couldn't face that.

Still fuming, he struck out on the road leading to the hills in the west. Then for some reason, he turned into a side street, a part of town he didn't know, tucked in behind the secondary school.

He passed a row of shops and stopped at a jeweller's. In the window display was a watch with a handsome black face, gold Roman numerals and a mesh band. It cost 300 rupees. Next door an electrical shop had several radios on display, including the latest transistors. That would be nice in the room. Could you get the BBC or just Radio Moscow? Two hundred and fifty rupees.

It was a warm night, so he picked up the bottom of his veshti and tucked it into his waist so that his lower legs were exposed to the air. Then he noticed a shrine built among the enormous exposed roots of a tree. It was a small concrete structure, painted dark blue and with an open front. A wooden sign on top said 'Mariyamman'. The goddess of small pox, both cause and cure of the disease.

Vijayan bent down and saw a dark granite statue about a metre high with a torn piece of cloth tied around the waist. A withered garland of tiny jasmine flowers hung from the neck, and vermillion shone on the forehead. Marigold flowers lay scattered at the feet among burnt-out candle stumps in shallow tin cups.

He looked hard at the statue. The shiny black stone, set off by the bright red dot and orange-red petals, was impressive. Tracing its smoothly sculpted surface with his eyes, he paused on the delicate lips and scoop in the cleft of the chin. Quality, he thought, unlike most things in this town. And it wasn't locked up behind a metal grill or hidden away in a temple. It was right here, on the street, open to anyone. Lots of people could ask for help and not just about small pox. He could, too. No one would know and it couldn't hurt.

A rat darted out from behind the shrine. It saw Vijayan and froze, thin nose quivering and tiny red eyes twinkling in the dark. Looking around, the rat considered its options and scuttled off towards the jewellery shop.

But how does one address a goddess? And what should he ask? Whether to accept Pandian's plan? What to tell the police? Money to buy that watch? He also wanted to know if he would get married. There's a lot he wanted to know, once he began to think about it.

It was past midnight when Vijayan reached the room and found the door locked. Relieved to be alone, he lifted his veshti, took the key out from the little pocket in his shorts and opened the unpainted door. It was pitch black and he remembered the bulb had burned out. Unrolling his mat, he slumped down with a grunt and folded his hands behind his head. Only six days left.

He heard voices as he climbed the stairs the following evening. Inside, Mani and Krishnan were talking to Raja, just returned from Madurai.

'Ah, welcome back,' said Vijayan with as much enthusiasm as he could muster. Raja acknowledged him with a little wag of his head and tried to smile but only revealed two rows of teeth held together by metal wires. His head of thick black hair and most of his face were still covered with bandages.

'It didn't go well, the operation,' said Krishnan. 'The bone didn't set right and his teeth are not lined up. The eye socket is all right. It's not broken after all, only badly bruised, like the rest of his face.'

'The doctor…' Raja tried to say through his teeth before Mani cut him off.

'Not now. Just rest,' he said and turned to Vijayan. 'His mouth is wired shut. Will be for several weeks, it seems. He can talk, but with a lot of pain. We'll have to feed him with a spoon.'

'How about a straw?' asked Krishnan.

'No. He can't suck and there's not enough space between the wires,' said Mani. Raja wagged his head in confirmation.

'Let's buy some spoons at Tip Top Fancy,' said Vijayan.

'He'll also need simple food. Dal and sambar, I guess. I'll ask my wife,' put in Mani.

'I'll do the same,' added Krishnan.

'What about his bandages?' asked Vijayan. 'They should be changed, probably every day.'

'We could take him to hospital,' said Mani, 'but we might have to wait hours.'

'And travelling there and back wouldn't be easy for him. He should rest as much as possible,' said Krishnan.

Raja tried to say something through his clenched teeth, but they didn't hear him.

'Right. We'll buy bandages, good ones, from that pharmacy near the roundabout and do it ourselves,' said Mani.

'Better get some antiseptic, too,' added Vijayan. 'And we'll have to keep everything clean.'

'Yes. We'll need one of those porcelain basins, some soap and towels. We can get hot water from downstairs,' said Krishnan.

The room became a hospital ward run by three nurses, who divided the day into morning, afternoon and evening shifts. At least one and often all three of them also spent the night with Raja.

Two days later, while on afternoon duty, Vijayan looked at the sleeping Raja and felt drowsy himself but remained alert. There were only four days left and he didn't know what he should tell Pandian. Or whether he should keep his promise to Murugan and talk to the police.

He had been thinking a lot about Velan's death, about how and why he had died. Struck with a machete, they said, but who had stood there, waiting with that heavy piece of steel? Was he really killed because he worked for Pandian? Maybe he was attacked like Raja, for some stupid reason.

Raja stirred and opened his unbandaged eye.

'Want some dal?' asked Vijayan, relieved to be taken away from his thoughts.

'No. Water.' He forced the words out through the metal grill on his teeth.

After guiding the water into Raja's mouth, Vijayan drew a clean towel out of the small aluminium trunk where they kept things for Raja and dabbed his lips and chin. With Vijayan's face so close, the young man examined him with his good eye.

'You don't look good,' he said. 'What's up?'

Vijayan leaned back and sat on his heels, folded the towel and laid it on the edge of the porcelain basin. Then he looked back at Raja, at his single visible eye, staring out from the white bandages.

'I'm in trouble, Raja,' he said without knowing why. 'It's nothing to do with money. Or politics. It's a problem with myself.'

Raja cocked his head a little to one side, and Vijayan pulled out his legs and crossed them. 'You see, I've never done anything worthwhile,' he said. 'Never, in my whole life.'

Raja started to speak, but Vijayan ignored him. 'Now I've got the chance to do something...something important that...'

'Tell me.'

'You see, I know what's right, but I've never done anything.' He wanted to tell Raja about his sister Meenakshi but didn't.

"And now you have a chance?'

'Yes. But it's dangerous and... I don't know if I can do it.'

'Take the chance. You're lucky to have one.'

'What do you mean?'

'I never had a chance. Except to paint walls. Fate was against me. From the start.' Raja struggled to enunciate through his wired teeth.

'From the start?'

'My father.'

'What?'

'Died in an "accident". Got drunk. Ran out into the road. That's what my mother said.'

'You don't believe her?'

'Doesn't matter. Ran off with another man. Haven't seen her since.'

'When was this?'

'I was six or seven. My aunt took us in. Me and my sisters. Her husband didn't like it. Used to beat us,' said Raja, out of breath.

Vijayan waited and he continued. 'I couldn't take it. Left when I was about ten. Stole some money. Went to Trichy. Worked on building sites. Then came here.'

'Where are they all now? Your sisters, I mean.'

'Don't know. Probably married. Somewhere near Trichy. That's why I'm saying this.'

'Saying what?'

'Take the chance. Whatever it is,' said Raja, slumping back in exhaustion.

Vijayan looked at him, his face battered for accepting food from the wrong person.

'All right. I will,' he said and stayed silent while this sunk in. Then he asked, 'You hungry?'

'Umm. Something different.'

'What?'

'Rice.'

Vijayan burst out laughing—Raja sounded like a five-year-old pleading with his mother, except his teeth were bared like a growling dog. Raja looked at him, confused, and then joined in with short snorts of laughter.

Vijayan got a plate of cold rice from the people downstairs, mixed it with dal and spooned the mixture into the space between Raja's two rows of front teeth. He had to position the spoon just right and then tip it so that the gruel slid off and into the gap. When it had worked its way through, he tipped in another spoonful.

Vijayan thought about what Raja said. He's got no family. Can't afford to wait, to see what's possible. He has to move ahead when he can.

Fifteen minutes later, Vijayan put down the spoon and spoke. 'What about the people who attacked you? We can go to the police.'

Raja shook his head no.

'Why not? We'll do it for you. We'll get them arrested.' Eager to act, Vijayan had put his cynicism to one side.

'No. They'll find me.'

'I see. Still I could…'

'No. You don't understand.'

'But…'

'You don't live my life. You try to understand. But you can't. You're a good person. You, Mani, Krishnan. You're my friends.' Raja stopped to catch his breath and continued, 'You've helped me. A lot. But you don't know me.'

'Raja, you know that I…'

'Better this way. We're friends. I can't live with your…ideas. They don't fit me. Who I am. A Pallar.'

Raja tried to smile through his metal grill while his single eye looked steadily at Vijayan.

'I see what you mean,' Vijayan said, though he didn't. All he knew was that they would never understand one another.

He filled the spoon again and lifted it to Raja's mouth. This realization hurt him because they had begun to treat each other as 'brothers.' Although he felt affection towards his nephew, Arun, he was too young, and he didn't spend enough time with him, anyway. And whatever he felt for Pushpa, it wasn't tenderness.

Besides they were family, while Raja was not part of his past. He was a stranger who had become a friend, like Mani. But Mani was his intellectual equal and sparring partner, while Raja was barely literate. Still, he had a kind of courage and his handsome face hid vulnerability. That's why he called him *tampi*, 'little brother,' and Raja called him *anne*, 'big brother.' They used these terms for others, too, but not with the same affectionate tone of voice.

What he didn't realize was that Raja's imperturbability came not from inner strength but from a diminution of expectation. That was something Vijayan would never grasp. He set goals, made plans, strove to achieve. The ideal always before him was Periyar, the energetic iconoclast he had met all those years ago in the railway station rest house.

Until then, Vijayan thought he knew about caste. It decided how people lived and died, who they married and where they lived.

But the old man had shown him that all this was in the mind. The edifice Vijayan had been trying to knock down turned out to be air. Only later did he grasp that this was precisely why caste was so powerful—it was more difficult to eradicate than, say, polio or illiteracy because it was an intangible idea.

That new understanding had set him at odds with the world around him. He began to register the unconscious codes of speech, body posture and clothing that underlay everyday encounters. Since he was not deferential by nature, it was easy to ignore some of these conventions, and it didn't matter much when he was young.

Later, though, people began to notice when he failed to follow the rules. Standing up when a man of higher status entered a room, for example, or gesturing towards his feet when introduced to him. Vijayan didn't always ignore these conventions since that would mean a life of constant friction. But he didn't always follow them either, because the daily drip of compliance would have eroded his self-respect.

His atheism, on the other hand, was less a revelation than a recognition that he had never believed in rituals and gods. Even the theatre and pageantry of it all failed to move him. Again, his unconscious non-belief didn't attract much attention until he left home.

While working in an office in Madras, his colleagues pitched in to buy a clay statue of Ganesh for a festival. When Vijayan failed to contribute five rupees, frowns appeared though no one said anything. On their way to lunch every day, they passed a Siva temple, where his colleagues made a barely perceptible bow, but Vijayan kept walking and was as conspicuous as someone out of step in a marching band. The others didn't notice until the fourth or fifth time and, again, while nothing was said, Vijayan felt they shut him out.

These rejections hurt him because he didn't think of himself as a rebel and didn't want to stand apart. Physical inclusion was important because it reassured him that he was like everyone else.

Vijayan put down the spoon and looked again at Raja's bruised face.

'Does it still hurt, *tampi?*' he asked, using the endearment.

'A little. The eye.'

'When are you going back to get your jaw reset?'

'Don't know. Might manage like this.'

'Didn't they say they would reset it?'

'Not sure.'

'What about the wires? When'll they come off?'

'Four or five weeks. They said. What's your opinion, nurse?' Raja's attempted laugh turned to a groan.

Vijayan smiled. Raja lowered himself on to his mat and lay on his back with a pillow behind his head to relieve the pressure on his face. His uncovered eye turned toward Vijayan. '*Anne*, get me a blanket.'

That's funny, Vijayan thought after he laid it over him. It's warm today.

Raja dozed and Vijayan considered again what he had said. Of course, he doesn't know the risk I'd be taking and I better…

Hearing steps come up the stairs, he expected to see Mani,

who would take over Raja's care.

'How's the patient?' boomed Perumal Tevar, leaning on his wooden umbrella as he stood at the door.

'He was sleeping,' said Vijayan without sarcasm. Raja opened his good eye and closed it again but remained awake.

'Well, I hope he's recovering. I haven't seen him since he was in hospital.'

'He's recovering. But the jaw wasn't set right. His teeth are wired and we have to feed him with a spoon. The good news is the eye socket wasn't broken.'

'Poor boy,' murmured Perumal Tevar, looking around the room. 'At least he's got good care. Anything I can do?'

'I don't think so. Except you can cheer him up with your company now and then.'

Perumal Tevar placed his umbrella in a corner and drew out a mat to sit on. 'Actually, I've come about that manuscript I mentioned the other day. It's ready for you to look at.'

'Right,' said Vijayan, who had forgotten all about it. 'It's not a good time now, with Raja and the shop. Muttusami's given me extra time off. But he's broken all his rules, so he's angry with himself.'

'I see. But it's not long. It won't take you more than a few hours,' said Perumal Tevar, dabbing the beads of perspiration on his bare chest with the towel hanging over his shoulder.

'Ah, length isn't the issue,' said Vijayan. 'It's your intricate phrasing and complex ideas that will require careful attention.'

'Well, then, come see me when you can,' conceded Perumal Tevar, too proud to catch the irony.

Raja opened his eye and sat up. 'Can't go. Must tell a story,' he said through his clenched teeth.

Perumal Tevar looked more closely at the metalwork in Raja's mouth. How can he talk? Or chew betel nut? he wondered. Distressed by any impediment to the proper functioning of the masticatory organ, he was speechless.

'Come on. At least one,' Raja pleaded.

'Well,' began Perumal Tevar, encouraged by the sound of his own voice, 'you know, don't you, that we Indians are about to send a rocket into outer space?'

When no one answered, he continued, 'It's true. You see, when the Americans landed a rocket on the moon, the Russians said, "We can do better than that" and landed men on the moon. Then the Indians said, "We can do better than both of you."

'"What's that?" the Russians and Americans asked. "We'll land men on the sun," the Indians boasted. "But that's impossible. It would be too hot," said the others. "We know," said the Indians. "That's why we'll land there at night." '

Raja choked on his laughter and Vijayan grinned.

'One thing still bothers me about all this, though,' Perumal Tevar said.

'What's that?' said Vijayan, expecting another joke.

'Is the moon a man or woman?' asked Perumal Tevar in earnest.

Vijayan bit his lip to suppress a smirk and admitted that he didn't know. When he promised to see him that evening about the manuscript, Perumal Tevar collected his umbrella and left.

Half an hour later Mani arrived to relieve Vijayan. 'Sorry. I couldn't leave the office when I wanted to. How is he?' he asked tilting his head towards the sleeping Raja.

'Not too bad. Perumal Tevar was here and cheered him up. He asked for a blanket, though.'

'Did he eat?'

'Yes. I even gave him some cooked rice, from downstairs. It seemed to go down easily.'

'We better get Chellappan and maybe Perumal Tevar to take over some shifts. I don't think we can handle this by ourselves much longer,' said Mani.

'I was thinking the same thing. I'll ask Perumal Tevar. I'm going to see him tonight anyway,' said Vijayan.

After Vijayan left, Mani told himself that his friend was beginning to act more normally and, looking at the sleeping Raja, thought he knew why.

Back at the shop, Vijayan got through the rest of the day on auto-pilot. Only three days left, he kept thinking as he composed his letter to Pandian.

'I am honoured,' he began but realized that was too self-regarding. Then he tried, 'I accept your offer with humility,' but disliked its false modesty. He settled on, 'I am prepared to do whatever is necessary to further the cause of...' The exaggerated language matched Pandian's commitment.

By the time he helped to close up the shop, Vijayan glowed with satisfaction at his skilfully worded letter. Muttusami noticed this and put it down to the elimination of his long-term debt.

As Vijayan walked toward Perumal Tevar's place, however, his contentment was eroded by doubt. Do I really want to do this? It is dangerous. And maybe I'm not up to it. Then Raja's face appeared in his mind and he revised the last sentence of his letter again.

A rickety wooden staircase led from the unpaved road up to a small verandah on the first floor of an old building. Perumal Tevar ushered him inside his room, and Vijayan surveyed the littered desk. A sun-bleached copy of Chambers English Dictionary, cheaply printed editions of traditional ballads, a well-thumbed SSLC Examination Guide, film magazines and newspapers, both Tamil and English.

For two hours they talked about revising the manuscript, chewed fried snacks and sipped brown sugary tea from ribbed glasses.

'I need to read through it again,' said Vijayan, as he rose to leave.

'Good. I think it's ready now. By the way, I'd like you to come with me to Madurai tomorrow.'

'What for?'

'I need to see a printer about publishing this. Two heads are better than one when talking business.'

'All right, but it'll have to be in the evening,' said Vijayan. 'I'm on afternoon shift with Raja.' Standing up, he glanced at the desk and saw an English newspaper he hadn't read. 'I'll borrow this,' he said and left.

11

Only two days to go, he repeated to himself trudging down the road that led to the hills in the west. Vijayan had awakened early the next morning and gone to bathe with the others still asleep. The thin fog that had settled over the fields was evaporating in the rising heat.

He hurried through his morning routine, hoping he could write his letter to Pandian in the room. When he got back, however, Krishnan was feeding Raja. It wasn't until late morning that he found a place to write. The most public place—a wooden writing desk at the post office provided for just such an activity—turned out to be the most private. Everyone was busy writing a letter and no one paid attention to him.

Standing at the high desk, he smoothed out the thin blue paper on its sloping surface. He began to write, but the scarred and scratched wood scrambled his handwriting. Finding a pamphlet in his shoulder bag, he slid it beneath the thin paper and quickly wrote the five sentences he had fixed in his head. As he was about to put Pandian's address on the front, Mani entered the post office with a bulky envelope. Vijayan stuffed the unaddressed letter into his bag and turned his back to Mani, but too late.

'How are you?' Mani asked in a casual tone.

'Okay.'

'Writing a letter?'

'Umm. To my sister,' Vijayan said weakly.

'I see,' said Mani, who knew that Vijayan never wrote to his sister and that, if he did, he would do so in the room. 'I'll take over from you this evening. Right?'

'Yes. Come at about five o'clock,' said Vijayan, pretending to fumble about in his bag for something.

When Mani had his back to him in the queue, Vijayan retrieved his letter. All he had to do was add the address. Glancing at Mani, he grabbed the letter Pandian had sent him and copied the address at the top: 3/C 2nd Cross St. T. Nagar, Madras. Having sealed his letter, he slid it into the slit in the wall marked 'Inland.'

That's done, he said to himself with a mixture of trepidation and relief.

Sitting in his room, Perumal Tevar was looking forward to the trip to Madurai. Vijayan interested the old man, who sniffed around any new acquaintance like a dog. This one, as far as he could tell, had a good knowledge of Tamil literature. More modern novels than ancient poetry, it was true, but that couldn't be helped. He had what the old man would almost call a passion for literature, though it seemed choked by other strong feelings. And that scowl of his—was he angry or just thinking hard?

Perumal Tevar's mind meandered as he gave tuition to the son of a man who had just opened a modern pharmacy in Melur. The lad was puzzling over verses in the Tamil version of the Rama epic. Knitting his brow into knots, he struggled to pronounce the words and missed the meaning altogether. He's the proverbial donkey carrying sandalwood, Perumal Tevar mused as he listened with irritation. 'All right. That's enough for today,' he barked and placed a reassuring hand on the boy's shoulder. Perhaps that's it, he reflected. Vijayan's scowl is just frustration.

During the hour-long bus ride to Madurai, Perumal Tevar noticed that Vijayan was in one of his moods. That pleased him because he knew his friend wouldn't be easily satisfied. Both were proud, stubborn men, but while that made Perumal Tevar vain, in Vijayan it bred discontent.

When they entered Galaxy Printing Works, Perumal Tevar scrutinized the printer—a wiry man pushing sixty, with betel nut stained teeth and tuffs of hair floating around the temples. Broken glasses, held together with tape, lay aslant on the bridge of his nose. No problem, was Perumal Tevar's silent assessment. Too dishevelled to be avaricious.

Indeed, up against Perumal Tevar's bluster and Vijayan's obstinacy, the printer had little chance. After small talk, Perumal Tevar placed on the table a parcel wrapped in a scarlet cloth. Unfolding it with ceremony, he lifted the manuscript to his eyes and held it out towards the printer, who had no choice but to accept the 274 foolscap pages as a blessing. Negotiations were brief. The editor would be paid 12 per cent of the sales price after the first 100 copies of a 500-print run were sold.

Walking back to the bus stand, Perumal Tevar's umbrella swung with extra swagger, and Vijayan's expression had lightened. Then he suddenly stopped and looked across the street at a police station. The scowl had returned.

'Not planning a visit, I hope,' said Perumal Tevar with a snicker.

'No, no. Just thinking about Velan. You see…'

'That's all over, my friend,' said Perumal Tevar, who only knew that his body had been found months ago. 'Don't worry about something that's passed. Now, as we were saying, that ballad about the seventeenth-century raja would…'

Vijayan fell back into step with the brisk pace of his older companion but responded to his enthusiasm with half-hearted replies. He was thinking hard about what would happen after Pandian received his letter.

Wait a minute! he said almost aloud, as Perumal Tevar crossed the street ahead of him. He had sent his letter to Pandian's T. Nagar address even though he had been told to use the one on Mount Road. He must have panicked with Mani near him in the post office and written the wrong address. Too late now, he consoled himself. Anyway Pandian's probably just over cautious. Nothing'll come of it.

Perumal Tevar stepped through the gap in a low-lying brick wall and they entered the bus station. Picking their way among the dangerously slow-moving machines, they found the bay from which their bus would leave. Two young men stood opposite talking in what sounded like English. Perumal Tevar took four long strides, drew himself up in front of them and asked in heavily accented but intelligible English, 'You are from England?'

'Yes, that's right,' said one of the tourists, looking at the barely clothed old man with a heavy wooden implement hanging in the crook of his elbow.

'Then you are also fishermen. Correct?'

'Excuse me? Fishermen?'

'England, Angleterra. Angles, anglers. The English are fishermen, I believe.'

And before the astonished tourists could reply, Perumal Tevar turned on his heel and marched back to Vijayan. On the bus back to Melur, Vijayan asked him how he knew English.

'I was taught by an Englishman. Most of us were in those days, even in small towns.'

'But I thought you left school early.'

'I did, but I learned some English before that. And then I practised on my own.'

'Practised?'

'Yes. I made up sentences and spoke them to myself. Over and over again.'

'Pandian should get the letter tomorrow. Tomorrow or the next day for sure,' muttered Vijayan as he walked to the shop early next morning. 'So I'll probably get his reply by Monday.' Retrieving the key from the shop next door, he opened up and made himself busy.

'How are you?' asked Muttusami cheerfully when he entered and saw Vijayan already at work. This is a welcome change, he added to himself.

'Not bad,' said Vijayan, turning around from the glass panels where he was rearranging piles of cloth.

'I've got to sort something out at the bank,' Muttusami said. 'Be back soon.'

Having tidied up and with no customers, Vijayan sat down on his stool. He couldn't stop thinking about when he would get Pandian's reply and what it would say. Or would someone just show up and take him to the 'training base'?

Resting on the cross support, his right leg started pumping up and down. He got up and walked the length of the counter, came back and began to play with the string dangling from the ceiling when his eye strayed to the newspaper he had borrowed from Perumal Tevar. It was *The Hindu*, the English-language paper, from two days ago. Smoothing out the front page on the counter, he read the headlines. **'British troops shoot demonstrators in Northern Ireland.' 'North Vietnam launches major offensive.' 'India withdraws troops from East Pakistan.'**

Turning the page, he scanned the national news about scandals in Delhi and the behind-schedule preparations for the Indian team going to the Olympics in Munich. The regional news had detailed reports on the new state government's education reforms, which Vijayan read with interest.

Then his eye snagged on a small headline: **'Three killed in Madras bomb blast.'**

> *Yesterday afternoon at about 3 pm, an explosive device was detonated in a residential building in T. Nagar, Madras. Preliminary reports suggest that three persons were killed. They were named as S.K. Pandian, M. Jeyalalitha and Subbiah Nadar.*

Vijayan gasped and read on:

> *According to local sources, Mr Pandian had lived at the address for the past four years. Ms Jeyalalitha and Mr Nadar are believed to be his associates. The explosive device has not been identified, although police believe that the explosion was deliberate. At present no motive is apparent and no one has been arrested.*

He stared at the black print, examining each word to make sure.

Then he swallowed hard. He knew who had killed Pandian. And he knew why they had killed him.

'I'd like some cloth, for a shirt.' Although he heard this polite request and looked up, Vijayan made no reply.

'Are two metres enough? For a long-sleeved one?' the man continued, now a little bewildered.

'Yes. That should be enough,' Vijayan managed to say. 'It depends on what kind of cloth you want. You see, we have...'

When the customer departed with his package, Vijayan looked at the newspaper on the counter. He folded it in half and smoothed it down with the heel of his hand. Folding it a second time, he pushed harder, again and again, and then left it on the counter. It wouldn't stay flat no matter how hard he pushed.

For the rest of the morning Vijayan played his part in well-rehearsed scenes. He spoke and he moved, but his face wore no expression. Muttusami noticed the change as soon as he came back. He's gone into himself again. Probably another debt, he surmised as he watched Vijayan drag himself around the shop.

By midday, Vijayan's whole body had tightened with fear. Would they come after him, too? They knew he had been in Madras and probably knew he had met Pandian. The man with the limp had even followed him here, to the shop in Melur.

He tried to keep calm, but his mouth was dry and his legs felt heavy. What should he do? He steadied himself by gripping the edge of the counter and sitting down on his stool.

'Feeling all right?' asked Muttusami.

'Ah, yes. I mean, no. Something I ate, I think.'

'Better go to the room, then.'

'Right. Right. I'll go lie down for a while.'

He walked slowly, one step, then another, but his mind was screaming. Suppose they find my letter to Pandian? It shows I'm one of his agents.

Inside the room, he collapsed on a mat, waking Raja.

'You're early,' the younger man said opening his one good eye.

'Not feeling well. Had to come back early,' Vijayan panted. The fear gripping his body had exhausted him.

'Right. Let's switch roles,' said Raja, baring his metalwork in a grin.

'Raja,' Vijayan began, still short of breath. 'You know what we talked about yesterday? Well, I did it. But today…'

'What, *anne*?'

'Today, the newspaper…' he started to explain but stopped. 'I'm not feeling good.'

Raja knew he was hiding something but said, 'Better sleep a little.'

'Okay.'

'Can you get me some cooked rice first?'

'Of course.'

When he had fed Raja and laid a blanket over him, Vijayan looked down. Something's not right, he thought—the colour of his face.

Although he, too, wanted to sleep, he knew he shouldn't. Inside the room, with Raja beside him, he felt safe, though his heart pounded and his body shivered. But he tried to think.

He realized that the newspaper, with the report of the bomb blast, was two days old and that he had sent his letter only yesterday. A letter to a dead man, he said to himself. Who reads those?

He could go to the police and ask for protection, but he doubted they'd take him seriously. He could tell someone about what had happened—Mani or Muttusami. That's sounds good, but could they protect him from someone who wanted to kill him? Pandian had influential friends. No. There was only one thing he could do.

Leave Melur, as soon as possible. They wouldn't find him at his sister's house in Virudhunagar. Having fixed this plan, his body relaxed and his heartbeat slowed. He also decided that no one in Melur should know where he was going.

'*Tampi, tampi*,' Vijayan whispered as he nudged Raja's sleeping body. When Raja opened his eye, he continued, 'I've got to tell you something. I'm going away.'

'Away? Where?'

'I can't tell you. And I can't explain why, not now, but…it's part of what we talked about yesterday.'

'I see. When are you going?'

'Tomorrow. I don't know when I'll be back. Maybe three months, maybe longer.'

Raja sat up and looked hard at Vijayan, who met his eye and said, 'When I do come back, you'll be better. Everything'll be better.'

'Right.'

'Until then, we have a secret.'

'Secret?'

'What we talked about yesterday. The chance to do something. I haven't talked about that to anyone else. Keep it just between us, okay?'

'Don't worry, *anne*. I'll keep it safe. Until you come back.'

'Good. I'm off to the shop, but I'll be back this evening.'

When Vijayan entered the shop, Muttusami saw a different person. 'Feeling better?' he asked, with no customers about.

'Yes. But I've got to…go away again.' Vijayan spoke without looking at his manager.

'What is it this time?'

'Sorry, but I can't say.'

'I see,' said Muttusami. 'We could always apply for emergency medical leave. That's allowed once a year. Can we say it's medical?'

'Well, yes, in a way.'

'Right. It's leave without pay. And you can rejoin with no questions asked.'

Vijayan wagged his head in agreement.

'Let's see now. How long do you need?'

'Three months, to begin with. Possibly more,' said Vijayan, still not meeting Muttusami's eyes.

'Three months! Listen, if you're in any kind of financial trouble, I can…'

'No. It's nothing to do with money.'

'All right. All right. It's not a financial problem,' Muttusami muttered, backing away and sitting down on his stool. 'It's a medical problem, like you said. You certainly don't look well, you know.'

'Well, it's a...serious problem,' Vijayan offered.

Muttusami considered this for a moment before asking, 'When do you want to leave?'

'Tomorrow.'

'Tomorrow? For three months! How am I going to run this shop by myself? I won't get a temporary assistant for at least a month!'

Vijayan looked at him but said nothing.

'Besides,' continued Muttusami, 'there's the paperwork we need to do.'

'Can't you backdate the letter?'

'Yes, all right. But who's going to help me in the shop?'

'Forgive me. But I have no choice. I have to leave Melur.'

'"No choice"? What does that mean?'

Again Vijayan stood without speaking. Muttusami looked at him and saw for the first time that he wasn't ill. His dark brown eyes stared like those of a frightened animal.

Muttusami stood up and smiled. 'All right, you rascal. I'll take care of everything. You might as well take the rest of the afternoon off and get ready to leave.'

'Thank you,' said Vijayan.

'By the way, where are you going?'

'I can't tell you that,' said Vijayan, hanging his head.

'No problem, no problem at all,' chirped Muttusami as he clapped a hand on Vijayan's shoulder. 'It's a medical problem. Just come back feeling better.'

'I will,' said Vijayan as he moved toward the street. 'Just one more thing.'

'What's that?'

'If anyone asks about me, don't tell them anything.'

'That's easy,' Muttusami chuckled. 'Because I don't know anything.'

'Yes. But don't say anything at all. I mean, about what you think you know.'

'Oh, I see. No, I won't say a word. Now, off with you.'

Vijayan took a step towards the street but turned around, put his palms together and raised them to the level of his chest, something he rarely did. 'Goodbye,' he said.

'Goodbye and come back soon,' said Muttusami, also raising his palms. He wanted to say something more but could only swallow hard. That evening, when he lit incense in front of the framed picture of Lakshmi, he mumbled a few words for his friend.

Fear and confusion drove Vijayan further into himself. He needed help, maybe protection, yet all his life he had built up a wall around himself. Now that protection had become a barrier.

Back in the room, Vijayan told Mani and Krishnan more or less the same story he had told Muttusami. They listened and didn't ask any questions. Raja lay on his side, listening.

Then they began to revise the schedule for Raja's care and find a replacement for Vijayan. This was a relief, allowing everyone to speak openly, as they had always done.

'Chellappan's agreed to help. He says he can come three times a week. In the late afternoon,' announced Mani. 'How about Perumal Tevar?'

They swung their eyes to Vijayan, who hesitated before saying, 'He's also agreed.'

'When can he come?' asked Mani.

'Ah, he said he'd let us know. He has to check his tuition schedule,' Vijayan said. He hated himself, not for lying but for neglecting something that would help Raja. His dissembling struck a false note that deflated the atmosphere. An awkward silence settled and no one picked up the thread of conversation.

Next morning, Vijayan knelt down in front of a small cardboard travelling case covered with a tan cloth. Inside he laid his two extra veshtis and shirts, underpants and vests, a handkerchief and a towel, plus things for bathing and cleaning his teeth. On top he placed his notebook, a collection of short stories, a compact English dictionary and a Tamil translation of Turgenev's *Fathers and Sons*. Over these he spread his cloth shoulder bag. His pen would go in his breast pocket, and ink he could buy anywhere.

It's not much, he thought, closing the case, but others had less.

The awkwardness of the previous night returned when Vijayan stood ready to leave in the morning. No one knew what the others were thinking, and no one knew how to express what he was feeling. It wasn't just Vijayan's mysterious mood and sudden departure. The future shaped by their shared ideals was less certain now that the limits of their friendship had been exposed.

Raja, who lay on his mat, too unwell to stand up, watched as his 'older brother' turned to step out the door. Vijayan gulped and gave him a little smile before climbing down the staircase His other regret was that he hadn't told Murugan he was going. Not enough time, he told himself.

Later that morning, Mani went to the khadi shop on his way to office. Muttusami looked up from his bookkeeping, greeted him and said, 'Vijayan's not here.' He assumed Mani knew this but was also conscious of his promise to Vijayan.

'I know. We said goodbye this morning,' said Mani, taking a seat on one of the stools. 'Strange. He left so suddenly.'

'Umm. He didn't look well,' said Muttusami.

'Took medical leave, he said, for three months,' Mani added.

'That's right.'

Mani discarded caution and plunged in. 'Did he say anything about why he had to leave? Where he was going?'

Muttusami looked at Mani for a moment and said, 'No, he didn't tell me anything.'

'Same as us,' said Mani. 'But he's in some kind of trouble. That's for sure.'

'Yes. Then, he's always been a little odd. Lost in his thoughts,' suggested Muttusami.

Mani smiled, thinking of the long hours spent walking with his friend at night. 'Anything happen yesterday? Out of the ordinary, I mean?'

'Nothing I can think of. Though he came in early yesterday, even before me.'

'And during the day?'

'During the day?' repeated Muttusami. 'Well, yes, something was different.' He didn't think mentioning this would compromise Vijayan.

'What?'

'I had to go to the bank and when I came back he looked different.'

'How?'

'Nervous, worried and…,' Muttusami searched for the right word. 'Shocked. Yes, he looked shocked.'

'Why would that be?'

'No reason I can think of. It was a slow morning. He had time to read his newspaper.'

'What newspaper?'

'I don't know. After he'd left, I found it folded up, over there,' Muttusami said, pointing to the far end of the counter.

'Where's it now?'

'I must have put it under here, for packaging. Might have used it already,' Muttusami said and bent down to search beneath the counter.

'Ah, here it is,' he said and handed the paper to Mani.

Mani spread it out on the counter and scanned the news, as Vijayan had done the day before. His eye also halted at the story about the bomb blast in Madras, but he read it quickly and moved on. Nothing there he could connect to Vijayan's sudden decision to leave Melur.

'I just can't understand why he left like that,' said Mani. 'I guess we'll never know. Unless he tells us.'

In Madras, T. Ramachandran was sweating. His pudgy body and heavy bag kept moving forward on his short legs, like a wooden toy on wheels. He liked delivering the post in T. Nagar, with its flowering trees and shrubs, clean-shaven men and women in expensive saris. Today he had a letter for the well-dressed man at 3/C 2nd Cross Street.

As he climbed the stairs to the third floor apartment, there was no police presence or any sign of what had happened a few days before. When he pushed the ordinary letter through the hole in the door, though, he smelled something acrid inside. Remembering that they both smoked, he began to climb back down. Then he noticed that the marigolds were withering in their pots. That's odd, he said to himself. They usually keep them well-watered.

12

It just fits, thought Arun as he pushed the pencil box into his satchel. The slender metal container slid in vertically between the tiffin carrier and history textbook. Sitting back on his haunches, he surveyed the neatly packed contents with satisfaction. He closed the flap, buckled it and swung the heavy load over his shoulder. Standing up, he adjusted the straps so that the satchel rode high on his back, its now sun-faded temple tower barely visible.

'C'mon! Time to go,' he shouted, standing by the door. His younger sisters, Vanni and Kalyani, were still scrambling about in the front room picking up things. Pushpa hurried out from the kitchen holding three parcels of fried snacks. 'Here's some muruku for you,' she said.

'Can't put it in now,' said Arun, disappointed but proud of his packing.

His sisters took the packets and stood up for the final inspection. Pushpa straightened the bows on their braids and adjusted their blouses and belts before smoothing down their skirts. As they picked up their canvas satchels, she turned toward Arun, comb in hand, but he was already out the door. The twelve-year-old led his sisters down the street, bending forward as if breasting a headwind on a cliff high above the sea. If he did turn around on the 20-minute march to school, it was only to make his charges hurry up.

Pushpa watched them from the doorstep until she heard her husband calling. She came back into the kitchen and saw he was where she had left him, sitting cross-legged on the floor bent over a plate of idlis.

'Give me some more chutney. Can't stand 'em dry,' he said tossing another chunk of steamed rice cake into his mouth.

Selvan was an expansive man, not fat or flabby but outsized, with ill-fitting arms and exaggerated shoulders. His high waist made him look taller than he was, and his bulky head seemed about to tip to one side.

Pushpa ladled on more coconut chutney, timing her movement to avoid his hand travelling at speed between plate and mouth.

'Arun's been stubborn. Getting above himself these days. Have you noticed?' she asked.

'Umm. Is he?' Selvan managed between mouthfuls.

'Yes. Of course, he's doing well at school and in sports. But he's not always courteous at home. To me.'

'I see. By the way, when is the kabaddi competition?' asked Selvan.

'Kabaddi! Kabaddi! That's all you care about,' she said, raising her voice. 'I'm talking about his manners.'

'He's all right. What about Vanni? Anything we can do about her teeth? She'll never get married with those things sticking out a mile!'

'Leave it. She's only ten, you know.'

And there they left it, for another day. Selvan rinsed his mouth and hands with water from a tumbler, letting the water trickle down into the shallow eating plate. Getting up with effort, he put on a clean shirt, slipped into his sandals and picked up his synthetic leather briefcase. It contained nothing, but he liked carrying it.

Watching him go out the door, Pushpa reflected that she had done pretty well, all considered. Her father's jewellery shop in Virudhunagar hadn't been much to boast about, and no one could say her brother's career had enhanced the family's status. Nor had her sister's child marriage.

Selvan was predictable, which his wife liked, and protective, which she accepted. But his only personal interest, beyond food and sleep, was kabaddi, the competitive game of tag that he had played as a boy and was now a national pastime.

Pushpa tidied up the front room, putting Vanni's toy dog, Arun's comic books and Kalyani's colouring book in the massive cupboard that stood against the wall. It was the only good piece of furniture in the house, an heirloom from Selvan's family, and she loved its dark maroon surfaces, it compartments, drawers, cubby-holes and shelves.

She was writing up the shopping list for the woman who went to the market for her when she heard a voice.

'Anyone home?' Vijayan called, stepping through the open door, travelling case in hand.

'Come in! Come in!' she cried getting up.

Vijayan looked tired. He wore his trademark disapproving expression, but the energy had drained away, leaving a pallid frown. And his observant eyes hardly moved.

'Have you eaten?' she asked.

'No. Just arrived from Melur.'

'Come. I'll make you some dosai.'

Turning to lead him to the kitchen, she glanced at the new travelling case, which he had put down. Not a short trip, then, but she wondered what the reason might be. She wouldn't ask him directly since she knew he wouldn't tell her anything important.

Drinking coffee afterwards in the front room, he explained that he had come to visit for a few weeks on medical leave, that Muttusami had said he looked rundown and needed rest. As he spoke, Pushpa heard an unfamiliar tone in his voice and worried that his illness was more than temporary.

While Vijayan was taking a nap in the back room, she considered the possible reasons for this sudden but not short visit. Maybe he lost his job. He won't like that, not one bit, she thought, referring to her husband. Or maybe he's in trouble with a woman. No, not likely, she said to herself with a knowing smile.

No matter how hard she tried to convince herself that nothing was wrong, Pushpa couldn't ignore the change in her brother's voice. Vijayan always spoke in a husky tone, but today his voice was higher, and the words seemed to stick at the back of his mouth.

When Selvan came home that evening, he found his brother-in-law lying on the floor, propped up on his elbows. Beside him stretched the shorter body of his son. He noticed Vijayan's clean but thread-bare veshti and, next to him, Arun's legs sticking out from his dark purple shorts. They both raised their legs, held them in the air for a few seconds and then let them drop back down to the floor, not in unison but in some kind of pattern. The rising and falling limbs disturbed Selvan, who turned away and took his briefcase to the bedroom.

When he heard his father's heavy step return to the front room, Arun rolled over on his back and said, 'Uncle's helping me with my history.'

Selvan and Vijayan exchanged brief greetings, with the latter still lying on his stomach and looking at Arun's schoolbook. After the family had eaten, the brothers-in-law sat on chairs, as the three children were put to bed by their mother.

'So, you're on medical leave?' asked Selvan swivelling his large head.

'Yes. Two weeks at least, maybe more,' answered Vijayan, leafing through the previous Sunday's newspaper.

'Anything serious?'

'Not really. Muttusami noticed I was "rundown." That's how he put it.'

After pumping him with more questions, Selvan doubted that Vijayan was ill. As a rule, he tried not to take much notice of his brother-in-law. Not a disgrace, but not exactly a success either, was how he summed him up. He appreciated that he was able to help the children with their school work, but Selvan felt an unease at the thought that he might influence them, especially Arun.

Although he never put it into words, not even to himself, the prospect of a prolonged stay in the house stirred in him a latent dislike of his brother-in-law.

Three days later, on a Saturday, Arun and Vijayan walked hand-in-hand toward the Imperial Cinema. Pushpa had not approved of the idea, but the twelve-year-old had anticipated that.

'Amma, can I go to the Imperial on Saturday?'

'Arun, you know your father can't take you on Saturday.'

'But uncle can, can't he?' said Arun, with a barely perceptible smirk. Pushpa had no answer, and Selvan, though not pleased, could think of no good objection either.

Inside the cavernous theatre, Arun sat next to his uncle watching the latest Tamil blockbuster starring Shivaji Ganesan. The forty-five-year-old matinee idol was in his prime, and Arun could hardly breathe as he watched the plump body slither from scene to scene, dance away from danger, sing songs of sorrow and finally win the girl who had never lost faith in her wayward hero.

When Arun and Vijayan filed out of the cinema almost three hours later, it was twilight. They didn't talk much as they picked their way through the crowded streets lit by paraffin lamps on pushcarts. The drama on the screen had overwhelmed them both, and each knew that to talk too soon would break the spell of their shared pleasure. Holding hands, they moved together, stopping to look at a shop window and then going on. Once or twice, Vijayan scanned the street for anyone with an unusual walk.

'Good, wasn't it, *mama*?' said Arun, after about ten minutes.

'Yes. It was.'

'I mean, he's so…strong and smart,' said Arun turning his face up towards his uncle.

'Well, he's a strong personality. But, I'm not sure…'

'I want to be like him. When I grow up, I mean,' Arun said.

'Oh, I see,' Vijayan said, not knowing how to respond.

'After school and all that. I want to be big and…handsome.'

'Oh, you'll be all that, Arun. But maybe you'll go to college. You could be a scientist or a doctor.'

'That's what mother says. But I can still be like Shivaji, can't I?'

'Of course you can. But first you need to work hard at school,' said Vijayan. 'Shivaji is a film star not…a real person,' he added, though this didn't sound right.

'What?' asked Arun, knitting his brow and shooting a look up at his uncle.

Before Vijayan could manage an answer they heard shouting in front of them. Edging to the inside of a circle, they saw a figure gyrating around with high steps and abrupt leaps. Yellow and black stripes rippled on its sinewy body as it crouched low and turned a whiskered face in one direction and then the other.

The tiger man, complete with long tail, paws and fangs, now stalked the crowd on all fours. It sprung forward and the spectators scuttled backwards; then it swung around and sized up another section of the crowd. Arun screamed with delight and held Vijayan's hand even tighter.

'Look, uncle! He's got tiger teeth!'

'They're not real, Arun,' said Vijayan. 'C'mon, let's go. I can't go home and tell your mother you were eaten by a tiger.'

'No. She might believe you,' said Arun with a crooked smile.

Then he screwed up his face into a tight frown, making his ears stick out, and said, 'And father wouldn't be happy with you, would he?'

Vijayan didn't reply but cast a sideways and downward glance at his nephew. He knows more than I imagined, he said to himself. A watcher, like me.

As they neared home, Arun looked up at Vijayan again and asked, 'Uncle, are you ill?'

'No. I mean, yes. I'm not feeling well. The doctor said I have exhaustion.'

'Oh, ex-haus-tion,' said Arun, feeling his way around the word with the tip of his tongue. 'Like at the end of my kabaddi games?'

'Yes.'

'When will you get un-exhaustion?'

'Two or three weeks, at least.'

'Good. Then you can see my match next week.'

'I'll look forward to that,' Vijayan said, tiring of the topic.

That evening, Vijayan joined the family in the front room after dinner. The men read newspapers, Pushpa helped Vanni with her maths, Arun copied a history lesson and Kalyani filled in her colouring book.

'Papa,' Arun called softly.

'Umm,' grunted Selvan, not looking up from his Tamil paper

'Uncle's going to come to the kabaddi competition.'

'I'm taking you to that,' said Selvan, raising his head.

'I know. But uncle can still come, can't he?'

'Of course,' Selvan said and returned to the list of commodity prices.

Vijayan went to the library most mornings, after coffee, to read every newspaper he could. He liked walking up the wide steps to the solid, red brick building constructed at the turn of the century with funds donated by a local merchant and now owned by the municipality. The spacious reading room, with its high ceiling and long windows, felt cool, even now in late April.

A month had passed since the initial report of the bomb blast in Madras, but he had found no further news. The police must know about Pandian's political activity, he thought, but if a CID investigation had begun, it was kept secret. He guessed that the government in Madras wouldn't want its support for Pandian's clandestine work in Ceylon to become public.

On the island itself, the political situation was worsening. In one paper Vijayan was alarmed to read that Tamil groups were openly advocating violence in order to create a separate homeland. No paper said anything about an alliance between Tamil and Sinhala dissident groups. That possibility, Vijayan suspected, had ended with Pandian's death. Armed resistance—and civil war—seemed inevitable.

One day, when he returned to the house at midday, Pushpa told him a Brahmin astrologer had come that morning and fixed the date for their mother's annual memorial ceremony. The ritual, she explained, would be held on a day in the dark fortnight of the moon that corresponded with the date of their mother's death in the lunar calendar. Vijayan tightened his lips but failed to suppress a sarcastic smile as he listened to her describe the astrologer's calculations.

'Next Tuesday's the day,' she announced. 'It'll begin early that morning and we need to prepare the day before.'

He knew what to expect and had done his duty, as the oldest son, in his case the only son, many times before. Summoned by his sister by telegram, he used to arrive the day before the ceremony, but now he was present for the planning and under her full command.

'We'll need that picture of mother,' said Pushpa. 'But I think I'll have it reframed. It's cracked and looks terrible. What do you think?'

'Ah, yes. Good idea,' said Vijayan, vaguely aware of what he was endorsing.

Pushpa went to the mahogany cupboard, yanked open one of its drawers and lifted out the framed photograph.

'See. It's not right,' she said and handed it to her brother. 'Take it to the bazaar and get a new frame.'

Vijayan held up the black and white photo. He always liked his mother's name—Kasturi. She was so young in the photo, only fifteen or sixteen, and just married. Sitting erect on a highbacked chair, she faced the camera wearing a dark sari with a light border, one end thrown over the left shoulder.

He couldn't help focusing on her arms. Falling in straight lines from the shoulder and bending horizontally at the elbows towards the viewer, they seemed to shield the timid body between them. Vijayan noticed the thin arms, with silver bangles ready to slip off the wrist, and the small hands, one on top of the other in her lap.

The Brahmin priest who came on Tuesday morning seemed remarkably young. His broad bare chest and thick black hair reminded Vijayan of a wrestler he had seen in a circus.

Sitting on the floor in the front room, he heaped up a mound of paddy on a large banana leaf, put a small brass pot on top and placed a coconut on the mouth of the pot. Next he propped the photograph up against the wall, framed it with a string of jasmine flowers and laid out another, smaller banana leaf in front of it.

Then, having lit camphor in a shallow brass lamp and placed the lamp on the leaf in front of the photograph, the young man chanted and rang his hand bell. Finally, he instructed Vijayan, Selvan, and lastly Arun, to toss jasmine flowers on the coconut and place balls of cooked rice on the leaf in front of the photograph.

Afterwards, Vijayan looked more closely at the photo. It was mounted on cream-coloured cardboard, with the words 'Sun Ray Studio' printed in florid red Tamil letters in the bottom right corner. It must have been taken in 1933 or 1934, after his parents had married and just before he had been born, in their old house in Virudhunagar.

It no longer existed, that house where he had spent his childhood. He was thirteen or fourteen when they had left its hard mud walls for the new house of reinforced concrete and glass windows.

The old house consisted of two windowless, rectangular buildings. The main one, for sleeping, faced the lane and was fronted by a narrow verandah built up from the ground and made of dried clay. Four steps, cut into the middle of the verandah, led up from the lane and into the single room, with a mud floor about ten metres long and three across.

Outside, along the back wall, another narrow verandah of dried clay led to a separate room. The door was kept locked and Vijayan never knew what was inside, until one afternoon when he was six or seven. He had come back from school and lay down on the verandah leading to the mysterious room. An hour later, his mother shook him hard and screamed, 'Don't sleep like that, with your feet towards the door! Do you hear? Never!'

His mother explained the next day. Inside was a trunk with a wedding sari and pieces of jewellery that had belonged to his paternal grandmother and great-grandmother. Pointing one's feet towards the door was disrespectful. If he did it again, she warned, he would have to pay a fine of 25 paisa, like anyone else who made the same mistake. Unlocking the door, she showed him a small brass pot in the corner. 'In there,' she said. 'That's where we put the money.'

Facing this little room, across an open space, was the second free-standing building. Similar in size and shape to the main building, it was the kitchen, where they also ate. Cold rice with water in the morning and hot rice in the evening, usually with vegetable curry or tiny dried fish. Sometimes, a glass of watered-down hot milk before bed. A biscuit with the milk was a treat. On special occasions, they had curry with mutton or bat meat or crabs, which were dug out of the dry paddy field bunds after harvest.

Vijayan remembered the cool verandahs with their smooth, brown surface. Shaded by the eaves of a clay tile roof, he could take a nap, play or watch the goings-on in the house and in the lane. He was often left alone on the front verandah, with his mother and sisters in the kitchen or courtyard. If his father came home late, as he often did, he might still be there after sunset, playing jacks with small stones.

Because that old house had no running water, his sisters spent a lot of time going to and from the municipal pipe, about half a mile away. Twice a day, early in the morning and in the afternoon after school, the two girls each brought back a clay pot full of water, balancing it on their heads.

Tall for her age and strong, Pushpa managed all right, but his younger sister, Meenakshi, struggled. Most of the time, Vijayan didn't notice the way her legs buckled at the knee when she walked. Seeing her stagger home under the heavy pot of water, however, he just wanted to look the other way. Children in the lane and at school missed nothing and called her 'gimp' and 'peg-leg.' 'She's still growing,' is what her parents said.

Then, one day, they could ignore it no longer. When the sisters were coming back from the water pipe, Meenakshi collapsed and her pot smashed on the ground. Their father realized it was serious and took her to the Mission Hospital in town and later to the municipal hospital in Madurai.

She had polio. Their father managed to scrape together enough money to buy a pair of crutches, while their mother made enquiries through their network of relations. A year later, aged eleven, she was married to a thirty-six-year-old uncle, with a few acres of cotton in an interior village.

Although Vijayan had always known about this marriage, he tried to pretend he didn't. He wanted to hide from it all, not just the abandonment of his sister but also the recognition of his impotence. He knew he couldn't have done much—being only fourteen at the time—but that was what he wanted to forget. His inability to prevent something he knew was wrong stored up the anger in him. It wasn't the only time that fury at the outside world turned inwards and stoked his sense of inadequacy.

13

Arun glided towards the line scratched in the dirt, trying not to attract attention. Suddenly he swerved and cut across the line, calling 'kabaddi, kabaddi, kabaddi' as he hunted his prey. Then he lunged and tagged a small boy on the arm, wheeled around and raced back towards the line, repeating 'kabaddi' again and again, without taking a breath. But before he crossed to safety, a tall boy caught and held him by one leg, while another wrestled him to the ground. Squirming to get free, Arun kept up the mandatory call of kabaddi.

'C'mon! Get across the line!' shouted his father from the sidelines.

Two more boys piled on top and crushed the air out of him. Gasping for breath, his kabaddi calls stopped and the referee shouted 'Out!' Arun trudged to the sidelines, head down, shorts dirty, vest torn.

Standing behind Selvan and others in the crowd, Vijayan watched with surprising interest. He had never thrown or kicked a ball in his life and disliked the notion of a team, yet he found himself riveted by Arun and the boys playing kabaddi. Not so different to bull-catching at Pongal, he thought. Less dangerous, but the same competitive drama. And all those gangly legs thrashing about beneath underdeveloped chests and resolute young faces struck him as comic.

When Arun came and stood by his father, Selvan put an arm around the boy's shoulders and said, 'You did well, son. Almost made it.'

'We'll still win, won't we?' Arun asked looking up.

'I hope so,' his father said and turned back to the game.

Vijayan stood by in silence. He didn't know the game well enough to comment and didn't want to say the wrong thing to the dispirited boy. Arun broke the ice. '*Mama*,' he whispered with quiet disappointment as he grabbed his uncle's hand and smiled up at him. 'I'm not like Shivaji, am I?'

'No, Arun,' said Vijayan. 'Not yet.'

Intent on the game, Selvan overheard but didn't comprehend this exchange between his son and brother-in-law.

As they walked home, with Arun and his father talking about kabaddi, a man going in the other direction slowed his pace and looked at Vijayan before passing on. Five seconds later, Vijayan turned around and confirmed that the man was walking normally.

It wasn't unexpected. Since he had arrived, Vijayan had known there would be an argument, and probably harsh words, but he hadn't anticipated the ferocity of his own anger. Late one afternoon, the children were doing schoolwork in their room, Pushpa was in the kitchen and Vijayan was reading in the front room. Vanni came out to get something and noticed a man standing by the door.

Pushpa didn't pay the washerman by the piece, as most people did, but instead paid a fixed amount at the end of each month. It was simpler this way, she reasoned. No need to keep a tally of every item of clothing and its cost. Although both parties suspected they were being cheated, the fixed payment eliminated the easily forgotten details that could ignite disputes.

Waiting outside the door, the dhobi stood with his towel tied around his waist, having removed it from his head out of deference. His knobby knees stuck out, almost poking through the thin covering of skin. Of the three local castes of washermen, he belonged to the lowest because he washed the clothes of other Untouchables.

He didn't say anything, but Vanni recognized him by his spidery whiskers and puckered cheeks. She went to her mother in the kitchen, got a ten-rupee note and was coming back through the front room, when Pushpa called, 'Don't forget. Put it on the step, not in his hand.'

Vijayan gripped the arms of the wicker chair and waited until Vanni had joined her sister and brother in their room before confronting Pushpa in the kitchen.

'How could you say that? Such backward ideas! In my own sister's house!'

His explosion stunned Pushpa, who took a minute to recover. 'What? What ideas?' she asked in genuine confusion.

'"Put it on the step, not in his hand." That idea!' said Vijayan, his voice rising with every phrase.

'Oh, I see,' said Pushpa. 'But that's not the problem, is it? No. It's you and your ideas. I'm just telling her to do what everyone does.'

'Everyone?'

'Yes, in case you haven't noticed, Mr Writer!'

'You're wrong, Pushpa! I for one...'

'Oh, yes! You're not like the rest of us, are you? Very special, aren't you? We know that, only too well. That's why you'll never get married!'

'Shut up! You're an ignorant woman!'

'Don't speak to me like that, in my own house.'

'All right, I won't,' he shouted and marched down the corridor towards the front room, almost knocking Arun down.

The children had heard the shouting, but only Arun had ventured into the corridor. Having withdrawn as Vijayan stormed down the corridor, he stepped out again and watched his uncle grab his shoulder bag and leave the house. By the time Arun reached the front door and looked down the street, he was out of sight.

When Arun came back to the children's room, Kalyani continued colouring in her book, but Vanni stared at him open-mouthed. Grimacing, he threw himself down on the floor. The angry words had pierced him, and the pain was compounded by confusion. What had happened? He knew he couldn't ask his mother, so he waited for his father to come home.

'He got furious, about Vanni paying the dhobi,' he overheard his mother explain to his father that night. 'Something about "backward ideas," not putting the money in his hand. Then he left.'

'Did he speak to Vanni? Or Arun?' Selvan asked.

'No, I don't think so.'

'Well, see that he doesn't. About any of his ideas, I mean. That's all I care about. He's your brother, so I'll leave it to you.'

'Right. I don't know where's gone. Or when he'll come back.'

'Oh, he'll come back, all right,' said Selvan with a little snort. 'He's got no money.'

'Well, he is ill. On medical leave and...'

'You don't believe that, do you? Something else is going on with him.'

'Could be. But what?'

'With him who knows?'

'One thing's clear. We'll never be able to find a bride for him, if he keeps acting like this,' said Pushpa.

Motionless and silent in a corner of the room, Arun copied out a long paragraph for his English lesson. While his hand formed the letters, his mind absorbed each spoken word like a raindrop into a still pond.

Arun understood a bit more, but why had his uncle had been so angry? Something about putting the money in his hand.

But she paid him the right amount. Maybe it was the dhobi. He was dirty.

Arun knew about castes. They were like families; some were like yours and some weren't. They did different work; some were rich, others poor. They all went to school. Well, most did. You married one of your cousins, or someone like that. Everyone did and it made sense.

'We'll never find a bride for him.' That bothered Arun more than the angry words about the washerman. Why won't his uncle get married? He wondered and then remembered that he was ill. Probably got a disease, he decided.

Vijayan spent that night in a lodge and in the morning went to the library as usual. Dozens of men, mostly older ones, were reading newspapers, while the younger ones flipped through magazines and a handful of women held books. Their silence made the high-ceilinged room seem larger, a space in which he could forget why he had come.

Two hours later, he gathered the newspapers together and stacked them on top of each other. Not quite right, he thought, picked up the pile and squared the edges against the table top. Easier than folding cloth, but he missed the feel of hand-woven cotton.

Someone coughed. He pushed the pile of papers to the centre of the large table and scrapped back his chair. 'What do they care what's happening in Ceylon?' he muttered under his breath and stood up. The middle-aged man in the next chair tapped his paper and asked, 'Did you see this? Senthil Nadar School won the municipal kabaddi competition last Saturday. Third time in a row!'

Arun left school early that day, claiming a family ritual as an excuse, and went to find his uncle. He looked in the library and the cinema, where he was let in for a few minutes without a ticket. Then he had an idea and went to the local khadi shop, but no one there knew his uncle's name or recognized his description.

Wandering in the fierce May sun, he passed the hospital, the post office and the bus station before entering the main bazaar. Now it was five o'clock, his satchel was heavy and his white shirt stuck to his back. Discouraged, he sat on a low brick wall that separated a row of shops from the dusty street.

Then he saw him looking at a shop window. Arun jumped up and started to run but stopped. His uncle's veshti and shirt were crumpled and unclean, the scowl on his unshaven face was darker than usual and his thinning hair stuck out in all directions. Arun wanted to call out but held back, unsure if he would embarrass his uncle.

Vijayan turned away from the twinkling display of watches and shuffled along the street toward the vegetable market. If he goes in there, thought Arun, I might lose him.

'Uncle!' he cried and leapt forward.

Vijayan wheeled around and saw the boy a few feet away.

'*Mama*,' Arun repeated and came forward. 'Let's go home.'

Vijayan would have said no but saw the determination in the boy's face.

Arun took his uncle's hand, and Vijayan steered the boy around pushcarts and shielded him from oncoming vehicles. When Arun tightened his grip, the pleasure that surged through Vijayan was unlike anything he had known since reading poetry to his mother as a boy. Withdrawing his hand, Vijayan placed it on the back of the boy's head and guided him home.

They exchanged words without saying much, until the house

came in view. Then Arun blurted out, 'Everything'll be all right, won't it?'

'Yes,' said Vijayan, though his moment of hesitation told Arun he wasn't sure. If only Arun were old enough, thought Vijayan, I could tell him everything.

Their entrance startled Pushpa, who froze, with her embroidery frame held in mid-air. But the amiability between uncle and nephew reassured her.

'Ah, there you are,' she said, recovering fast. 'You must be hungry. Come into the kitchen.'

No one said a word about the day before, either then or later. Vijayan and Selvan barely spoke to each other anyway, but now even conventional greetings were dispensed with and all communication passed through Pushpa. Arun noticed that his father began to pay more attention to his sisters and him and that his mother and uncle interacted with icy courtesy. While he sensed that his uncle was the centre of it all, he didn't understand why.

With every conversation, and almost every word, the strings connecting the family were pulled further and further apart. Arun felt something would snap and, even worse, knew he could do nothing about it. Then he decided to rely on an old trick.

'Amma, can we go to the cinema?'

'No, Arun. You know we can't this Saturday,' Pushpa said.

'But with uncle, I mean,' he persisted, knowing this was dangerous territory.

'No…uncle is very tired. It's not a good idea for him to spend so much time in the cinema.'

'But…'

'Arun! No means no. Don't ask again!' Pushpa barked and walked towards the kitchen.

So, uncle is the problem, Arun concluded. He's not good for me.

Vijayan retreated further into himself. He continued to help Arun and the girls with their school work but spent more time in the library, where he read everything on Ceylon, including that it had been renamed 'Sri Lanka.' He also tried to write short stories in order to earn money because the cash Muttusami had given him was running out and he wasn't going to ask Pushpa and Selvan for any.

Although Arun felt powerless, he did contrive to alter one thing. He began to walk home from school along a different route, a longer one that took him past the library. He knew that Vijayan spent most of the day there, and one afternoon he ran into him leaving the building. After this apparent coincidence, they followed an unspoken plan and met at roughly the same time and walked home together.

Routine set in, deflating the tension at home, and before long the whole family found themselves bumping along in a bus. No one objected to Pushpa's idea of an outing to the waterfalls at Courtallam, especially since it was mid-June and the temperature had risen to 40 degrees centigrade. Vijayan, however, was surprised when he saw that they were joined by his Aunt Kamala, her husband and three of their children. Although Kamala was their father's much younger sister and lived in the same town, the two families were not close.

Accompanying Kamala on the outing were her eighteen-year-old daughter and two sons, aged sixteen and fourteen. Vijayan looked at them as they rode along in the bus and realized he hardly knew them. In the daughter, Thangamma, he failed to recognize the two-year-old child he had held in his arms on one of his rare visits to Virudhunagar, for his father's funeral.

The waterfalls appeared in the distance as the bus disentangled itself from a small town. There were nine falls, the highest plunging for sixty metres, but all they could see were white streaks down the black mountain face.

When the bus pulled into the parking area, several hundred visitors had already arrived, mostly large families, tour groups, college students and pilgrims from all over India. They bathed in separate groups—women and older girls in saris, men and boys stripped to their underpants. All luxuriated in the cool created by the falls and the green hills encasing them.

Some chose to bathe in the placid pools or under the gentler falls, but most edged their way along the narrow concrete platform towards the main falls, gripping iron railings as they advanced. Each year, a dozen or more people ventured on to the slippery, black rocks below and were swept away.

Selvan held on to Arun and moved under the deafening high falls. The boy squealed with delight, but they could endure the ferocious battering for barely ten minutes before nature beat them into a retreat. Then Vijayan's uncle and two nephews huddled close together and let the water crash on to their heads and shoulders. Vijayan stood nearby, yet alone, letting thick sheets of water seal him in and the thundering downpour silence his thoughts.

Vanni and Thangamma took their turn, shrieking with excitement and clinging on to each other as the water pounded down. Looking at them, Pushpa recalled her childhood, while Vijayan saw Meenakshi, their younger sister, who had been the same age as Vanni when she collapsed carrying the water pot.

Retreating, they changed into dry clothes and laid the wet ones in the sun. Then they bought small baskets of fruit and flowers and headed for the nearby Siva temple. Vijayan said his sandals needed repairing and went to find a cobbler among the stalls lining the approach to the falls.

When he rejoined them, half an hour later, Pushpa eyed him and asked, 'Did you get them fixed?'

'Yes. They're fine now,' he replied, holding her gaze. 'Did you get what you wanted, too?'

'We offered prayers and asked for Siva's blessings, for the children and for you,' she said without hesitation.

Pushpa, Vijayan and their aunt retrieved the large plastic-mesh baskets they had left with a shopkeeper and had him fill their thermos flasks with hot tea. The boys, commissioned to reconnoitre a place for the picnic, found a grassy area, flat but with small outcrops of rock.

Selvan, Arun, Vijayan, his uncle and his two nephews sat down on woven mats, while Vanni and Kalyani occupied a corner. Pushpa, her aunt and niece, Thangamma, placed a shallow plate in front of each person and walked around, ladling food on it from containers.

Stepping behind Vijayan, Thangamma slipped on a rock and would have fallen had he not shot up his hand, which she instinctively grabbed. Vijayan turned to see if she was all right, and she lowered her eyes to avoid his. Nothing was said, but Pushpa saw that Thangamma wore a faint smile and thought that Vijayan did, too.

'Where's Arun?' Pushpa asked a few minutes later.

'They all went off, there,' said her uncle, waving vaguely towards the forest slope behind them.

'Go after them,' Pushpa said to her husband, who sighed and set off.

After ten minutes, Pushpa turned to Vijayan, 'Where are they? Better go look.'

'Okay. I'll try down by the bazaar,' he agreed and headed towards the line of shops that led to the falls. He found Arun and the other two boys watching a man perform for an admiring crowd. Sitting on the ground, he riffled a pack of playing cards and fanned them out in a half circle in front of him. Then he leaned forward, opened the door to a little wooden cage and a parrot strutted out. Green with soft rose colouring around its neck, the parrot paraded around the cards, holding its head high. Arun nudged one of his cousins and whispered, 'Look. Its wings are clipped.'

Stepping carefully, the parrot circled the cards and stopped. It turned its head to one side, then to the other, bent down and picked up a card in its beak. Arun watched the parrot return to the man and drop the card in his outstretched palm. Holding the card against his forehead, the astrologer closed his eyes, mumbled a few words and finally placed it on the ground face up. The six of hearts.

'This is the red card, with six red faces,' he said in a sing-song voice. 'Like our youthful Murugan, lord of beauty and wealth. The parrot chose because the parrot knows. And so the cards do tell what is and what will be...'

'Come along, all of you,' ordered Vijayan, shaking Arun's shoulder and looking at the other two. 'Hurry. Your mothers are waiting.'

The three boys looked at each other, dropped their heads and followed Vijayan out of the crowd.

'Uncle,' said Arun. 'Don't tell mother where we were. Okay?'

Vijayan said nothing, so Arun pleaded, 'Please don't tell her.'

'All right. But what am I going to say?' asked Vijayan.

'Ah, that we were playing games.'

'Right. But you have to promise me something.'

'What?'

'That you'll never go to an astrologer again.'

'Why not?'

'Because they are ignorant...charlatans.'

'What's a charlatan?'

'Someone who lies and deceives.'

'But he was trying to tell the truth, wasn't he?'

'No, Arun, he wasn't. He was using the parrot and cards to fool people. To get money from them.'

Arun considered this for a moment and said, 'He didn't tell a lie. Maybe the parrot chose the wrong card. But the man didn't lie.'

'All right, clever boy! Do what you like,' Vijayan snapped and strode ahead. Watching Vijayan's back weave through the crowd, Arun wondered if he had said something wrong, like his mother about the washerman.

After tea and sweets, they all climbed aboard the bus to take them back home. On this special tour, the usual division of men and women in a bus gave way to groups sitting together, with the sexes separated within each group. Chivvying her party like a mother hen, Pushpa managed to get Vijayan and Thangamma seated in the same row with the aisle between them.

Unable to see much outside, and without a book or newspaper, Vijayan looked straight ahead. The evening sun slanted in through the windows and illuminated the interior so clearly that he could count the black hairs sticking out of the ears of the man in front. Then his eyes strayed across the aisle, where Thangamma was laughing at something Vanni said. She felt his attention and turned towards the window, but when she turned back their eyes met. She blushed and Vijayan looked away.

He didn't think she wasn't attractive. Thin, with small eyes and wiry hair, but he liked the way her cheeks rose up in soft mounds. And he was intrigued because of the roles they were playing in a game so deftly arranged by his sister.

As she raised her arms to battle with her windblown hair, Vijayan noticed the shape of her small breasts. He was still a virgin. His only sexual experience had been with a prostitute in Madurai and it had not been a success. She might be on the thin side, but those firm shapes hinted at a young body. Quickly he turned to Arun and asked about his next kabaddi competition.

He was still smiling, though, and the watchful Pushpa thought she knew why.

She waited until the next day, when they were alone in the house.

'Nice trip to Courtallam, wasn't it?' she began.

'Oh, yes. Very nice,' Vijayan ventured, afraid of what was coming.

'What did you think of aunt's family?'

'Pleasant. The boys were well-behaved, even if they ran off for a while.'

'And the daughter, Thangamma?'

'Oh, I don't know. I didn't really speak to her.'

'You don't have to speak to someone to have an opinion.'

'That's true,' he conceded. 'Well, she seemed a nice girl.'

'Yes. Vanni and she got on well,' she said.

'Umm, they did laugh a lot,' he said, wondering if he was off the hook.

'She's educated, you know,' Pushpa continued. 'Finished high school and did a year at Lady Doak College in Madurai.'

'I see. That's good, for her, I mean,' he said, feeling the trap close in.

'And for her future husband, too,' she said, moving in for the kill.

'Pushpa! Drop this, all right?' said Vijayan.

'Okay. Okay. It's just that I thought you and she enjoyed each other's company. That's all,' Pushpa said, beating a tactful retreat.

'That's enough,' said Vijayan, raising his voice and going to his room at the back of the house.

He was beginning to feel content in this dusty, provincial town. Reading in the library, walking home with Arun, trying to write stories, occasional trips to the cinema—it was enough. He didn't need to talk to Selvan, and he could get along with Pushpa as long as they avoided certain topics. Scanning the street for someone with a limp no longer seemed necessary.

Then a letter arrived. It was addressed to:

Sri Vijayan Naidu,
c/o Srimati Pushpa Naidu,
Near St. Stephen's Hospital,
Virudhunagar

He didn't recognize the handwriting, but it had a Melur postmark. Opening the inland letter, he saw it was from Muttusami:

Dear Friend,
I am well and hope the same for you. I write to you at your sister's address, hoping that this letter will reach you.

I have two important pieces of news. Otherwise, I would not have written.

First, a man came to the shop two days ago and asked for you. I told him that you were on medical leave. He asked where you had gone, and I said that I didn't know. Then he wanted to know when you would return and about your family. I said I knew nothing. He did not believe me, but he spoke politely and soon left the shop.

He was not a local person and spoke with an unfamiliar accent. He was in his forties or fifties and dressed like a man from Madras.

Vijayan could hardly breathe. Sitting on his bed, his head fell forward and the letter slipped from his hand. Then he took a deep breath through his nose, raised his head and picked up the letter.

The other news is about Raja. He has not recovered. In

fact, he is worse. His jaw has not healed and his eye is not right. Also, he does not eat properly. Mani has taken him to Madurai for an examination.

We must trust in God for his recovery.

With love,
Muttusami

He had to go to Melur and see Raja. Although Mani and the others were looking after his 'little brother,' he wanted to be with him. But it was too dangerous. Pandian's killers were looking for him there.

Muttusami had done well not to reveal anything, but they would eventually trace him to Virudhunagar. Someone might tell them where his sister lived. Or they could get information about his family from the head office in Madras. It was only a matter of time.

He had to leave Virudhunagar, but where could he go this time? A village would be too small. Madurai was too close—someone might recognize him. It had to be somewhere he could blend in and also find work.

'Muttusami needs me to do some work in Madurai,' Vijayan told Pushpa. 'It might be several months. I don't know.'

'But you're on medical leave. And you don't look well, really.'

'I'm fine. Your cooking's done wonders,' he said with a forced smile.

'I'm worried about you. Is there something wrong? I don't mean…'

'Pushpa, I'm all right. Honestly.'

She looked hard at him, hurt that he wouldn't confide in her, and said, 'Arun will miss you.'

'He's growing up, isn't he? He'll be a young man soon.'

'When must you leave?'

'Tomorrow morning.'

'Why not pay a quick visit to Aunt Kamala this afternoon? I know...'

'Pushpa! We agreed not to talk about that.'

'It's only polite, that's all.'

'I'm leaving in the morning.'

That evening he sat in his room trying to make plans. How would he earn money? Should he tell Muttusami where he was going?

Arun watched him from the corridor. He knew Vijayan was going away and worried that he was to blame.

'Oh, there you are,' said Vijayan.

Arun edged his way into the small room, still uncertain until Vijayan waved him over to the bed and made room for him.

'Will you be gone long, *mama*?'

'Not very long. A few months probably,' Vijayan said, as he reached over and brushed the hair from Arun's forehead.

'Will you come back and visit?'

'I'll try.'

Arun's face suddenly lit up. 'Can I come see you in Madurai?'

'You'll have to ask your mother,' said Vijayan, though they both knew what she would say.

'There're good cinemas in Madurai, aren't there?' Arun asked with more hope.

'There are,' said Vijayan, starting to fight back tears. 'But you must work hard at school. Will you promise me that?'

'Yes, uncle, I promise,' said the boy, his eyes seeking reassurance.

'And you won't become like Shivaji? Not at least for a year?' Vijayan asked lightly.

'Yes. But I'll only wait one year.'

'Gone, has he?' asked Selvan the following evening, with the family gathered in the front room. He spoke to no one in particular and without raising his eyes from his newspaper. When Arun remained silent, his sisters looked up from their school work and Pushpa confirmed that he had.

'I'd like a veshti with a red border,' said the chubby-faced man as soon as he entered the khadi shop in Virudhunagar.

While the young clerk wrapped it for him, he spoke again. 'I'm looking for a friend, whose family lives here.'

'Yes.'

'His name is Vijayan, Vijayan Naidu. He works in a khadi shop, near Madurai, so I thought you might know him.'

The clerk considered this for a moment and said, 'No, I don't know anyone by that name. Wait a minute and I'll ask the manager.'

The manager came back with the clerk. 'Vijayan Naidu? Is that your friend's name?' he asked.

'Yes. Do you know him?' asked the customer, his cheeks puffing out.

'No. But a few days ago, a boy came in here asking for the same person,' said the manager.

'What kind of boy?' asked the stranger, whose accent the manager was trying to identify.

'Well, I don't know. About twelve years old, I guess.'

'Anything else? I would very much like to find my friend.'

'Let's see,' said the manager, raising his eyes towards the ceiling and squinting. 'Right. He was wearing the uniform of Senthil Nadar. That's a middle school here. And he said his name was Arun.'

'Arun from Senthil Nadar Middle School,' repeated the other

man. 'That's very helpful. Thank you and goodbye.'

'Don't forget your package,' cried the clerk, running after the customer.

14

Vijayan looked out above the tops of the coconut and palm trees, whose thick fronds hid much of the bustling town below. Beyond, the mountains rose up sharply, making them appear closer than they were.

They won't find me here, he said to himself, watching a deep purple spread over the rocky slopes. Circling crows cawed and traffic horns screeched, but no human voices reached him.

He had been in Nagercoil for nearly a month but had still not found a job. At first it had been difficult even to get around because it is a town without a centre. The old 'Snake Temple,' which gives Nagercoil its name, is nestled low in the Brahmin quarter where its squat walls are a landmark for no one. A clock tower built at the turn of the century stands at a junction that long ago ceased to be a hub. Rather than spreading out from a nucleus, the town had sprung up as separate neighbourhoods, mostly along the main road and on its low hills.

He almost went further, to Trivandrum on the west coast, but he decided on Nagercoil. He liked the local patois, a mixture of Tamil with Malayalam words with a distinct nasal intonation. 'It's easy to speak Malayalam when you need to,' he had heard people say. 'Just pinch your nose and use Tamil.' It seemed to work.

He had also known where he would stay. The olive green walls of the Pioneer Kumaraswamy Mudaliar Lodge rose up like a fort behind the municipal park. The park, with its withered gardens and cracked fountains, stood as a monument to failed civic ambition, while the lodge had been built by the entrepreneur who brought electricity to this southern tip of India. Halfway up a hill, set back from the road, its tiled entrance facing west, the PKM lodge felt cool even in the heat of the day.

Standing now on the terrace and looking at the mountains, Vijayan's face grew a scowl. Where could he find a job? He had avoided the khadi shop, which would be the first place they would look for him. The several bookshops turned out to be stationery stores with schoolbooks and dictionaries, and none was interested in a new employee.

Coming down from the roof and entering his room, Vijayan threw himself down on the bed. He had enough money for one more week; then he would have to return to Virudhunagar.

The following afternoon he sat in the Indian Coffee House, with its white wicker chairs and middle-class clientele. Spending money on good quality coffee was an indulgence he allowed himself, though soon it wouldn't be possible. Looking around at the waiters with their flashy green turbans and wide purple sashes, he had an idea. It seemed ridiculous, but by the time he had finished his coffee, he knew he would try. His enquiry about employment received a cold rejection.

Back at the PKM, something in Vijayan's voice prompted the man at the desk to speak when he asked for his key.

'Everything all right?' the man asked, key still in his hand.

'Yes, fine,' said Vijayan.

'New to Nagercoil, aren't you?'

'Well, I've been here before, but...'

'We have a lot of people like you. Educated but no job.'

Vijayan looked at him and said nothing.

'What kind of work can you do?'

'Well,' began Vijayan, who didn't like this man but had no choice. 'I've worked with a small publisher, in a bookshop and...a cloth shop.'

'No publishers around here, and not many bookshops either,' the man said, rubbing his shiny forehead like a crystal ball.

'Yes, I've tried them. No openings.'

'But we do have cloth shops.'

'I've been to half a dozen,' said Vijayan, starting to resent the man's kindness.

'Have you been to the one near the post office?'

'Near the post office? No. I'll try there tomorrow.'

'I'll take you there myself. You see, I know the manager. He's my wife's cousin. He's the manager, as I say, not the owner. But let's see.'

Next morning, the manager at the Maharaja Emporium had only two questions for his prospective employee.

'Can you measure and cut cloth?'

'Yes,' Vijayan answered. Looking at the long bolts of brightly coloured cloth on wooden racks, though, he wondered if he could carry them to the measuring table and back.

'What about letters? Can you write business letters?'

'Yes.'

'All right. You begin tomorrow.'

Walking out of the shop, Vijayan felt himself expand and glide down the pavement. It was only half-day, 3 p.m. to 8 p.m, and only for three months, replacing someone who had gone on a pilgrimage to Siva temples across India. The pay wasn't as good as in Melur and the atmosphere wasn't as congenial either.

'You'll have a 30-minute tea break at 6 p.m. That's all,' the manager had said. 'Don't be late and don't talk to the customers more than is necessary.' But he would have enough money, at least for three months.

He fell into a routine. After tea and idilis in the morning, a walk took him up the hill to a prosperous residential area, with the Magistrates' Court and the High School. In a wooden shack, at a sprawling junction, a man sat hunched over a sleek black machine. As he worked the treadle, the tailor never failed to spot Vijayan and wag his head in greeting. After fifteen minutes, he found himself in the countryside. It reminded him of Melur. Only here, in this sliver of land wedged between mountains and ocean, the air was fresher.

The rest of the morning was spent in the library, reading and working on his writing, rewarded with a good coffee. At midday, he ate at a modest private house that had been converted into a sort of restaurant. Although the price was higher than the usual 'meals-ready' places, the rice was stickier and tastier. Afternoons and evenings he cut cloth and answered letters at the Maharaja Emporium. Back at the PKM, he stood on the roof terrace watching the mountains change colours.

As July slipped into August, the temperature dropped and rain fell more frequently, but only for an hour or so. Once a week he allowed himself a visit to the cinema. People began to recognize him—in the library, where he ate, at the Maharaja Emporium, at the PKM, on his walks. He missed the conversation and physical company of others but remained aloof. Friendship might lead to unwelcome questions.

The man approached Senthil Nadar Middle School with a determination that disguised the wobble in his walk. He was guided to the headmaster's office by a barefoot peon in a khaki uniform. Entering the outer office, the man gave his name and stated his purpose to the secretary behind a bare metal desk. He was asked to sit down and only then did the secretary scrutinize the visitor. Light blue polyester shirt, pressed trousers, closed-toe leather sandals. Clean-shaven, puffy cheeks. And not a local man by his accent.

'I'll inform the headmaster,' the secretary said after ten minutes and disappeared through a swinging door with a sign that read 'Sri Sundaralingaswamy Nadar, S.S.L.C., B.A., B.Sc, Headmaster.'

'Sir. There's a Kumara Pillai to see you.'

'Who is he?'

'Well-dressed, educated. Probably from Madras, sir.'

'What does he want?'

'To see one of our pupils, he said, sir.'

'Which pupil?'

'He didn't say, sir.'

'Oh, all right. Show him in. But make him wait another fifteen minutes.'

When the visitor was ushered in and offered a seat, the headmaster picked up a large paperweight and dropped it on a pile of papers. Kumara Pillai watched snowflakes float down over a blue pond and green forest.

'I understand you've come about one of our pupils,' began the headmaster, still fiddling with things on his desk.

'Yes. That is…'

'What's the pupil's name?'

'Arun Naidu.'

'And your business with him?'

'His uncle is my friend from college. You see, I haven't seen him for years and now I'm in Virudhunagar. I remember him saying his family lived here and that he had a nephew named Arun.'

'And why come to our school?'

'Well, I simply thought my friend's family would send their son to the best school in town,' said the visitor with a smile obscured by the folds of his fleshy face.

'Just so. Just so,' said the headmaster, picking up the

paperweight, turning it over and placing it down again. As both men waited for the snowflakes to fall, the headmaster administered two swift jabs to the metal bell on his desk and said, 'My secretary will help you find the boy. Good day.'

Kumara Pillai told the secretary he would wait until the lunch break rather than disrupt lessons. Very considerate, thought the secretary, who later instructed a peon to bring the boy.

'Arun, this gentleman knows your uncle. Did you say a college friend, sir?' asked the secretary.

'Yes, from Madras,' said Kumara Pillai.

Arun looked from the secretary to the visitor and did not smile.

'You may take one hour off to speak with him,' the secretary said.

'Come, Arun, let's have a cup of tea,' said the man.

Arun didn't speak, knowing something was wrong.

'Here we are,' said Kumara Pillai, leading the boy into a modern-style snack bar and taking a table. 'What would you like? Ice cream? Fanta?'

'Just tea,' said Arun, looking down.

'Are you sure? Why not some cashews, too?'

'No thank you,' said Arun, still avoiding eye contact.

Having ordered, Kumara Pillai pulled his chair close to the table and said, 'Well, now, Arun. How is your Uncle Vijayan?'

Arun tried to think fast. His lips parted but no words came out.

'Have you seen him lately?' prompted the man, leaning over the table to within a few inches of the boy's face.

'No. No, I haven't seen him lately,' said Arun, who found it easier to repeat words.

'I see,' sighed Kumara Pillai, falling back in his chair. 'Doesn't he visit you often?'

'No. He doesn't visit us often.'

'And who are "us"? Your father and mother?'

'Umm.'

'And do you have brothers and sisters?'

'Umm.'

'And where do you all live?'

'We all live…near the grain market,' said Arun, not knowing if he should have said this. 'Ah, I have to return to school now.'

'There's still time, Arun,' said Kumara Pillai, looking at his watch.

That's what's wrong, Arun realized. His expensive watch was not what his uncle's friends would wear.

'But, you see, I have an extra lesson. I missed one last week,' he lied, looking at the man for the first time and with a fierce stare.

On his way home from school that afternoon, Arun concentrated hard. Should he tell his parents about this man? Somehow he had to tell his uncle in Madurai. Trying to work things out, he kept his eyes downward in order to measure each step. Otherwise, he might have noticed a man in a light blue shirt.

Vijayan caught a bad cold and stayed in bed for two days but struggled to the Maharaja Emporium on the third. He couldn't afford to jeopardize his position, although the manager seemed pleased with his performance. Special orders were given to him now and he was asked to draft letters. Best of all, he no longer had to carry the heavy bolts of cloth between the rack and the measuring table. He spoke little with colleagues, and when work was slow, his mind drifted to Melur and to Raja.

'Hey!' shouted the manager. 'What are you doing? Cutting pieces for an elephant?' He had been asked to cut two pieces of yellow cloth, each one metre long, but the heavy metal shears had kept moving so preoccupied was he by his thoughts. Now they clattered to the floor, and the shop went quiet as he bent down to pick them up.

Walking to work the next day, he saw a crowd around a booth set up in front of the park. Over the booth a neon sign flashed on and off, showing a roaring tiger with two rifles crossed behind it. Above the door of a second, larger structure a sign in Tamil read 'Tamil Eelam: Struggle and Victory.'

'Tamil Eelam.' Vijayan said the words to himself and had to admit they had both euphony and substance. He knew *eelam* was the old Tamil word for Ceylon and that groups used it to underline their historical claim to the island.

Names are everything, Vijayan reflected. That's probably why they change. We call it 'Ilankai,' up north they say 'Lanka' and now they've added the Sanskrit word 'Sri' to give it status.

Vijayan walked to the booth, where five or six young men in modern shirts and trousers were handing out pamphlets. 'Come and see the exhibition!' one shouted. 'This is their struggle; this is our victory. Our Tamil brothers and sisters in Eelam are suffering, but they are fighting back. Learn about their history, about our history.'

Vijayan looked at the speaker, no more than twenty years old, whose cold glass eyes reflected nothing.

Inside the building, Vijayan saw black and white photographs and maps on two long walls. Going closer, he realized they were only poorly reproduced xerox copies. In one, taken with the camera close to the ground, bodies lay on a deserted street, face down. The caption read: 'Martyrs slain, Colombo, 5 April 1972.' Another showed a young girl, possibly nine or ten, rigid with fear, with a caption: 'Interrogation of Ampal, Vavuniya, 8 May 1972.'

These were the images of 'Struggle', while those on the opposite wall, labelled 'Victory,' showed people waving banners in demonstrations, men in military uniform giving speeches and children smiling in a 'Tamil Freedom School.' Vijayan's eye was drawn to a picture at the end, in which young soldiers stood at attention with their rifles held out for inspection. Their forest green uniforms were unfamiliar, but in their faces he saw young Tamil men and women.

Newspapers had carried reports of secret camps in Tamil Nadu where militants received training. Vijayan hadn't put much faith in these stories, but now he wondered if that was where he would have been sent.

A series of maps near the exit were crude but effective. In blood red they showed the extent of Tamil control of the island at different points in history. Only the northern tip was red in 300 BC, while more than half the island was in 1000 CE. By 1800 the Tamil area had receded to the northern tip, east coast and central highlands, and in 1972 it had shrunk to half that area. In the last map, 'Future Tamil Eelam' covered the entire northern and eastern parts of the country.

Clever, thought Vijayan. There's enough truth to convince people it's accurate. He knew that medieval Tamil kings, with their tiger insignia, had controlled the northern half of Ceylon. But he also knew that half-truths led a charmed life in accounts of the island's history.

Outside, Vijayan approached one of the young men handing out pamphlets.

'Excuse me,' he said.

'Yes, sir,' came the reply so briskly that Vijayan would not have been surprised if the young man had saluted.

'The last map of Tamil Eelam. I mean, will it be part of Ceylon? Or a separate country?'

The man trained his opaque eyes on Vijayan and said, 'Tamil Eelam will be an independent state. Tamil Eelam will be a free nation. Tamil Eelam will...'

'Yes,' cut in Vijayan. 'But how will it be separate from Ceylon? Is there a natural boundary? A river or something?'

The young man hesitated a moment before resuming. 'Tamil Eelam will be an independent state. The oppressor state of Ceylon will not...'

'But how will the boundary be maintained?'

Again a pause, only three seconds but long enough for the man to recall his catechism: 'The boundary between free Tamil Eelam and the oppressor nation Ceylon will be determined by the United Nations.'

'Good, very good,' said Vijayan, who turned and left. The UN? he chuckled to himself. That'll make it a success.

Only Pushpa was at home that morning.

'Good morning, madam,' said the man standing on the steps that led up to the verandah. 'My name is Kumara Pillai. I'm an old friend of Vijayan's, from Madras.'

'Oh. Come in,' said Pushpa, somewhat surprised at the visitor's neat appearance. So unlike most of her brother's friends. He stepped into the enclosed verandah, while Pushpa stood a few steps back, at the entrance to the house. The woman who did her shopping would be back soon, so she didn't feel alone.

'I haven't seen your brother in years,' said the visitor. 'And I thought I'd look him up while I'm passing through.'

'He's not here now, I'm afraid,' said Pushpa.

'Oh, that's a shame. But he does move around a lot, doesn't he? Where is he now?' he asked, keeping his small eyes steady.

'In Madurai. He's doing some work for his office,' said Pushpa. 'I don't know when he'll return.'

'What's his address there?'

'He didn't say. That's my brother, you know,' said Pushpa with a little laugh of indulgent pride in her brother's casual habits. The man frowned and she noticed beads of sweat on his face

'I see. Well, perhaps I'll be more fortunate next time I'm here. Please tell him that I called,' said Kumara Pillai, who turned to leave.

'Yes, of course. I'll tell him…when I see him,' Pushpa said without enthusiasm. Watching him go back down the street, she felt a relief she didn't understand.

That evening, while Arun and Vanni did their school work and Kalyani played with her crayons, Pushpa told her husband about the visitor.

'What did he want?' Selvan asked.

'To see Vijayan. I just told him he was in Madurai. But he was odd.'

'Doesn't surprise me. Not in the least. That brother of yours has always had strange friends,' he said indifferently.

'I know. That's just it. This man was…well, too neat and normal,' said Pushpa.

'Did he have a Rolex watch?' asked Arun, lying on the floor.

'What? A Rolex? Yes, I think so. How'd you know?'

'He came to school yesterday. To see me.'

'What? Did he walk home with you?' she asked.

'No.'

Pushpa considered this and then asked aloud, 'Then, how did he find the house?'

'Probably followed Arun,' Selvan said, with alarm in his voice

'Mother, who is he?' asked Arun.

'Uncle's friend. A friend from Madras,' she answered.

'He's not. I know it!' cried Arun.

'Calm down, Arun! Of course he is. Your uncle knows lots of people,' said Pushpa.

'He's not his friend! He's not!' Arun was now standing up and shouting.

'That's enough! Be quiet!' ordered Selvan. Arun screwed up his face and was about to burst into tears but went slack and slumped onto the floor.

That night Arun listened to his sisters' soft breathing in the bed next to his. That man was lying, he was sure of it. Not just the watch but something else, which he tried hard to remember. As he dozed off, it came to him: the secretary had said he was a 'college friend.' Uncle didn't go to college.

He had to warn Vijayan, but his parents wouldn't believe him.

He couldn't go to Madurai and didn't know where Vijayan was in that big city anyway. Then he realized he could write a letter to Melur, to the shop and ask them to forward it.

Although Vijayan passed the photo exhibition each day on his way to the Maharaja Emporium, he didn't go in a second time.

He would have liked to study those maps again but not if he had to meet the young men's unseeing eyes.

As the weeks passed, he retreated more and more into himself. He wanted companionship, but everywhere he went—to work, the PKM, the library—he avoided people. The rain fell a little more each day and he curtailed his walks. Even the roof terrace was wet at night.

There was no news from Melur and none from Virudhunagar either. No one knew where he was, but still he was afraid. Unlike the confused panic that had driven him from Melur, it was the conviction that he was in danger.

He wanted to go to Melur, to see Raja. But he wouldn't go;

it was too risky. Despite his ideals, he always put himself first. He knew that, but now, with Raja in trouble, he confronted it for the first time, and it drove a dagger into his heart.

They were always looking at him. Even in shops. Yesterday at the dry goods place, people around him at the counter chatted away among themselves, about someone's stupid daughter's marriage and the cricket scores. When it was his turn, he fumbled in the pocket of his tunic.

'I've left my purse at home. I'll…I'll come back,' he said sheepishly. Suddenly everyone stopped talking and looked at him. Their eyes followed him all the way to the street, more in disbelief than disapproval. How could anyone be so stupid? he heard them thinking.

The Maharaja Emporium was no better. Vijayan worked separately from everyone else, at the long cutting table in the back. He could see them all, the sales assistants, but couldn't hear them. Whenever he looked up, he felt they were looking at him, talking with their heads close together. 'Ignoramuses!' he swore under his breath and cut too much off a piece of silk, which he nonchalantly pushed off the table and into the cuttings bin.

'How's that piece coming?' The manager's voice sliced into his thoughts.

'Fine. Almost finished.'

'What's this?' the manager asked, fishing the large, perfectly good piece out of the bin.

'I don't know. Must have slipped off,' said Vijayan, stumbling for words.

'Don't get careless. You've started well, but remember it's only temporary,' the manager said and walked away.

Leave me alone, you sharp-eyed little shit, said Vijayan to himself.

His cold became worse. In the mornings, a rasping cough bent him double and rattled through his chest. He gave up his walks altogether, and soon getting to the library became a struggle, so he spent most mornings in bed.

The short walk to Maharaja Emporium was dispiriting. Passing through the park, he saw only broken benches and neglected fountains. The patter of voices on the street grated like metal against metal. Although he didn't feel it every day and it didn't last long, an unhappiness had crept into him.

The heavy wooden shutters crashed back and forth on their hinges. He awoke with a start and lay awake, wondering what had happened to him. In January he had been organizing meetings, writing stories, discussing politics, chatting with people in the shop. The shop. He missed the glass-fronted cupboards and the ribbed texture of khadi, even its dry, musty smell.

He decided to write to Muttusami. It wasn't a good idea, but he needed contact with someone in Melur and Muttusami would be discreet.

Muttusami was frustrated. The central office in Madras was still processing the paperwork to sanction a temporary shop assistant. His letter, sent five months ago, had passed through the offices of the Under Secretary for Employment, the Assistant Commissioner for Planning, and the Deputy Commissioner for Provisioning.

Despite all his years of experience, Muttusami still fumed at the bureaucracy. That's when he realized how much he missed Vijayan. He'd have a few choice words to say. Muttusami had found Vijayan difficult to understand, often withdrawn and seldom punctual, but now his contrary nature would be welcome.

Fussing about the shop that morning, Muttusami had no time to look through the pile of post that had arrived. Anxious for a letter from central office, however, he glanced at it and noticed a thin blue inland letter with familiar handwriting.

My Dear Friend,

I trust you are in good health.

I am writing after several months to receive news about all of you in Melur. I hope that Raja has recovered and is working again. I know that Mani, Krishnan and Perumal Tevar are taking good care of him. My main regret in leaving Melur is that I could not do the same.

After leaving you, I spent two months in Virudhunagar with my sister and her family. Things did not work out there, so I have now moved to Nagercoil, at the address given at the top of this letter. Do not give this address to anyone, even our friends in Melur.

Here I am able to work and make some money.

Unfortunately, the circumstances which necessitated my departure from Melur have not changed. I do not know when they will change and enable me to return.

My greetings to all our friends. You can explain that you heard about me through my sister. Again, do not tell them where I am.

With affection,

Vijayan

Muttusami read it through again and frowned. The tone of the letter upset him, and he didn't have any good news to send back.

Pushpa liked the cooler weather brought on by the rains in Virudhunagar. Not that it was a proper monsoon, like the one in Kerala that summer when she visited a friend. But now, in early September, the winds were carrying moisture down from the western mountains and the scorching sun was blunted by clouds.

She sat alone in the house, with her embroidery on her lap, looking at the vaporous light through the verandah She picked up the circular wooden frame, selected one of the needles, the one with the red thread, and bent her head. Back and forth she worked the needle, pushing it through the canvas and pulling it out the other side, again and again, until the colour spread and a rose petal took shape.

I could invite them for Navarathiri, she thought, putting the frame down. Yes, she could help the girls with the dolls. Pushpa picked up her embroidery again and completed another petal but then stopped. The problem, she realized, was how to contact Vijayan.

Frowning, she bent over her work once more and concentrated. I know, she said to herself after ten minutes. I'll write to the shop in Melur and find out where he is. What's the manager's name? Muttusami? Yes, that's it. She held up the frame and smiled at the tiny rose.

15

He looked again at the square file box on his desk. Pasted on its gunmetal grey cover was a piece of white paper with a typed title:

Crime Branch-Criminal Investigation Department, Madurai
Superintendent of Police, South Zone
Case No. CB-CID 2124/M/14

Picking up the box with both hands, he decided it wasn't very heavy and opened its hinged lid. Inside were three documents and a plastic bag containing material evidence.

He didn't rush things because he felt in control. Colleagues misunderstood this as dullness and considered him no threat to their careers. He didn't care. He had joined the Madurai division of the state Crime Branch more than twenty years ago and had now reached the rank of Inspector. His father had been a weaver, from a family of Muslim weavers, in a small town near Coimbatore. Inspector Ali might not be ambitious, but he had unshakable confidence.

He read the documents, one at a time, word by word, taking notes in a separate notebook. All three were in English, which he could read, especially since many of the words were used in police work. Nevertheless, he read with care because he wanted to absorb every detail.

Holding the bottom right hand corner of the crinkled carbon copy between thumb and index finger, his eyes moved along the lines of type at an even pace, until he turned the page with a flick. If he stopped to make a note, he first placed a finger on the word where he was to resume.

The first document was from the Inspector General of Police, Crime Branch-Criminal Investigation Department, Madras. It had been sent last week to all regional deputy superintendents of the CB-CID in Tamil Nadu. Dated 4 September 1972, it read:

> *On 14 April 1972, the Hon. Minister of State, Hindu Religious Charitable Endowments, received an anonymous letter. The writer claimed that the murder of S.K. Pandian and two associates in Madras in the prior month had been perpetrated by agents of the government of Ceylon.*
>
> *The letter also stated that the deceased Pandian had a network of seven more associates working in Ceylon (viz. Appendix). Two of these associates have been murdered, one in Ceylon and one in Tamil Nadu. Preliminary reports indicate involvement by the Military Intelligence Corps in Colombo. Further investigation is to be carried out by regional CB-CID officers, who will report directly to the Inspector General of Police.*

Ali turned to the list of Pandian's agents. The man killed in Tamil Nadu was P. S. Velan of Kelalavu, Melur Taluk. None of the remaining five men on the list resided within the jurisdiction of the Madurai Crime Branch. Ali put the file down on his desk and ran his upper teeth over his curled lower lip.

So that's it, he said to himself. I've got to find out who killed this Velan.

At first Vijayan didn't hear. He had walked into the lobby of the PKM and picked up his key from the man at the desk. He didn't respond to much these days. The weather remained chilly and rainy, and his interaction with others had shrivelled to courteous grunts, even with the man at the PKM, who had helped him get his job. Now they hardly spoke. Four times a day—twice when leaving and twice when returning—they enacted a silent pantomime with the key.

'A letter for you,' the man said again.

Surprised to hear him speak, Vijayan stopped at the foot of the stairs and turned around. 'Letter?' he asked in a breathy voice and retraced his steps.

It was not the usual thin blue envelope but a large beige one. By the time he reached his room and opened the door, he had recognized Muttusami's handwriting. It had to be from him anyway. No one else knew where he was.

The flap on the back had been taped down so he had trouble opening the envelope without tearing it. Two letters spilled out, one written on paper from a school exercise book and the other on foolscap. Glancing at the first and seeing it was from Arun, Vijayan smiled and then grimaced. He decided to read the second one, from Muttusami.

> *Dear Friend,*
>
> *I am well and wish the same for you. Thank you for your letter. Nagercoil is a pleasant town, although the weather can be cold. I am glad that you have found some work.*
>
> *I have three pieces of news for you. First, your nephew Arun's letter is enclosed. Second, your sister has also written and asked for your address. What should I tell her? Lastly, I must tell you that our beloved Raja is no more.*

Vijayan couldn't breathe. He read the last sentence again and twisted his face into a mask of pain. Grabbing the edge of the bed, his body shook with convulsions. Five minutes later he straightened up and read further:

He died two weeks ago from an infection. Mani believes the infection came from the operation on his jaw.

He was buried outside Melur on the Nattam road. We hired drummers and gravediggers who carried him to the ground. I insisted that a priest accompany us. Mani would not agree to a ceremony in Sanskrit, so Arumugasamy did it in Tamil.

Raja's body was wrapped in a cloth and covered with marigold flowers. We lit candles and put his sleeping mat into the hole.

We all wished you had been here. Many things are changing in Melur. I hope you will return soon.

With love,

Muttusami

A steady drizzle had begun and a cold wind blew in through the window. He folded the letter, pressing hard with the heel of his palm, folded it again and pressed harder. Again and again he folded and pressed, until he squeezed it into a small ball and smashed it with his fist. He sat still until the pain drained out of him. Exhausted, he picked up Arun's letter and read:

Dear Uncle,

I am well and I wish the same for you.

A man came to school and spoke to me. He also came to the house. He said he was your friend. I do not believe him. His name is Kumara Pillai. He wanted to know where you are. I did not say that you are in Madurai. But Mother did. I do not like this man.

Where are you in Madurai? Come home soon.

Love,

Arun

Good boy, Vijayan thought. He had expected that they would trace him to Virudhunagar. Telling Pushpa he was going to Madurai had paid off. But Kumara Pillai would soon discover he was not at the khadi shop in Madurai and search for him elsewhere. There was no reason for Kumara Pillai to think of Nagercoil, but he had already proved resourceful and he knew Vijayan by sight.

The rain had stopped and the sun streaked the watery air outside. He slid both letters inside his writing notebook and left the room. Handing in his key, he was about to say something to the man at the desk, but shifted his eyes to the large calendar on the wall behind him. The man watched Vijayan walk out of the lobby and wondered what had been in that large envelope.

Fear and remorse drove him as he walked through the park. He hadn't been there at Raja's death. Abandoned him, just like his younger sister. Making no effort to avoid the puddles, he splashed through the fractured reflections of trees and sky. At least there's Arun, he consoled himself as he emerged through the gap in the low railings and joined the flow of pedestrians.

Maybe I'd be a good father, he reflected. Or at least not a bad one. He was less sure about being a husband and preferred not to think about it. Except sex. He had almost no experience—only that disaster in Madurai years ago—but he had desire. He knew that after the outing to the waterfalls.

He measured and cut cloth, packed parcels for the post and wrote business letters. Although he hardly spoke, no one noticed because he was always withdrawn. Silently he composed letters to Pushpa and Muttusami, revised and rewrote them in his head. Once or twice he reached for his fountain pen in his breast pocket before he remembered where he was.

That night, in his room, he wrote a short letter to Muttusami, telling him to write back to Pushpa and say that he was moving around from town to town. That she could contact him through the shop in Melur. Then he wrote to Arun:

Dear Arun,

I am very well. I hope that you are doing well in school…

He tore it up. How could he send a letter to Arun without Pushpa knowing? Still, he wanted to see the boy, to let him know that he was right to doubt the stranger. He would have to go himself. It was dangerous—Kumara Pillai might still be in Virudhunagar—but he had to see someone he loved.

Inspector Ali put aside the directive from the Inspector General of Police and picked up the second document. It was a carbon copy of the report filed by the officer sent to investigate the discovery of Velan's body. Its three pages were held together by a rusted pin at the top left corner.

Date: 28 March 1972
Station: Melur, Madurai District
Officer: Additional Sub-Inspector N. M. Joseph

Time and place: On 4 January 1972 a body found in culvert on Melur-Nallampatti Road, Melur Taluk. The spot is estimated 500 metres from Kelalavu village.

The corpse found by one T. Sattiyamurthi, day labourer. He proceeded to Melur Police Station and reported this discovery at 15:00 that day.

Examination of body and place: I went to scene on 5 January 1972. I am guided to place by same Sattiyamurthi and I arrived at 11:30 hours. A small crowd is convened, includes R. Murugan, brother-in-law of deceased.

Body was male, decomposed, lacerations and abrasions on head.

I examined scene and found one purse, probably belongs to man. Purse contains coins and notes.

Interviews at scene:

1. *T. Sattiyamurthi, Paraiyar male, 32, of Kelalavu. He declared he found body when working in nearby field. He noted water flow in culvert not correct. He saw leg under bridge. He told co-workers and then proceeded to Melur police station.*
2. *Nallatampi, Pallar male, 55, of Nallampatti. He said he working with Sattiyamurthi and informed of body. He thinks deceased is P.S. Velan, Paraiyar male, of Kelalavu.*
3. *R. Murugan, Paraiyar male, 41, of Kelalavu Elder brother of deceased's wife. He informed he heard about body and came to scene. He also said body is P.S. Velan. He informed Velan not seen for 5 weeks prior. He said purse not belong to Velan.*

Body disposal and identification: Body removed on 6 January 1972 and transported to Madurai Government Hospital. On 7 January body identified as P.S. Velan.

Later interviews:

16 January, Kelalavu. Deceased's widow, Alamelu, stated her husband worked at iron factory near Melur. He had no enemies. He was often out of station. He gone to work on bicycle one morning and did not return. She did not know exact date. R. Murugan, brother-in-law of deceased, informed that deceased was CPM organizer.

Other villagers divulged deceased had debts. They say he was drinker. He owed money to C. Periyaswami.

25 February, Aritappatti. C. Periyaswami is primary school teacher and CPM organizer. He agreed Velan owed him large debt. He denied killing or assaulting deceased.

22 March, Kelalavu. Widow is now dead (suicide). R. Murugan is not helping. He refuses questions.

Ali put down the report and picked up the plastic bag that contained the only physical evidence from the crime scene. The object found near the body was an ordinary man's purse, made of a stiff, red synthetic fibre in a mesh pattern. Common enough, Ali thought, except for the five interlocking circles, the emblem of the Olympics, on one side and the words 'Mexico City 1968' on the other. He looked at the report again. He had remembered correctly: the brother-in-law said it did not belong to Velan.

Ali reread the three pages of faded type and raked a hand through his short, grey-flecked hair. Not enough evidence to bring charges. That was obvious. Ali didn't doubt that ASI Joseph had tried to identify suspects, though he also knew that most officers relied on getting a confession, often coerced, rather than on collecting evidence. Murugan, the brother-in-law, would have been in Joseph's sights from the very beginning. Ali had to admit this was reasonable. An argument with an inebriated, debt-ridden Velan might have driven Murugan to murder his sister's husband. A similar combination of drink and money, plus rivalry as political organizers, might also have led Periyaswami, the other creditor, to attack Velan.

Ali put the file box down and leaned back in his chair. What ASI Joseph doesn't know, he reminded himself, is that Velan was one of Pandian's agents. And probably killed by the same people who killed Pandian. Ali reached for his notebook but stopped.

Before making any more assumptions, he needed to see what the medical officer had found.

The report was signed by Dr B.S. Subramanyam, Chief Medical Officer, Government Hospital Madurai, and dated 9 January 1972. While reading the typed report, Ali summarized it in his notebook:

1. *Body identified as P.S Velan on 7 January 1972 by R. Murugan (brother-in-law) and Vijayan Naidu (friend)*
2. *Murugan from Kelalavu, daily labourer*
3. *Vijayan from Virudhunagar, works in Melur khadi shop*
4. *Identification by ring on finger*
5. *Body decomposed after lying in water 4-6 weeks*
6. *Time of death: late November 1971*
7. *Cause and manner: head trauma; homicide by heavy instrument or instruments. Cerebral contusion. Skull intact but many lacerations. Lacerations also on shoulders and upper torso.*

Ali leaned back again and relaxed into a thin smile. It was another concise and uncomplicated post-mortem. During twenty-two years in Crime Branch, he had seen scores of them, all following the template established a hundred years ago. The regulations for his own work, the Criminal Procedure Code of 1861, he knew by heart. Picking up his inspector's cap, with its wide brim and badge, he turned it around until he spotted something and then rubbed it off with a moistened fingertip. Right, he said to himself. I'll start by interviewing Velan's relatives and friends.

16

Pushpa took the dolls out of the box, one by one, and placed them upright on the table. She lined up the gods and goddesses in one group, the people in another and the animals, fruits, trees and houses in a third. The carved wooden pieces ranged in size from four to ten inches, the tallest being a special pair of male-female dolls. Then she counted them, ninety-six in all. Most had been given to her by her mother, though Pushpa had bought several in Madurai years ago.

Navarathiri, the festival of Nine Nights, was only two days away, and she loved setting up the dolls. Aunt Kamala and her niece, Thangamma, were coming to help with the dolls and preparing the food.

'Anyone home?' Hearing a voice, Pushpa turned towards the verandah. Vijayan took a few steps inside before she recovered enough to speak.

'Come! Come! How are you?'

'Not bad.'

She looked at him and saw that he was exhausted.

'Then you…I mean, did Muttusami tell you?' she asked.

'Yes. He wrote to say you'd asked about me,' said Vijayan, sitting down. 'So, I thought I'd come.'

'Wonderful. Navarathiri starts in two days and you'll…'

'Pushpa, I can only stay overnight. I have to go back tomorrow.'

'Oh no, you don't,' she chided him. 'I know those khadi shops are the centre of the universe, but this is special.'

'You don't understand...'

'I understand everything, little brother,' she declared with arms akimbo. 'You're staying for the start of the festival. For one thing, you need some good food. You look ill. Come and eat something now.' She turned and led him into the kitchen.

That evening Pushpa and Vanni dusted each one of the dolls with strips of cloth torn from a bed sheet. Selvan and Vijayan sat a few feet apart holding up their newspapers like shields. Arun lay on the floor pretending to do his school work, while Kalyani, bored with her crayons, began to bother him. Vijayan wanted to speak to Arun, but Selvan kept everyone under surveillance. Pushpa nursed her private plans, and Arun tried to penetrate everyone's thoughts.

Turning to her brother, Pushpa asked, 'Do you know someone named Kumara Pillai?'

Arun looked up and caught Vijayan's eye.

'No. Why?' he asked, trying to sound calm.

'He came here looking for you. About a week ago.'

'He went to Arun's school, too,' said Selvan.

'I don't know any Kumara Pillai. What does he look like?'

'Well-dressed, average height,' said Pushpa.

'Anything else?' prompted Vijayan.

'He wore a watch. A big gold one,' piped up Arun.

'Said he was your friend. From Madras,' added Pushpa.

'What'd you tell him?' asked Vijayan.

'That you'd gone to Madurai. Like you said. You are in Madurai, aren't you?' asked Pushpa, putting down a doll and looking straight at her brother.

'Yes, of course.' His deflated voice barely carried across the room.

'So why's he looking for you?' Selvan asked with irritation.

'No idea. Sounds like he's not completely honest,' Vijayan

said. The suggestion hung in the air for a moment, waiting for someone to bat it away, but no one spoke and they all resumed what they had been doing. When Vijayan picked up his paper, he glanced at Arun, whose anxious eyes were trained on him.

Although she walked in behind her mother, Thangamma's sea blue sari caught Pushpa's eye. Set off by a cream-coloured choli, its sheen dazzled in the subdued interior light. She's taller than I thought, Pushpa said to herself as she greeted her visitors with effusive and genuine enthusiasm.

'What a beautiful sari,' she said and reached for the girl's hand. Thangamma bent her head and let her outstretched arm be raised to waist height. When she straightened up and looked at Pushpa with a faint smile, the older woman smiled back and kept smiling until her whole face lit up. Watching this near-wordless exchange, Vanni wrinkled her nose.

Thangamma's mother bustled into the kitchen and set down two huge plastic-mesh baskets. Pulling out coconuts, papayas, bananas, banana leaves, strings of jasmine and her favourite betel nut mixture, she first pushed a hefty wad of paan into her mouth. Then, when her jaws were moving up and down like well-oiled pistons, she set to work arranging the food and puja items.

By early evening, Pushpa and Vanni had set up a wooden structure at one end of the front room and spread white cloth on each of the nine steps. Then Vanni, Kalyani and Thangamma began to arrange the dolls.

The main goddesses—Durga, Lakshmi and Saraswati—in gleaming reds and yellows went on the top step, next to Ganesa. Below them stood blue-faced gods and long-bearded saints, followed by caricatures. Vanni laughed as she picked up the pot-bellied merchant and put him next to the woman carrying firewood. Rajas, washermen, drummers and farmers stood next to houses, trees and bullocks. Arun grabbed a soldier and tried to fit him in, but only knocked over a postman. Monkeys, horses, birds and fruit were displayed on the bottom three steps. Below them, on the floor, a tiny temple was encircled by a blue pool of water.

Arun retreated to a corner. He always liked putting up the dolls with his sisters and mother, but this year was different. He knew he wasn't wanted. It was all right, though, because he shared a secret with Vijayan. Ever since his uncle had bought him that satchel, things had begun to change. He still wore shorts, but he knew he wouldn't always.

The room was filling up with girls of all ages, some with their mothers and aunts, chatting and admiring the dolls. Standing by the entrance to the room, Vijayan watched Thangamma's brilliant blue weave through the bustle and clamour. When Arun slipped up to his uncle and took his hand, Vijayan looked down and said, 'Let's go for a walk.' Thangamma hadn't noticed Vijayan, but she followed Pushpa's eyes and saw him leave the house with his nephew.

Fingering her slender gold thali, Pushpa surveyed the display of dolls. She moved one of the goddesses, stepped back, cocked her head to one side, stepped forward and put it back in its original place. The girls had done well.

Only two dolls remained—the special pair her mother had given her when she was married. The husband and wife dolls stood together on a little platform, their stiff arms reaching just below their ample hips. Lines chiselled into the soft red wood picked out jewellery and facial features. Pushpa didn't dress up her pair of wedding dolls, as others did, because she liked the cut wood surface to show.

When she handed the husband and wife dolls to Thangamma and whispered something, the young woman giggled and placed them on the top step next to Ganesa.

On the concrete floor, in front of the doll display, stood three brass oil lamps, each with a cone rising from its circular base. Pushpa lit the cotton wicks, decorated the goddesses with strings of jasmine and beckoned her aunt to sit down next to her, facing the dolls. By now the room was packed. Few families had dolls of such quality, or in such numbers, and Pushpa had let it be known that everyone was welcome. As she and her aunt began to say prayers, the women and girls sitting behind them whispered to each other and fidgeted with their saris and half-saris.

Then Pushpa and her aunt started to chant to Durga, and the others behind joined in. Their combined voices grew louder and louder, and soon the clapping began. Two or three women swung their heads from side to side, while others swayed back and forth at the waist. Selvan got up from his chair in the bedroom and closed the door more firmly.

In the cool night air, Vijayan and Arun walked beyond the street lamps to the outskirts of town. Vijayan wished he had brought a towel to wrap around his head and wondered how much Arun's jumper cost. They talked about school and the Nine Nights festival until Arun stopped and looked up at his uncle.

'Did you get my letter?'

'Umm. It was a nice letter.'

'But you didn't write back.'

'No. I decided to come in person. Isn't that better?'

'Yes, but…'

'Arun, what exactly did that man ask?'

'He wanted to know where you were. Said he was your friend.'

'Did you notice how he walked?'

'Walked?'

'Yes. Did he walk funny, with a limp?'

'I don't know.'

When Vijayan was silent for a minute, Arun blurted out, 'Will you come to my kabaddi match next weekend?'

'No, Arun. I can't.'

'Why not?'

'I have to go back…to work.'

'Where is that? I won't tell anyone.'

'It's not one place. It's many places.'

Returning in the pitch dark, Vijayan and Arun heard the women's voices before they reached the house. Drawn to the warmth and sounds inside, they headed towards the front room but stopped at the entrance, transfixed by the chanting and clapping. Arun looked into the crowd and saw a blur of swaying bodies and flushed faces. Then he saw Vanni, packed in with a group of girls her own age. Her intense face and parted lips made him look away with embarrassment.

Vijayan spotted Thangamma, sitting near the front, her head bobbing up and down as she clapped to the chanting. Although her face was hidden from him, he saw the blue sari shimmering in the lamplight. Suddenly she turned and looked at him. Neither could hold back a smile.

Vijayan took Arun's hand. 'C'mon. We'll come back later, when the food's ready,' he said and led him to his room at the back of the house

'Navarathiri was nice, wasn't it?' said Pushpa as Vijayan stood ready to leave in the morning.

'Umm.'

'Thangamma was a great help.'

'And her mother, too.'

'All right. All right. I won't mention her again. So, when will you come back?'

'Not sure. I'll try to let you know. But I might just show up.'

'That's fine. Just don't let it be too long. Okay?'

'Okay,' he said and walked out the door.

Waiting for the bus to pull out, he stared through the window and asked himself why he was going back to Nagercoil. He wouldn't mind staying at his sister's. Then someone in the crowd, a man in modern shirt and trousers, caught his attention. As the bus pulled away, removing him from view, Vijayan stood up and leant over the seat behind him, craning his neck to look out through another window. But the figure had disappeared.

The weather had turned cold in Nagercoil and Vijayan's cough became a fever. He had dragged himself to the government clinic for an injection and antibiotics, but now it was early afternoon and he had to go to work.

He found the lobby of the PKM filled with North Indian pilgrims on their way to Kanyakumari. Seeing his unsteady step and haggard face, they parted to let him walk through them like a condemned man. Water was splashing up the steps and through the steel-mesh gates drawn back at the entrance, forming puddles on the tile floor. He tightened the towel around his head and stepped into the wet forecourt.

As he edged down the hill towards the park, he slipped and broke the thong on one of his sandals, so he had to slide forward on that foot instead of lifting it. At the gate leading from the park to the main street, he slipped again but managed to grab a railing. The rain increased and he had to go even slower.

When he entered the Maharaja Emporium with a mud splattered veshti and soaking shirt, customers and shop assistants stopped talking and watched the shivering figure make its way to the back of the shop.

'Here, dry yourself,' said the manager, handing Vijayan a thin towel.

'Thank you. I think I need a tea.'

'Right. Get one for everyone. No umbrella? Take one from the corner,' suggested the manager.

He's in a good mood, Vijayan said to himself. The Navarathiri festival should happen more often.

On his return, Vijayan was told that his position would be extended for another month, and possibly more. No explanation was offered, and he wanted to believe that the man on leave had found more temples to visit. The more temples the better, he chuckled to himself.

Drugged by antibiotics and warmed by the tea, he began to feel better and let his mind wander. Maybe the Maharaja Emporium wouldn't be too bad. I could live in Nagercoil. Of course…

The telephone rang and all eyes turned towards the shiny black hump on the manager's desk. He picked it up, listened, scanned the shop, said a few words and replaced the heavy receiver in its cradle.

'Vijayan, there's someone to see you. At the PKM,' he announced across the shop. 'Take the rest of the day off.'

Vijayan froze. Numb on the outside, his heart racing inside, he stumbled out of the shop. It must have been him at the bus station in Virudhunagar.

Sunlight trickled through heavy clouds as he made his way back to the PKM. He could escape, jump on a bus and go anywhere. But he was tired of running. Besides, he asked himself, what's he going to do? Shoot me in the lobby?

Through the park and up the hill, his broken sandal strap flapped annoyingly with each step. Turning in through the gate and into the spacious forecourt, he stopped. What if he wants to take me somewhere? He started to retreat, but a black Ambassador taxi sped by and forced him back inside the compound. Not knowing what else to do, he kept going forward, up the steps and into the lobby.

A man stood up and approached, followed by a younger man, both in uniform. 'Vijayan Naidu?' he asked. Vijayan said nothing and he continued, 'I'm Inspector K. Ali, Crime Branch-CID, Madurai. I need to ask you a few questions.'

Vijayan stared speechless for a moment before he said, 'A few questions?'

'Shall we talk in your room?'

'Yes. In my room,' said Vijayan, still unable to respond properly.

He collected his key from the astonished man at the desk and led the way up the stairs. Ali told the younger man with him to remain in the lobby.

Vijayan fumbled nervously with the key, turned the heavy lock and gestured for the Inspector to enter. Ali put his cap on the table and sat on the chair, leaving the bed to Vijayan. Unzipping a thin plastic briefcase, he took out a notebook and placed it on his lap. Then he unclipped his pen from his shirt pocket and pushed down on the top. On the third try, the tip shot out.

'This is an informal interview. You're not under suspicion.'

'I see.'

I've come to ask you about P.S. Velan. You knew him, didn't you?'

'Yes, I knew him.'

'Tell me about Velan. What you know about him.'

Vijayan looked at the man opposite. He was in his fifties, short and stocky in a pressed khaki uniform, clean-shaven, short hair with flecks of whitish-grey. Vijayaṇ's eyes kept returning to his insignia, three small silver stars above red and blue ribbons on each shoulder. A tan braid hung from his left breast pocket and looped over his left shoulder. He stored up the details to tell Arun later.

'He came to the shop often,' said Vijayan.

'The khadi shop in Melur?'

'Yes.'

'Why did he come?'

'Well, he was my friend, acquaintance really. He was a CPM activist. But I guess you know that.'

'Go on.'

'All right. He'd come in and we'd talk about politics…in Madras. That's all.'

'What do you mean "that's all"?'

'Ah…we didn't talk about anything beyond Madras.'

'What about Velan? Was he involved in "anything beyond Madras"?'

Vijayan remembered his promise to Murugan, to tell the police about the letter and what he knew about Velan. He swallowed hard and cleared his throat. 'Velan was a CPM activist, but he also worked in Ceylon…supporting the Tamil cause there.' He stopped, unsure how much to reveal.

'We have information about his activities in Ceylon. He worked for a man called Pandian. Is that right?'

Vijayan was startled but managed to respond, 'Yes.'

'And how do you know this?' Ali put down his pen for the first time and looked straight at Vijayan.

There was silence, so Ali repeated his question, 'We know, but how do you know?'

'I was given a letter written to Velan. I have it here.'

Vijayan took the crumpled letter out of his notebook and handed it to Ali.

'How did you get this?' asked Ali, after reading the brief message.

'Murugan, his brother-in-law, gave it to me. When I went to see him, after Velan's death.'

'Right,' said Ali, placing the letter in his briefcase. 'But what about Pandian? How do you know him?'

'I met him. Well, he came to Melur and…then I went to see him in Madras.'

'Why was that?'

Vijayan hesitated but said, 'He tried to recruit me, to work in Ceylon.'

'And did he succeed?'

'No. Well, yes. I said I'd think about it. I came back to Melur and wrote saying I'd do it. Then he was killed.'

'You know what that means.'

Again silence. 'You're a potential target for the people who killed Pandian,' said Ali.

'Yes,' Vijayan said and looked straight at the Inspector. 'That's why I'm here in Nagercoil. No one knows.'

'No one except Muttusami in Melur.'

'I see. That's how you found me.'

'He was reluctant, but it's a murder investigation. He understood.'

Vijayan considered this for a moment and said, 'Something else. I've been followed by someone, a man who visited Velan's village before the murder. Then he came to Melur, to the khadi shop. And he followed me in Madras, when I met Pandian.'

'Who is he?'

'He calls himself Kumara Pillai. He found my sister's house in Virudhunagar, too. Even went to my nephew's school.'

'What does he look like?'

'Average height. In his forties, I think. Fleshy face.'

'I see,' said Ali, writing this down.

'But the most important thing is, he walks with a slight limp.'

Ali continued to write and Vijayan watched, wondering if the man at the bus station in Virudhunagar had been Kumara Pillai. Now he wasn't sure.

'And Velan? What happened on that last day? When he came to the shop. It was a Friday, right?'

'Yes, Friday. The demonstration was a week later, on Saturday.'

'And how did he seem? Anything different?'

'I don't think I can remember. It's been almost a year.'

'What did you talk about?'

'The demonstration. He wanted my support.'

'That was all?'

'Yes, I think so.'

'Did Velan drink a lot?'

'He did drink. I'm not sure how much.'

'Did he have debts?'

'Debts? I really don't know. Maybe. That's not unusual, is it?'

'No. But not everyone gets murdered.'

Ali closed his notebook, put it in his briefcase, replaced the pen in his pocket and stood up.

'Is that all?' asked Vijayan.

'For now. I may want you to come to Madurai. I'll let you know. And I'll tell the police here in Nagercoil about this man, the one who's following you.'

'What'll they do?'

'Probably nothing,' admitted Ali. 'But it means that you can go to them, if you need to.'

When they parted outside in the forecourt, Vijayan asked the question that had been in his mind from the beginning.

'Do you think the people who killed Pandian also killed Velan?'

'Possibly. But one thing bothers me.'

Vijayan looked at him and Ali explained, 'Why would they

kill Velan first, before Pandian? Pandian was the leader, and they knew where he was all along.'

17

Vijayan slept for twelve hours and woke without a fever. The cough was gone, too, so he decided to go for a long walk. Passing through the park, he continued down the winding main street, past the redbrick clock tower and towards the old market at Kottar. Head down, he shuffled along, trying to make sense of what he had learned.

The Inspector isn't convinced Velan was killed by agents from Colombo, he summed up for himself. But I'm a target for whoever killed Pandian. And the man with the limp might be here in Nagercoil. If he is, he probably knows I met Ali. Vijayan couldn't decide if that meant the man was more or less likely to act.

He was standing in front of St. Xavier's church on the outskirts of Nagercoil. The four-hundred-year-old stone facade and bell tower looked as pristine as if they'd been built last year. Admiring the white filigree windows beneath the ochre tiles, he wondered if he were safe. If I see Kumara Pillai, he reassured himself, at least I can go to the police. He decided to enter the church but the door was locked.

On his way back, Vijayan thought about Raja, the other murder in Melur. He hadn't really been killed, but in a way he had. And, unlike Velan and Pandian, he hadn't died for a cause. It had been squalid and stupid.

I wasn't there to help him, he fumed. Let him down, just like Meenakshi. His face blackened as his anger burst out in a half-strangled scream, 'It's wrong, all wrong!' People stepped aside while he stumbled along, seething with disgust.

Pushpa wasn't sure what to do next. When she had tried to discuss it with Selvan, he had flung out his hands in exasperation. She felt there had been wordless contact between them during the Navarathiri celebration. Yes, she was sure of it. But Vijayan was so private and defensive. I have to do this carefully, she warned herself. One wrong move and the whole thing will collapse. In the end, she decided to put it to him directly.

Inspector Ali fell into his chair and took out his notebook. It was the end of October and he had been working on the case for six weeks. Looking over his notes, he saw once again that he hadn't made much progress. He had begun by working through a long list of people to interview, seventeen in all. All of Velan's friends and relatives, except the printer, who had spoken with him on the evening he was killed.

He had, however, managed to establish the day of the murder as Friday 25 November. The leaflets on the back of Velan's bicycle announced a demonstration for Saturday 3 December, and the printer had confirmed what Murugan and Vijayan had told him—that Velan had been in Melur on Friday, a week before the event.

Ali brushed a hand back and forth over his stubbly hair. He had assumed that Velan had been killed by agents from Colombo, perhaps even the same people who had killed Pandian. That's why he had been assigned to the case in the first place. Now he wasn't sure.

The two killings were not consistent. One man was hacked to death with a machete, while the other was the victim of a sophisticated operation with explosives. Also, why kill Velan first? Killing Pandian would have been enough to stop Velan. And was

Velan such a threat that he had to be killed at all? No, it didn't make sense.

Then there was Kumara Pillai, the only positive lead he had. Although Ali had requested a surveillance check on him, it might take months to get any information, even assuming that Kumara Pillai was his real name. He might not be Velan's killer, but he appeared to be implicated.

Ali looked out the window and squinted. Suppose Velan's killer wasn't from Ceylon. Suppose he was from Melur or thereabouts. He looked again at ASI Joseph's report. It highlighted debt and drink, casting suspicion on Periyaswami and Murugan. Sipping his tea, he read over some of the notes of his interviews with these two men.

'Did Velan owe you money?' he had asked Periyaswami.

'Yes.'

'How much?'

'Four hundred rupees. He borrowed it a few months before… he died. But he didn't pay any of it back.'

'Did he have any enemies?'

'No, I don't think so.'

'Anyone in the CPM who might've wanted him out of the way?'

'No. It wasn't like that at all.'

'You never quarrelled with him?'

'No. He was my friend. We were comrades.'

Periyaswami had been forthcoming, almost too affable. Murugan, on the other hand, had kept a tight lip.

'Why did Velan have so many debts?' Ali had asked him.

'Don't know.'

'Why would he need extra money?'

No answer. 'C'mon. You're his brother-in-law. You lived in the same village. Next door. Tell me, why did he borrow so much?'

'Don't know.'

'Did he use it for CPM work?'

'Maybe.'

'Did he need it for his work in Ceylon?'

'Ceylon?'

'You found a letter written to him about Ceylon. Isn't that right?'

'Oh, yes. The letter.'

Ali could get nothing more from him. Both he and Periyaswami claimed to have been at home on the night of the murder, and although their wives backed this up, Ali had only been able to interview the women with their husbands in the same room.

If Velan had been killed by a local person, Ali didn't doubt that greed might be the reason. He didn't discount lust or jealousy, but this case didn't appear to involve passion. Money was the more likely motive, he thought, but would someone kill another man for a few hundred rupees? Yes, he admitted to himself. Just as someone might murder his brother-in-law in a drunken brawl.

Ali looked at his list. Fifteen people interviewed and little gained. Only two names remained without a line drawn through them, both male cousins, one in Melur and one in Singampatti, about ten miles away. He decided to go to Singampatti first.

Pushpa's letter, redirected from Melur, reached Vijayan in Nagercoil at the beginning of November. The man at the desk in the PKM gave him a look as he handed yet another letter to this mysterious guest. Looks as ordinary as a millet stalk, he thought, watching Vijayan climb the stairs. But then again, he reminded himself, not everyone who carries a bowl is a beggar.

Vijayan opened the letter in his room:

Dear Younger Brother,

We are all well here and we wish the same for you. I do not know where you are, so again I am sending this letter to Muttusami in Melur.

Arun continues to study well and plays kabaddi almost every Saturday. Vanni and Kalyani are fine. He is also healthy.

I am writing because I have decided to open discussions with Aunt Kamala's family about a possible matrimonial union. As of now, nothing has been said or decided. But if I do not hear from you within two weeks, I will assume that you do not object to my beginning the discussion on this important matter.

We all hope that you will visit us again soon.

Love,

Pushpa

Vijayan wasn't surprised. He knew it was coming. His only surprise was that he had no objection.

His mind was racing so fast that he almost didn't see the covering letter from Muttusami. It was also brief. Mani had been transferred to another office, in Trichy. Krishnan had another child and was now a junior manager in his bank.

He stood up and moved around the small room, looking at things. Notebook, books, ashtray and candle on the table. Calendar and shoulder bag hanging on the wall. He adjusted each one in turn, straightening and squaring them, an inch or two. Mani gone. That was a blow. He might never see him again.

Yes, he decided, he would marry Thangamma and go back to Melur with her. It would be different, without Raja and Mani, but he had to accept that. First, though, he had to be sure it was safe.

It wasn't yet midday, so he went to the library. In Ceylon,

he read, five policemen had been killed in an explosion that destroyed a rural police station. Vijayan thought of Pandian, and the two people who had died with him. Tamil students in Ceylon were supporting an armed struggle, and one headline shouted: 'Civil War!' Vijayan remembered the vacant-eyed youths at the exhibition near the park a few months ago. Then he saw Velan's mutilated corpse. He threw the papers down and left.

The jeep made good time weaving in and out of morning traffic. Even though it had no special lights or siren, the insignia and the word 'Police' on the side were enough to persuade most drivers to give way. Once it left the northern suburbs of Madurai and reached the countryside, however, it bumped over potholes and slowed down on the twisting turns of the narrow road that threaded through green fields towards Singampatti. Bicycles and bullock carts grudgingly gave way to the blaring horn of the jeep with its uniformed passenger.

The driver knew better than to expect any small talk. Inspector Ali always stared straight ahead and barely acknowledged the man next to him. Today was no different except that he kept working his lips back and forth, as if trying to slot something into place.

Earlier that morning Ali had received a telex from Crime Branch in Madras:

> *Kumara Pillai departed Madras for Colombo on SS Chidambaram 2 November.*
>
> *Regret unable to detain.*

He might return, and he might have been responsible for Pandian's death. But for the time being, at least, he wasn't following Vijayan or any of Pandian's agents in Tamil Nadu. And his departure strengthened Ali's suspicion that Colombo had not been behind Velan's murder.

Singampatti was a handful of huts and houses on boulder-strewn land surrounded by paddy fields. A large, flat slab of rock, tilted at an angle, made for a perfect surface to thresh and dry the harvest.

As the jeep approached, a few goats scampered away and a squatting man put aside the basket he was weaving. Manikkam was in his fifties, with hollow temples and pinched cheeks, but his eyes were bright. Notified that the police were coming, he wore a clean shirt and veshti.

Ali followed him into a one-room mud-brick house, where a folding metal chair was set up in front of a low wooden stool. A laminated tray, with an image of a chubby baby, had been placed on the stool and filled with biscuits. The Inspector sat down, opened his briefcase and took out his notebook. He bit on a biscuit, checked his notes and looked up. Manikkam stood nearby, clutching a fan to beat away the flies from his visitor. His wife gave the Inspector a glass of tea, stepped back and stared.

'You are the cousin of P.S. Velan?' Ali asked, already knowing the answer.

'Yes, sir.' Manikkam spoke with a squeaky voice.

'His mother's brother's son, is that right?'

'Yes, sir.'

'When did you last see Velan?'

'I don't remember. A few weeks before he died.'

'Where did you see him?'

'In Melur, at the GBTS. He...'

'The Government Basic Training School?'

'Yes, sir.'

'Why did you go there?'

'That's where I work, sir.'

'What's your job?'

'Different things. Mostly chopping wood for the kitchen.'

'Did Velan often visit you at work?'

'He didn't come to see me, sir. I mean...'

'What do you mean?'

'I mean he came...to see his friends.'

'Who were his friends there?'

'Some of the teachers, sir.'

'Which ones?'

'He knew Alagarswami, the Tamil teacher. And Karim, who teaches maths. He knew a lot of them, sir.'

'Who else?'

'Dandapani, the games master, sir.'

'Anyone else?'

'I don't know, sir.'

'Did he borrow money from any of them?'

'I don't think so, sir. I'm not sure.'

Sensing that Manikkam was keeping something back, Ali asked, 'Do you know who killed Velan?'

'No, sir. How would I know?' Manikkam's thin voice was running out of air.

'Do you have any suspicions?'

'No, sir.' Manikkam hesitated and looked down when he said this, but Ali decided not to push him. He would wait for another time, when Manikkam wasn't expecting him.

Mr T. Navajeevan, alias Kumara Pillai, landed in Colombo early on the morning of 3 November 1972. Four days later he submitted his confidential report to the Military Intelligence Corps. It contained the following details:

1. *S.K. Pandian ran a network of agents based in Tamil Nadu and Sri Lanka who worked contrary to state interests.*
2. *P.S. Velan, one of his agents, was under surveillance from 13 to 19 November 1971. He was later killed; assailant unknown. His body was found in early January 1972.*
3. *S.K. Pandian was eliminated, along with two accomplices, in Madras on 28 March 1972.*
4. *Three more of Pandian's agents, Sivakumar Nadar, T. Kannan and Vijayan Naidu, were under surveillance for different periods of time from February to October 1972. They were found not to be a threat to state security.*
5. *S.K. Pandian's other agents remain unidentified.*

Inspector Ali arrived at the Government Basic Training School, accompanied by local officer Joseph. They explained to the principal that they needed to talk with one of the kitchen staff, ignored his offer to send a peon to fetch the man and set off across the large open space between the office block and the mess hall.

A group of students in their late teens and early twenties were playing volleyball in the dying sunlight of a late November afternoon. A burly man sat on a bench under a tree smoking a cigarette, as he talked and laughed with several students.

Suddenly he stood up. 'What the hell are they doing here?' he snarled. The boys looked over and saw two policemen advancing toward the mess hall. 'Is Manikkam working today?' the man asked. When the boys said he was, the man swore and started to move towards the hall but stopped.

Speechless, they all watched the drama unfold. The policemen entered the building and emerged three minutes later escorting Manikkam between them. Even the volleyball players stopped to watch the silent procession of khaki and white cloth move across the clay-coloured earth. Manikkam caught a glimpse of Dandapani glaring at him and quickly looked away, but he felt the other man's eyes on him until he was driven off in Ali's jeep.

'What's that all about?'

'Two policemen?'

'And one an Inspector!'

The boys' excited speculation was cut short by the games master. 'Probably caught that little bastard stealing food from the kitchen, that's what,' Dandapani snorted and stomped off to his staff quarters on the other side of the compound.

Dandapani was confident that Manikkam didn't know anything, but he was Velan's cousin. He recognized Joseph from the Melur police. Not especially bright. But who was the other one, the Inspector? He didn't like this one bit. Still, he'd better sit tight.

The jeep slipped under the 'Police Station Melur' signboard that arched between two crumbling concrete pillars. Joseph grunted at the desk sergeant inside, who barely looked up from his magazine, and led Ali to a small room with a metal desk, four wooden chairs and one window. The officers sat down, and Ali gestured for Manikkam to do the same, but he remained standing.

'You are not a suspect. But you can help us find out who killed Velan. Are you ready to help?'

'Yes, sir.' Manikkam's voice creaked like a door.

'Good. Now, we know Velan needed extra money for his work with the CPM. Is that right?'

'I'm not sure, sir.'

'I'm telling you it is true.'

'Right, sir.'

'He also needed money for his work elsewhere. In Ceylon. Isn't that true?'

'Ceylon? No, sir, I don't know anything about that.'

'Okay, we'll put that to one side. Now, from where did Velan get that extra money for his CPM work?

Manikkam's eyes darted sideways.

'He borrowed money from his friends at the GBTS, didn't he?'

'No, sir,' said Manikkam quickly.

'How do you know he didn't?'

'Because…because…'

'Because what?'

Manikkam bowed his head.

'Manikkam! You're not a suspect, but if you withhold information, you may be charged with perverting the course of justice and go to jail. Do you understand?'

'Yes, sir.'

'Now, then. Where did he get that money?'

'From Dandapani.' Manikkam's whispered words were almost inaudible.

'From who?'

'Dandapani, sir. The games master.'

'How did Velan get money from him?'

'I…I can't, sir. He'll hurt me.' Manikkam's eyes pleaded with the Inspector.

'Listen to me, Manikkam. You are cooperating in a police investigation and therefore you are under police protection. No one can harm you.' Ali had used this half-truth many times and it never failed.

'We won't let anyone hurt you,' he repeated. 'Now tell me about Dandapani and Velan.'

Less than half an hour later Ali had Manikkam's story.

On the first Saturday of every month, in the late afternoon, a bullock cart from the government godown in Melur would pull up at the back of the GBTS mess hall. Under the tarpaulin were sixteen 50-kilogram sacks of paddy, one sack of onions, several baskets of tomatoes and vegetables, some ginger root and tins of cooking oil. Enough to feed the boys at the hostel two meals a day for a month. The goods were unloaded and stored inside the kitchen by the driver, supervised by Dandapani.

When the bullock cart left, four of the 50-kilogram sacks of paddy would still be under the tarpaulin, to be sold on the blackmarket. Ali later learned that those sacks would have added about 325 rupees to Dandapani's monthly salary of 400.

'Dandapani made sure the bullock cart came on Saturday afternoons,' Manikkam explained. 'It was the cook's half-day off. No meal was served Saturday evening and no one was around.

'If I happened to be there, chopping wood or something, he told me to leave. But once, about five or six years ago, I was sitting against the kitchen wall, around the corner. He didn't know I was there.

'When the driver had unloaded the sacks, I heard Dandapani say, "Four still there, right?" I didn't hear what the driver said, but I stuck my head around the corner and saw Dandapani give him some money.

'After that, I knew. I didn't tell anyone, though.'

'Did anyone else at the GBTS know?' Ali asked.

'No, sir. The boys were always complaining about the poor meals, the small portions. But the principal didn't take any notice.'

'Did you tell anyone about this?'

'No, sir. I was scared of Dandapani. What he'd do if I said anything.'

'Then what happened?'

'Well, it must have been about four years ago. We were walking home from Melur at night. Velan and me. We'd been drinking.

And that's when I told him about Dandapani and the paddy.'

'What did Velan say?'

'Nothing, sir. We never talked about it again.'

When Ali let Manikkam go, he issued orders. 'Don't go back to the GBTS. Stay in Singampatti until you hear from me. I'll arrange everything with the principal.'

Alone in his office that night, Ali nibbled his lower lip and reviewed his notes again. Velan had known about Dandapani's embezzlement for three years. Why was he killed after all that time? Ali told himself there was only one answer. He had been right that the motive was money. But it wasn't debt.

The jeep purred through the GBTS compound gate and pulled up under the tall tamarind trees. Ali got out, walked a few metres and stood between two rows of staff quarters. Each concrete building had a latticed verandah in front. Not bad, he reflected. Better than the old police quarters.

No one was about, but he knew where Dandapani lived. Mounting the steps, he took off his cap and rapped on the verandah door.

'Is your father home?' he asked quietly when a young girl came to the door, her mother visible in the background.

'Papa!' the girl shouted and skipped inside.

Minutes later Ali sat opposite Dandapani in one of the front rooms with a small metal table between them. 'The Inspector and I have some private business to talk about,' he had said to his wife, telling her to take their daughter to a neighbour's house.

Ali began. 'That's a nice daughter. Any more children?'

'Another daughter, older. She's having tuition now.'

'No sons. That must be a disappointment, for a games master.'

Dandapani didn't reply.

'I think you know why I'm here,' Ali said, shifting his tone.

'No, Inspector. I do not,' said Dandapani, crossing his arms on his chest.

'I am here to ask you about your embezzlement of funds from the GBTS.'

'My what?'

'You stole 200 kilograms of paddy each month, food intended for the hostel here.'

Dandapani stared but said nothing.

'You kept it and then you sold it, on the blackmarket. How much profit did you make?'

'This is ridiculous! Who told you this?' He was agitated but in control.

'You thought it was a secret, didn't you? Nice little earner, stealing food from the boys.'

'Someone's told you lies, Inspector. You shouldn't believe everything you hear.'

'You're right. I don't believe everything people tell me.'

'Well, then, since it's a lie, we've nothing to talk about.'

'But this is not a lie. You've been defrauding the government for years. Stealing paddy and selling it since 1968.'

'You can't prove that!' Now he was shouting.

'Oh yes, I can. And I will prove it. In court.'

'How?'

'I'm not obliged to tell you that. But I will say that the evidence is substantial.'

Dandapani considered this and remained silent.

'But I'm not here to charge you with fraud. Not yet.'

'I see. Then why are you here?'

'To ask you about a murder.'

'Murder?' Dandapani batted the word away, but his face tightened.

'Yes. The murder of P.S. Velan.'

Dandapani said nothing.

'He knew about your embezzlement, didn't he?'

Again no reply.

'He knew about it and he needed money. So he blackmailed you.'

Dandapani glared at Ali.

'He blackmailed you. Then you killed him.'

After a moment's silence, Dandapani challenged him, 'What makes you think that?'

'This,' said Ali, taking from his pocket the purse found near Velan's body and placing it on the table. They both looked down and saw the Olympics symbol of linked circles.

Ali raised his head and said, 'It's yours, isn't it?'

The other man's face twitched.

'Isn't it?' Ali demanded.

'No. It's not mine.'

Ali stared hard at him. 'You knew Velan, didn't you?'

'I hardly knew him.'

'But you did know him, didn't you?'

'Sort of.'

'Did you see him often?'

'Not very often.'

'Like the first Saturday of every month?'

'What?'

'You heard me. The first Saturday of every month when you paid him to keep quiet about your stealing. Not just the driver. But Velan, too.'

'I don't know what you're talking about.'

'Yes you do.'

'I know you police donkeys. You make up something and try to pin it on someone.'

'I've enough evidence to charge you with fraud. And I'll get enough for murder, too!' Ali was so enraged he almost believed his boast.

Ali was about to leave when Dandapani's teenage daughter returned from her tuition and bounded into the house. Seeing the policeman, she stopped halfway. 'It's all right, Veena. The Inspector is an old friend. He's going now,' said Dandapani, putting his arm around her shoulders and drawing her close.

Relieved, she looked around and saw what was on the table. 'Oh, papa! You found your purse!' she cried with a big smile.

'Yes. Good luck, isn't it?' Ali said. 'I found it on the road and brought it back to him.'

Dandapani decided not to run away but didn't know how he could face his daughters. He was in his front room, trying to work out a plan, when Ali returned with an arrest warrant, took him to Madurai and placed him in custody. After a week of interrogation and sleep deprivation, he confessed.

'When did Velan first approach you?' Ali asked.

'About four years ago. He wanted fifty rupees a month. Otherwise he'd talk.'

'Did he say how he'd found out?'

'No. At first, I thought it was the driver. But I paid him ten rupees each month to keep quiet. He was scared of me, anyway.'

'Did you pay Velan the fifty?'

'I laughed at him. Fifty rupees a month! But then he showed me a piece of paper. He had details about the paddy sacks, dates, the driver's name. Said he'd go to the GBTS principal, to the police, the newspapers.'

'Then what did you do?'

'I paid him, the little cunt. Fifty every month. Then he raised it to hundred. And last year he said he wanted 150. A hundred-and-fifty! I was only getting about 325 myself from selling the sacks. And I was doing all the work, taking all the risk.'

'Did you pay him 150?'

'No. But he threatened me again, that he would tell everyone. I was going crazy. I'd lose my job. But I couldn't go on paying him. Not month after month. It wasn't the money—I would've still made about 175. I just couldn't let the bastard get 150 for doing nothing!'

'Then?'

'I couldn't go on like that. It was eating me up. It wasn't right!'

'So, you killed him,' prompted Ali.

'It was the only way. I found out when he cycled home, what days, what time.'

'And that night?'

'I got there before him and waited. Where the road dips down, with trees on both sides. Like a tunnel.'

The details of the vicious attack on Velan, provided by Dandapani, were included in Ali's report.

'There's a telegram for you,' said the man at the desk. 'From Madurai,' he added as he handed over the small square envelope. Vijayan looked at his name and address printed in the cellophane window on the front, crossed the floor and climbed the stairs. Watching him, the man again wondered who Vijayan really was. 'Letters, telephone calls, a police inspector and now this telegram,' he muttered. Reaching to hang Vijayan's key on its hook, he stopped, arm still outstretched. I know, he said to himself with a shiver of excitement, he's a secret agent.

Vijayan sat on his bed and looked at the yellowish-brown envelope. He guessed it was from Ali, since only he and Muttusami knew where he was. Then he realized that it could also be from Kumara Pillai.

He ripped it open and read the typed message:

Come immediately. Important news.
Inspector K. Ali
Madurai CB-CID

The Criminal Investigation Department was housed in a three-storey concrete building, separated from the busy road by a shoulder-high perimeter wall, its severity relieved only by straggly papaya trees in the compound. At the entrance, Vijayan was frisked by a sleepy solider with a rifle that might have seen duty in the First World War. After climbing two flights of stairs, he was told that Inspector Ali was out and no one knew when he was expected back.

Vijayan wandered around the city centre, where he used to work, but he couldn't concentrate. Wedding processions going in and out of the massive temple gate tower surged around him like bleating sheep. He was about to scream at them to get out of his way when he heard the whining oboes and booming barrel drums. Despite his aversion to temple ceremonies, his body tingled with the recognition of familiar music.

The yawning soldier let him through again, and fifteen minutes later Vijayan was ushered into Ali's office. It was smaller than he had imagined, only a wooden desk with neatly stacked files, a metal filing cabinet and two chairs. The single window was near a corner.

'I've got some news for you,' Ali began. 'Good news.'

Vijayan fidgeted in the hard wooden chair. He had been wondering what to expect. Had they arrested Kumara Pillai?

'We know who killed Velan,' said Ali. 'Do you know a man called Dandapani? The games master at the GBTS in Melur.'

'Dandapani? Yes, a little,' said Vijayan, puzzled.

'Velan had been blackmailing him. He knew that Dandapani was committing fraud, stealing paddy sent to the GBTS kitchen.'

'Fraud?'

'Yes. Every month he kept some of the paddy sacks, sold them and pocketed the profit. He'd been doing this for years, but Velan found out and demanded money to keep quiet. At first Dandapani paid him off. But when Velan kept asking for more and more, Dandapani decided to get rid of him.'

Ali let Vijayan absorb this.

'You mean,' said Vijayan after a few moments, 'that Dandapani killed Velan?'

'That's right. He waited for him by the road, jumped out from behind the trees and hacked him to death.'

'How did you find out?'

'A purse.'

'Purse?'

'Dandapani's. It must have fallen out during the attack. The Melur police found it and included it in the report passed to me.'

'How did you know it was his?'

'I didn't. I guessed. It had the Olympics symbol on it, with the circles. Who would choose a purse like that?'

'A games master.'

'Yes. You see, I'd already found out that Velan knew about Dandapani's fraud. So, it seemed logical.'

'Logical?'

'That the two were connected.'

'I see.' Vijayan thought for a moment and asked, 'But what about Pandian?'

'We're still investigating that. But we think it was an agent, or agents, from Colombo.'

'And Kumara Pillai?'

'That's the other thing I wanted to tell you. He's gone back to Ceylon. Last month.'

'Are you certain?'

'Yes. We know the boat he took and the date.'

'But why…'

'We don't know his motives, or those of his bosses. Presumably, they felt the threat had been minimized.'

'But they…he followed me all over. Melur, Madras, even Virudhunagar.'

'He followed you, yes. But maybe he decided you weren't so dangerous after all,' said Ali, with a little smile.

Vijayan considered this before declaring, 'The threat's not over. Tamil groups in Ceylon are more organized, arming themselves and…'

'Yes, attacking police stations,' Ali said. 'We're aware of that, but it's not our jurisdiction. It's another country, isn't it?'

Vijayan was about to challenge this convenient moral boundary but only looked down and then out the little window. He couldn't see anything except another concrete building.

When he looked back, Ali was reading a file. Vijayan rose, thanked the Inspector for confiding in him and shook his hand. Vijayan rarely did that, but this time it seemed right.

18

Pushpa sensed something had changed as soon as she saw him standing inside the door.

'Come in! Have you eaten?' she called.

As Vijayan came closer, his body looked lighter and she saw that his eyes had recovered their dark brown lustre. Turning to lead him towards the kitchen, she noticed his travelling case. He's come back, she said to herself. Something must have happened.

'Why not change your veshti?' she called over her shoulder as she went into the kitchen. Although he had put on a clean one when he left Nagercoil that morning, it was splattered after his walk from the bus station. He had forgotten how a sudden downpour could turn the streets of Virudhunagar to mud.

When he didn't reply, she understood and said, 'Take one of Selvan's.'

Later, sipping coffee in the front room, Vijayan felt himself unwind. Velan had been killed for blackmailing someone, not for working with Pandian. That was over. Yet he had nearly gone to Ceylon, where civil war threatened, and he could not forget the blank-eyed men at the photo exhibition.

He wanted to tell Inspector Ali about the attack on Raja. Placing the small ceramic tumbler on the low table, he began to stack the newspapers in a neat pile. But there was no case, no evidence. Only blind prejudice. And a death that had burned a hole in him.

'I've spoken to aunt and uncle about Thangamma,' Pushpa broke into his thoughts.

Vijayan made no reply and she continued, 'You remember I said I would. In the letter. If you didn't object.'

'I remember.'

'They have agreed! And she has also given her consent.'

He stopped fussing with the things on the table.

Pushpa went closer and stood in front of her younger brother. 'Vijayan!' she cried. 'This is good news! I am happy, very happy!'

Vijayan stayed silent.

'Say something! Don't just sit there like a deaf mute!'

'They have agreed? Yes, that's good.'

He looked up at her and their eyes met, hers brimming with joy and his moistened by a mixture of relief and loss. Neither pulled away, and although they remained in separate worlds, they both felt that the barrier built up between them since their sister's death had crumbled away.

'We'll do the horoscopes soon. Of course, we can't have the wedding for a while. I was thinking August-September would be best. What do you think?'

'All right, but I...'

Pushpa cut him off and plunged into a recital of details, arrangements and decisions, exchanging horoscopes, choosing the astrologer and making the formal proposal to Thangamma's parents. She strode around the room, talking to herself. 'And we'll get that priest who did Kalyani's naming ceremony. What's his name? Subramaniam something?'

'That's just it, Pushpa.' Vijayan raised his voice to get her attention.

'What?'

'There won't be any priest.

'But...'

'But nothing. I won't agree to a wedding conducted by a Brahmin. That's all.'

'Well, I'll have to talk about this with aunt and uncle.'

'And there won't be any dowry. Nothing beyond kitchen things, some clothes and two pieces of jewellery. Only two. I've thought about it and this is my decision.'

'Vijayan! Don't be so rigid. You're going to ruin this before it starts.'

'Then it won't start.'

'Anyway, all this has to be discussed with them. So...'

'Fine. Discuss it with them, but this is how it will be. No Brahmin and no dowry.'

'Then it's not a proper marriage!'

'Yes, it is. They changed the law recently. You can have a simple ceremony without a Brahmin.'

Pushpa was about to say something when he cut her off. 'We can have a non-Brahmin priest, if you insist. That's my only concession.'

'I see. You've worked this all out, haven't you?' said Pushpa, eyeing her brother with an irritation that concealed admiration. While his intransigence was predictable, his serious planning impressed her.

'All right,' she said, unable to hide her delight. 'I'll talk it over with them.'

Arun came bounding up the steps, swung the bulky satchel off his shoulder and let it crash to the ground.

'Uncle! When did you come?' he cried and ran to Vijayan, who reached for his hand. They were face to face, the boy standing and the man sitting.

'How are you, Arun?'

'Good.'

They looked at each other for a moment. Then Arun furrowed his brow and asked, 'Is your work in Madurai over?'

'Yes, it's all over now.'

'Then you'll live with us?'

'No, Arun. I'm going back to Melur.'

'But why can't…'

'Arun! Your uncle has a job in Melur. That's why,' said Pushpa.

'Don't worry. I'll come back and see you, often.'

'How often?'

'I don't know, but I will.'

'Your uncle will be coming to see us a lot now, Arun,' said Pushpa.

Walking up the main road from the bus station, Vijayan saw that little had changed in Melur. The same shops with battered wooden shutters and the same tea-stalls with men on wooden benches, smoking beedis and holding thin glasses. Women bought vegetables and put them in jute bags. Dogs scavenged on the roads and were scattered by a passing bus. People came in from villages, on foot and on bicycles, converged at the roundabout and threaded themselves into the mid-morning lives of a small market town.

Little more than a year had passed since Velan's death, and only nine months since he had left, but Vijayan was a stranger in this familiar place. Although nothing surprised him, he felt no connection with anything or anyone. He had built up defences all his life, relaxing them only when in the room he had shared with his friends, and then Velan's death had taken away even that sanctuary. Something had happened in Virudhunagar, with Arun, with Pushpa and with Thangamma, but in Melur the barriers remained.

'Welcome!' Muttusami's spontaneous greeting broke through

his isolation. Vijayan smiled and entered. He was accepted here, in the shop, accepted without words or explanations.

The shop hadn't changed, but Vijayan had to reacquaint himself with it. Sitting down on a stool, he ran his hand over the warm wooden counter. In the light reflecting off the glass-fronted cabinets, he saw a stack of shirts fanned out like a pack of cards and frowned.

'You're looking better than when you left. But that wouldn't be hard,' said Muttusami with a throaty chuckle.

'You, too. I mean, you're just as busy and…'

'As ugly as ever?'

'No. No. It's just that everything's the same.'

'Not everything. This is Sadasivan, by the way,' said Muttusami, nodding towards the temporary assistant, who had been watching from the far corner of the counter.

'You got my letter?' asked Vijayan.

'Oh, don't worry about that. You can start on the first of the month. Main thing is to find a place to sleep.'

'The room…'

'It's still there, but your friends aren't. Krishnan decided to give it up.'

'I see.'

'He's been promoted, some manager position in the bank. And he's got another child. I told you in the letter.'

Vijayan acknowledged this with a little wag of his head.

'And Mani's gone. Off to Trichy.'

'Right.'

'And…well, you know.'

'Yes. I know.' Neither of them wanted to mention Raja.

Vijayan's hand sought the string hanging from the ceiling and began to wind it around his finger. 'I need to eat something,' he said and tossed the string away.

Turning right outside the shop and right again down the lane, he came to the outside stairs that led up to the room. He stood on the bottom step and looked around. The door at the top of the stairs was locked, but the shutters overlooking the lane were open. Trying to imagine Raja's jet-black hair flopping over his young forehead as he leafed through a magazine, he saw instead a wired mouth and battered face.

Vijayan spent the night in Perumal Tevar's room on a mat wedged between a metal desk and a wall. The sagging clothesline and betel juice-streaked walls set him thinking about where he could find a place to live after the wedding. We'll need two rooms, maybe three, he said to himself. He liked planning and he liked saying 'we.'

Perumal Tevar's bonhomie took Vijayan out of himself, but when they took walks, his chatter recalled Mani's silence. As they strolled north out of town one evening, his formidable umbrella swung back and forth like a pendulum.

'And another thing. You must start those meetings again. The Rationalist Society,' he commanded. 'They were the only good thing in this town.'

Vijayan had considered this and was thinking about topics for a meeting. 'Tamil poetry and politics in Ceylon' might be good.

They both looked in through the compound gate as they passed the Government Basic Training School. Beyond the large open space, Vijayan could see a corner of the mess hall. News of Dandapani's arrest had surprised everyone, except Perumal Tevar.

'He was a rogue. First class. But why did he do it? That's what I want to know,' he said and glanced at Vijayan.

Vijayan guided Muttusami to a tea-stall, the one near the roundabout with the comfortable blue benches. It was mid-afternoon, with few customers. They sat side by side and looked straight ahead.

'You know that inspector? The one who came looking for me?' Vijayan began.

'Yes.'

'He told me what happened. Why Velan was killed.'

When Vijayan finished the story, Muttusami looked puzzled.

'But why did the inspector want to see you?' he asked.

'He thought I might be in danger. I'd been in contact with someone recruiting people to help the Tamil movement in Ceylon. The Colombo government killed him and they were following me.'

'So…that's why you had to leave?'

'Yes.'

'Who else knows this?'

'Just you and Inspector Ali.'

'What about Murugan?'

'I'll tell him.' Hearing this, Muttusami looked at his friend from the corner of his eye.

'Oh, one more thing I wanted to tell you,' Vijayan said.

'Umm.'

'I'm…you see, Pushpa's arranged it all.'

'C'mon, Vijayan, say it,' said Muttusami, who now turned to face Vijayan.

'Yes. I'm going to get married. My cousin.'

'Excellent news. Then we'll have to see about getting you a promotion,' said Muttusami with a broad smile.

Two weeks later, around the time of the Pongal festival, Vijayan finally found a single room. He couldn't really afford the 75 rupees per month, but Muttusami loaned him some money in the belief that his monthly pay would rise. Although small and less than clean, the room was on the ground floor with a backyard space for cooking and washing. The owners lived upstairs with their daughter and her children, while the lorry driver son-in-law rarely spent nights at home. It was also near the edge of town, where the paddy fields started to stretch out towards the rocky hills. It's quiet, Vijayan thought. Good for writing.

In early February, after weeks of negotiations, the marriage agreement was confirmed in Virudhunagar. Vijayan remained in Melur, so the groom's party consisted of Selvan, Pushpa and Arun. Selvan presented Thangamma's parents with a brass tray of betel leaves, betel nut, bananas and flowers, while Pushpa gave them a silk sari. Money passed hands. A Brahmin priest conducted the ritual with coconuts and prayed to Ganesa to remove any obstacles that might arise in the coming months. A date in late August was fixed for the wedding, and they all sat down to a feast.

Back home that evening, Pushpa was thinking aloud about what she should do to ensure that nothing went wrong. Her main worry was Vijayan.

'Let's see. We'll have to buy him a new pair of sandals. Black, I think, with a closed toe. And a silk veshti, a shirt and...'

'A watch,' said Arun without looking up from his schoolwork.

'And a watch,' Pushpa repeated unconsciously.

'I know which one,' said Arun.

Pushpa looked at her son and wondered what else he knew.

Vijayan received Pushpa's letter with news of the confirmation and the date for the wedding. Looking around the spare but now spotless interior of his room, he worried how he and Thangamma could live there. He had a pretty good idea of the things they would need, and her parents would give her most of those. But there would be other things, surely, that she might want. And when they had children?

Caressing his high forehead with his fingertips, he decided that he wouldn't borrow any more from Pushpa and Muttusami. He would earn more. Maybe write something popular for the magazines.

The customers continued to come in from town and the nearby villages, farmers chewing betel nut and government employees in trousers. He showed them veshtis and lungis, towels and shirts. He measured and cut khadi and silk, three and a half metres for a regular shirt, three for a short-sleeved one. Playing with the dangling string, he planned his magazine essay and worried about the future.

Krishnan, Kantan and Chellappan stopped by to catch up on all the news, which Vijayan gave them in an abbreviated version. Once or twice a week Perumal Tevar entertained everyone with his stories. But familiarity only highlighted absences. When Vijayan left the shop, he no longer went down the lane to the room. The Rationalist Society never met again. No late night walks with Mani. No Raja.

Vijayan was alone in the shop, half-heartedly reading an old newspaper, when he heard a noise outside. Looking up, he saw nothing and turned back to the paper. Then he recognized the spluttering sound coming from next door and stepped out. A group of ten or fifteen men were looking at the loudspeaker mounted at the corner of the electrical shop. Although he could barely make out the crackling words of the broadcast, one sentence was enough:

> *E.V. Ramasami Naicker, leader of the Justice Party and social campaigner, has died at the age of ninety-four.*

He leaned against the opened shutters to steady himself and listened.

> *Periyar, 'The Great One,' as he was known, established the Self-Respect Movement. He often said it had only one aim: to restore pride to the Dravidian people based on their true history. Self-Respect was only possible, he argued, in a casteless society, where...*

Vijayan staggered back inside the shop, landed on a stool and gripped the edge of the counter. Everyone knew this was coming, yet it hit him hard. He felt a part of him, the best part, was gone, and he wasn't sure how to regain it.

Next day, as he approached the Tip Top Fancy store, Vijayan noticed an old man standing near the entrance. His threadbare veshti was folded up above his knees, and he wore no sandals or shirt, not even a towel over his shoulder.

'Out of the way!' The words, spoken as one speaks to children and animals, jabbed at the man, who bent his head and withdrew. Vijayan stepped forward but before he could say anything, the speaker had marched down the road. Avoiding eye contact with everyone inside, Vijayan bought a bar of soap and walked out. Now the old man was squatting at the edge of the road, his knees sticking out like a skeleton. Passing him, Vijayan tried a thin smile of sympathy, but the man only squinted in the sun.

Next day he opened the shop before Muttusami arrived. As he began to rearrange piles of cloth in the cabinets, a shrieking horn made him turn around. A bus swept by, throwing up a funnel of dust and debris that hung suspended in the air and then dispersed.

Sitting down, he glanced at the shop entrance where the sunlight had crept up over the third step and now lay in an oblong patch on the floor. He looked again and noticed that the top half had begun to slide forward; by lunchtime, he calculated, the top and bottom would align themselves and form a perfect rectangle. That's it, he said to himself. I'll write an essay on the chimera of caste. That was the only way he could respond. He wasn't Velan, or Pandian, or Inspector Ali.

Yes, he told himself, I'll expose caste 'as a mist that befogs the mind.' He was firming up this promising opening sentence when a man entered the shop.

'Two veshtis. One plain, one with a green border.'

'Right,' said Vijayan as he turned around and faced the glass-fronted panels.

Acknowledgements

I would like to thank Aruna Ghose at Rupa for a critical reading of an earlier version of this book and for guiding the final version through to publication.

The poem on page 41 is adapted from a translation of a poem by Subramania Bharati (1882-1921).

The poem on page 48 is A.K. Ramanujan's translation of a classic Tamil verse from 100-300 CE (*The Interior Landscape*, Indiana University Press, 1967, p. 37).